The Van Helsing
Conjecture

Evelyn Chartres

(Nom de Plume)

2025

Ottawa, Ontario

ABOUT

Clara Grey was a hunter forged by faith, an angel cast out of Heaven, and a goddess haunted by voices of the vanquished. She exists in a world fraught with peril, where every shadow hides something that goes bump in the night.

Once a legend among the ranks of a secret order of hunters, Clara finds herself adrift. She thirsts for closure until a fleeting echo from the Roaring Twenties reveals a potential path back.

Allied with creatures she once hunted, Clara must venture out alone to reach the order that defined her. But as divine foes and her pasts intersect, will she find an army to reclaim the night or end up in a graveyard?

Before you turn the page, heed this: In the hunt for closure, even an angel may lose their way.

While part of a series, The Van Helsing Conjecture stands on its own, inviting new readers into a dark fantasy saga of hunters, angels, and perilous nights, with no prior tales required.

CONTENTS

ACKNOWLEDGEMENTS

I wish to thank those who helped make this novel a reality.

Amy Queau, who took on the challenge of getting this cover made. The end result turned out even better than I hoped!

Thank you, Mark Schultz, for the edits and review. While nothing is perfect, I'm certain that the biggest offenders were purged.

Last, I wish to thank J.G. MacDonald. She's the brave soul who read my work in its development. You are my shining star in the night, proof that I'm not navigating these waters alone.

Evelyn Chartres (*Nom de plume*)
theportraitofawoman@gmail.com
http://evelynchartres.com

A NOTE ON SLANG

The Van Helsing Conjecture uses slang from the Roaring Twenties to reflect the main character's formative era. For your convenience, a Lexicon has been added at the end of the book.

A copy is also available online. Either click on or scan the QR Code, or type in the link below:

http://bit.ly/3XBXrFd

A NOTE ON BACKGROUND CHARACTERS

The Van Helsing Conjecture is part of a series and character names will come up even if they are not actively involved in this story. A Biography of Background Characters is available at the end of the book to help new readers or situate those returning to the series.

A copy is also available online. Either click on or scan the QR Code, or type in the link below:

http://bit.ly/4fz0Ij6

CHAPTER 1

SACRED HUNTING GROUNDS

A woman walked alone through the forest. Her steps left deep impressions in the hard-packed snow. The large backpack hanging from her shoulders weighed her down, pushing her ever closer to the brink of exhaustion. With every laboured breath, a heavy cloud of fog streamed from her mouth.

There was nothing out of the ordinary about hiking in the woods, other than doing so during the witching hour. The full moon was high in the sky, illuminating the path before her. The trees had shed their leaves long ago, giving her a clear view of the silvery forest ahead.

The hiker had grey eyes, with brown hair tied into a ponytail. Neither detail would turn heads. She blended into crowds, went unnoticed, with her passage immediately forgotten. The latter turned out to be a feature.

Something made a *whoosh* as it flew by her left ear. The pause in her movements was nearly imperceptible, dismissible as a trick of the eye. It was more than enough to alert her attacker that their prey was onto them. *That was close!*

There came another *whoosh*. She turned to evade but was too slow. The golden arrow buried itself into her backpack and made a dull *thud* as it struck a ballistic plate.

"Shit!" the woman swore before transitioning into a run.

The surge of adrenaline in her veins helped her to ignore the weight. Given the season and ample moonlight, she was dangerously exposed—

On either side, there came a *thunk*, along with splintering wood. She chanced a glance and caught an arrowhead protruding through the other side of the trunk. There came another *whoosh*, and this time it flew high. *Dammit! Does she ever run out?*

The hiker ducked behind a large tree and dropped her pack. Before the dull *clank* rang out from the woods, the prey was already headed deeper into the woods.

All the while, the woman's jacket deformed near her shoulder blades. The distortions grew until they tore clean through at two points. What came out was a congealed mass of bone and newly formed flesh. Shortly thereafter, the mass took on the shape of wings, with black feathers filling in the expanse.

Her transformation was not restricted solely to growing a pair of wings. Like a butterfly emerging from a chrysalis, the woman grew more beautiful with every breath. Her sharp facial features, elfin ears, and steel-grey eyes that turned heads for the better part of a century were visible.

She dodged another arrow, and another, but the third flew true. Her wings instinctively shifted to block the projectile, but it went through and through, causing a golden liquid to splatter on the virgin snow.

While a hit, the wing was enough to deflect the arrow from striking her neck. Tired of running, she ducked behind a tree and withdrew two pistols from holsters under her jacket.

The winged woman peeked around the tree trunk. Those steel-grey eyes scanned the horizon... *Nothing.*

"Figures," the woman mumbled.

A branch snapped from behind. She turned around, quick as a viper striking its prey, but that was not enough. Two arrows hit their mark, one passed through her left calf. Another struck her left wing before embedding itself into the tree. *This one is fast!*

"Well. Well," the teenage beauty said. "If it isn't Clara Grey, the angel who prefers to toil with the *humans* than defend Heaven."

Teen applied to her appearance only. Like most of the gods and goddesses of old, this one happened to be older than civilization itself. Back in her day, she would have been of marrying age, whereas any man who asked for her number today risked prison time.

The goddess featured the *perfect*, female physique, along with dark, braided hair, and elfin features that Clara attributed to the old gods. That being said, that golden bow and arrows were the biggest clue as to who she was dealing with.

"I could say the same thing about you, Artemis," Clara said, before chuckling. "Why aren't you up there *servicing* your one true *God?*"

At the mention of *God*, the goddess betrayed her emotions with a facial tick. On the day of her death, Clara encountered another goddess who had a similar reaction to that name. *Two points don't make a pattern.*

"How dare you—" Artemis hissed.

"How dare I what?" Clara asked. "Travel through the woods?"

Clara loved to rile up her opponents. Sure, the goddess held the proverbial high ground, but why let her bask in it?

"How dare you flaunt that name!" Artemis yelled.

"The god who discovered how to draw power from immortal souls?" Clara guessed.

"How did you—" Artemis asked.

That smirk on Clara's face gave away that this had been a shot in the dark. Unlike the goddess, Clara landed a blow on her first try.

"Well, these won't work," Clara said, and holstered her pistols.

She winced as the wing tore further which worsened the bleeding. Clara knew going in there would be no way to get out of this situation unscathed.

"Insolent whore, you killed my sister!" Artemis yelled.

"*Sisters* more like," Clara quipped. "They got what they deserved. Besides, Blue Eyes always thought you were a pretentious twat."

Hecate was the goddess who ended Clara's life. Those three personas reflected in statues and mosaics turned out to be distinct entities occupying the same vessel. Like most siblings, they were often in conflict with one another. *Now, they keep me company.*

"If you think you can just steal my bow——" Artemis said.

"I came along on a hunt…"

Clara focused until time *slowed* around her. In reality, she was speeding up her reaction times while the world moved on as it always did. This enabled her to move faster than the eye could see.

"Really?" Artemis asked. "You just happened to stumble onto my personal hunting grounds? Armed to the teeth?"

As time slowed down, the words Artemis spoke stretched out and lowered in pitch. Clara hated holding conversations in this state, but the payoff was often worth the aggravation. She could dodge bullets, if need be, although this ability was ironically, time limited.

"Young men have gone missing in the area for decades… That's not exactly subtle. Besides, I said that I came *along* on a hunt," Clara said.

She spoke in a well-practised timbre that appeared normal to anyone listening. *If I slow down time too far, I'll run out of breath before uttering the first syllable.*

"Along?" Artemis asked, before catching sight of Clara's grin. "...you were the—(*bait*)!"

That was Clara's cue. She shifted her focus to the mass of fur and muscle converging on their position.

While it had the eyes of a wolf, and ran on all fours, this was not an animal. *Why else would vampires stick to the cities?*

"Now!" Clara yelled, as Artemis lumbered toward the werewolf.

Clara's change in focus had a simultaneous effect. While she returned in sync with time, the werewolf was given a dramatic boost. Werewolves were naturally fast, but this one streaked across Clara's vision as though a speeding bullet.

A tree splintered and collapsed onto itself. While no one was near; its impact made the ground tremble. *That's my gal!*

Clara spotted the furry beast with its jaw locked onto the goddess's midsection. The werewolf repeatedly shook her head violently to the left and right. Those fangs tore through flesh and covered the forest floor in a splatter of golden blood. When done, the werewolf let go of the motionless lump. The werewolf then transitioned onto its hind legs, poised to strike. *Oh shit!*

Now was the time for Clara to intervene.

"Julia!" When the werewolf paused, Clara added, "You don't want the side effects of her death...trust me."

There was hesitation in those eyes, but the werewolf took a few steps back. Clara broke the shaft of the arrow that kept her pinned down. Despite the pain, she forced her wings to fold in.

"Killing a god or goddess imbues the killer with some of their powers... along with a transfer of their personas. Effectively, Artemis would haunt you for eternity, and I wouldn't wish that on my worst enemy," Clara said. *Which is exactly why I have four, unwelcome guests in my head.*

Unable to communicate effectively, Julia sat like a dog and whimpered. Clara took that as a sign the message was received loud and clear.

"They think they are above us," Clara said. "Pawns in their petty games."

Clara's eyes glowed blue. From the tip of her index finger a bolt of blue energy made the air crackle. The scent of ozone permeated the air, along with that of burned flesh and hair.

The sight of Clara flicking her *evil* switch must have triggered something in Julia's mind. The werewolf whimpered, and after seconds of watching a goddess being turned into charcoal, she looked away entirely.

"Consider this my electric—*(cure)*," Clara said.

"*Stop! Julia's had enough,*" Silver, the dominant persona of the Hecate triumvir, said.

All that was left when Clara ceased her attack was a mound of smouldering ashes. She took a deep breath to find her centre and spotted the troubled werewolf. Realising the effect her cruelty had on the other, Clara approached with an outstretched hand.

"I'm sorry…" Clara said. "It had to be done."

Julia shrank away as though the touch of an open hand would set her aflame. In that moment, the werewolf must have understood just what '*all in*' entailed.

"I…"

Clara stopped cold when Julia turned away. The sight of it was nearly ridiculous, as these creatures were feared by both hunters and vampires alike. These were animals of myth and nightmare, standing at least three metres tall, with claws that felled trees. *The literal stuff of nightmares.*

Alas, Julia recently escaped from a human trafficking facility. Werewolves were formidable under the full moon but still mostly human for the rest of the lunar cycle. Clara could not imagine what happened to her during those two weeks in captivity. *It could have been days had I saved her myself at the expense of the mission.*

"Do you need some time alone?"

The werewolf nodded, and Clara choked on her breath. *I didn't want to make things worse.*

"Can you find your way—"

The werewolf turned her head at an odd angle, and Clara could have sworn it cocked an eye. Had this been a defiant teenager, the fallen angel would have understood precisely what this was… *At least she still has her sass.*

"*Nor is she holding a grudge…*" Ethereal, another one of Hecate's personalities, said in a tone that sapped the excitement from a successful deicide.

Everything that Ethereal said was cold and emotionless. Each syllable leeched the joy from the room, as though death herself had spoken. *Goddess of ghosts and necromancy, but thankfully not song and dance.*

Those words left a bitter taste in Clara's mouth, but Julia did not know that extraction from the facility could have been sooner. Instead, they sent another asset, Grace, at great personal risk to empower the werewolf to free herself and the others held there. Now was certainly not the time to tell her. *Will it ever be?*

"Okay," Clara said. "Take all the time you need. You know how to reach me if you want to talk…"

The werewolf cocked her head to the side as though questioning the finality of those words. While Julia said nothing about her time in that compound, Clara also did not delve into the events surrounding her visit to The Grand. *Even though the events were livestreamed to help grow my audience.*

Clara had a lot of emotions she had yet to come to terms with that *incident.* It was more than a hotel nestled in the Rocky Mountains that served as a haven for things that went bump in the night. She died there at the hands of a goddess and did so to rid the world of her greatest foe. Later, she was lured back to meet her sister, who had been turned by a vampire. It was not an especially warm family reunion. *Thus, the reason for me not wanting to talk about it.*

"I… I can't imagine they will let this one stand," Clara began. "Artemis still had connect(*ions*)—"

There came a bright flash of light, powerful enough that the werewolf shielded her eyes with those massive paws. Clara did not react, the divine light of creation was something she was all too familiar with. *Julia's lucky that she's not human.*

There came a *snap* of someone's fingers and just like that the forest went dark. Other than feeling drained of energy, Clara waited for Julia to recover before saying anything.

"Go!" Clara exclaimed, with wild eyes. "I won't be able to hold them off for long."

The large eyes of the predator opened wide. Even through the fur, Clara could see those massive muscles twitching. Fight or flight, and in this case the werewolf chose the latter and bolted for their camp.

Clara waited until the werewolf was out of sight before saying, "That took a *lot* out of me."

"Well worth the cost," Silver said. "There *are* three of them."

Clara betrayed her emotions by moving her head back noticeably. She would have been mad as a hatter to assume there would be no response from above. *How else could Artemis maintain her sacred hunting grounds without arousing suspicion?*

When the great *détente* was threatened, leading to a potential war, they sent a single, human-born angel to intervene. *Speaks volumes on their priorities.*

In this case, they sent three, and as judged by the light of creation, at least one was an archangel. *They aren't fucking around anymore.*

Clara looked at Silver, the goddess of the moon and crossroads. She too was young and the embodiment of perfection, with her skin ever aglow with silver light. While she was used to dealing with the goddess, she rarely did so face-to-face.

"How long?" Clara asked.

"For letting me stretch out my legs?" Silver asked. "They'll remain in that state until the sun rises."

The primary source of power for an angel was the light of God. Thus, the sunlight would be enough for them to break free. Until then, they were slowed down to a level Clara could not fathom. *Every second in our time means a year for them...*

"Thank you," Clara said. "You're the bee's knees tonight."

"We are all in this together."

That statement reflected that the goddesses Clara killed were now a part of her. For the moment, Hecate and Bastet were her guests, but Artemis was sure to make an appearance. *Hecate is looking forward to their reunion.*

"Still up for setting Heaven aflame?"

"I—We wouldn't miss it for the world..."

The more Clara gleamed about Heaven the more she was convinced that a scorched-earth approach was the best option. It was not the paradise it was made out to be, and angels were at best the unwitting jailers of souls to be drained of their power.

Right behind Silver there were three angels. They had been created in the image of God himself, so it came as no surprise they looked like Greek gods. Front and centre in his white armour and white-hot sword was Gabriel. *They sent down their general to deal with me?*

In this state, they may as well have been statues, and her sauntering past them would leave an imprint on their eyes that would last comparatively for decades. While Clara could manipulate time, she lacked the finesse that Silver displayed.

"I'm jealous..." Clara confessed.

"Eons of practice..."

"I wouldn't discount talent…"

Clara left it at that and set her eyes upon the jailers of heaven. Sending them down here was tantamount to declaring war, unless the act was sanctioned by both sides of the wager. *Whoever the other party is.*

Silver said nothing, seemingly happy to be free of her sisters while regaining a measure of autonomy. While they clamoured for more independence, Clara sensed that Hecate as a whole enjoyed running the roost.

"Do I have to walk out? Or can I—(*teleport out of here*)."

Silver placed a finger against her chin and cocked her head. This informal exchange was refreshing compared to their initial encounter. They tormented her for over a year, whispering in her mind, sowing doubt and fear, all to weaken her emotionally. *I hope this becomes the norm.*

"I'll have to stay behind while you do," Silver said. "I'll rejoin before you hold a convocation."

Silver could not exist for long independent of Clara. Tactically, she understood why, because teleportation would disrupt Clara's focus and give the angels an opportunity to break free. Silver was like a spring under tension, it was only a matter of time before she snapped back into place.

"That's why you're my favourite…" Clara said, with a wink.

From the depths of her mind, there came the sound of dry heaving, and she also caught someone doing a Bronx cheer. Silver must have been aware of her sisters' actions and laughed.

"I needed this," Clara whispered.

Without another word, Clara grabbed her backpack, focused on their campsite, and vanished.

* * * *

Clara popped in by the dying fire. She was unsurprisingly alone. Even at a full run, Julia needed an hour to make it back to camp. *A little bit longer and I might've considered taking a nap.*

For some reason Clara felt fatigued, which was abnormal for her. While she could push through it, the idea of resting her eyes for an extended period of time was tempting. *That'll have to wait.*

"Right… she asked for time alone," Clara said, while pushing back an intense wave of sadness. *What's wrong with me?*

Julia could be a powerful ally, but it was the scars unseen by the naked eye that took the longest to heal. Both their wounds were deep, even if the nature of them diverged greatly.

"I can't push her away."

Nor could she rush the process. Clara needed to show some patience and head back *home.* A vampire named Evelyn would be more than happy to see her. *The feeling is mutual.*

"The problem is, I never want to leave… Right."

Clara fed the fire some fresh logs, struck down her tent, and packed. She left behind a small, red bag, by its larger red cousin given to Julia in the early summer. This one contained more money, cards, and a secure phone. *Along with a note.*

"She may look like Red Riding Hood, but she really is the wolf. I should've taken her shopping instead of going on a hunt."

With everything in hand, Clara visualised herself being home. *It's time.*

CHAPTER 2

VANILLA AND SEX

The scent of vanilla invaded her dream, and a smile crept over Clara's face. It brought her right back to her mother's kitchen. She imagined herself running down the steps, skipping over the squeaky one, and found herself face-to-face with the treats her mother was making.

"*Why are you up?*" Her mother, Theresa, asked.

Clara always slowed down like a tomcat on the prowl, hoping that her sisters would sleep long enough to miss this opportunity.

"*Do I smell vanilla?*" Clara asked.

Her mother smiled, this was their ritual which always ended with Clara getting a cookie or treat.

"*Don't tell your sisters,*" *Theresa would say.*

As was the custom, Clara grabbed the treat and took a bite. Her mother's sweet confections never failed to put an impossibly large smile on her face. Every morsel brought her one step closer to heaven.

"*I won't, Mama,*" Clara would reply, while crumbs rolled off her lips.

Before the memory of that taste fully formed in her mind, a cool, soft hand rolled up Clara's tummy and stopped at the base of her breasts. *Just a minute longer…*

* * * *

Clara had no desire to awaken from that dream, but her training as a hunter kicked in. Her eyes fluttered open as a tear streaked down from the corner of her eye. The scent must have conjured up that beautiful childhood memory. She looked down to find a full head of black hair resting on her shoulder. *She must have finished early with her latest piece.*

She loves the heat. Whereas Clara loved that Evelyn was always cool to the touch. The vampire's heart beat strong and true, while her breathing was deep. Clara had yet to meet another vampire who could mimic human vital signs as well as Evelyn could.

To put it mildly, they had a complicated relationship. In reality, they should be enemies instead of lovers, but they worked well together and their goals were aligned. *For the moment.*

Evelyn was a vampire born under the reign of the Sun King. A woman with piercing, green eyes, prominent cheekbones, pale skin for a human, and black hair.

Her most alluring feature was that smile. One that promised so much if one surrendered entirely to her. Clara would swear on the Bible that this vampire very much delivered on that promise… *and so much more.*

Despite her origins as a courtesan in Paris, Evelyn was classically trained. She was quick-witted, and embraced her passion for the arts. Her studio, deeper within this building, held a trove of paintings and sculptures that were either welded or carved. Each and every one of them rivalled the works of masters.

Clara realised they were in Evelyn's room. There was always the odour of paint hanging in the air, as did vanilla, and since returning from the sacred hunting grounds, sex. *It's starting to feel more like making love.*

She may not have been around as long as Evelyn had been, but this former flapper had plenty of sexual partners, both men and women. The Roaring Twenties was more than music, architecture, makeup, and fashion. They had petting parties, along with slang to gauge the interest and consent of a potential tryst… *It was the best time of my life.*

But that was just barneymugging. Hunters learned to weaponize sex, using such skills to gain intelligence, to lure targets, or manipulate people to meet their objectives. While Clara had sex for fun, it never approached the tenderness and emotional component Evelyn had shown with her. *That's the problem.*

Clara was not sure how she felt about being with a vampire. Let alone someone who mastered hiding their emotions behind an impenetrable mask. Admittedly, she could not imagine vampires living long without that specific skill.

To be fair, Clara did the same, which made daily interactions interesting. Neither knew what the other really felt, but during these brief glimpses Clara sensed that Evelyn did love her.

"*She told you so!*" Ethereal said, to dampen the mood.

"Words are often used to mask lies," Clara replied, in her mind.

"*Shut up,*" Silver said, to her sister. "*I've seen how she looks at you. She's different around you.*"

"*Do you think so?*" Clara asked.

Her heart skipped a beat at the thought of capturing the heart of another. The fact this berry was more fun than a night at a clip joint certainly helped. *She's the only one who seems to understand me.*

"*It's obvious,*" Sparky said, the third persona of Hecate.

This was the goddess of magic and the nickname came from her powers. This particular sister was thin-skinned and quick to act. When those eyes glowed blue, that meant Sparky was on the verge of striking. *She always talks as though she's had one espresso too many.*

"*It's easy to get lost in what might have been,*" Sparky added, and Clara visualised the goddess nodding her head repeatedly like an over-caffeinated squirrel.

"*Instead of looking at what you have,*" Silver said.

"*Or realising you're in bed with a creative, intelligent, and ruthless monster…*" Clara said.

When the sisters did not reply, Clara smiled momentarily before slipping back into sleep.

* * * *

Clara's phone chirped, the single pulse vibrated through the nightstand. While it was barely audible, it was enough to wake her up. Her sense of hearing was sharper than that of a human.

Her eyes shot open and quickly used visual cues to sort out where she was. The scent of vanilla was further away and she noticed that Evelyn was cocooned in the bed sheets. *That makes things easier.*

She moved her wings out from atop of her. It was tricky to get a good night's sleep with black-feathered wings. While she could not wrap herself in blankets like Evelyn was doing, they did keep her warm at night.

Because Clara had no desire to wake Evelyn, she sat up slowly, manoeuvred to the end of the bed, and tucked in her wings. She stretched out her arms, yawned silently and pressed her feet onto the cold, marble floor.

Clara grabbed her phone and confirmed it was for the reminder. Part of her was disappointed there was nothing from Julia, but it had only been a week.

To further avoid waking up the vampire, she walked on the tips of her toes towards the en suite bathroom. At the halfway mark, doing her best to be quiet as a mouse when the cat was lurking about, two words shattered her reality.

"Good morn—" Evelyn said. "Aie!"

Clara turned around quicker than photoflash powder took to ignite. There was Evelyn with her fangs extended and a drop of crimson on her lips.

"Why are you bleeding?" Clara asked.

"*Aucune idée*," Evelyn replied in French without realising. (*I have no idea.*)

"Didn't you feed last night?" Clara asked in a perfect, Parisian accent.

Evelyn smiled upon hearing the French. All the while, her fangs retracted, and she healed the cut without shedding another drop.

"*Oui*," Evelyn replied, before changing back to English. "She was positively scrumptious."

That was the key detail that did not fit in with the puzzle before her. Evelyn could stretch out her feedings longer than any other vampire known, which made cohabitation easier. *The fact that she leaves them alive is the only reason this works.*

"Do you want some company?" Evelyn asked, while those emerald-green eyes twinkled.

Clara smirked, but her phone reminded her once more that she was up for a singular reason. *We ran out of hot water last time.*

"I can't think of a better way to start the day." Before Evelyn could leap out of bed, Clara added, "I have to be somewhere in an hour."

Evelyn pouted long enough to tug at Clara's heartstrings and stuck out her tongue. Both knew of the appointment, but the vampire never passed on an opportunity to tease. *She's hard to say no to.*

The vampire stretched out her arms letting the sheets glide off her chest. This gave Clara a full view of that bare chest and those tight and perky breasts. *Very hard to say no to.*

"I'll be waiting," Evelyn teased.

Clara gulped, paused for a moment, but nevertheless found the strength to drag her feet towards the bathroom.

* * * *

Heat from the water radiated into her back, which made Clara moan. Her back and joints had been sore for the last few days for reasons that eluded her. She closed her eyes, revelling in the soothing heat. After taking several deep breaths, Clara reached for a sponge and her body wash.

The act of bathing had changed a lot since she was a child. Being the youngest meant she was the last one to bathe, and by then the water was lukewarm at best.

What was once a luxury reserved for the wealthy was available even in roach-infested hotels. However, Evelyn did not skimp on this water closet; the white marble, brass fixtures, and glass panels of the shower were a testament to that.

There were three jets focused on her back and one raining down from above. This shower was like being pampered at a spa. When Evelyn was there to *help*, Clara considered this room to be Heaven-adjacent.

She rubbed the sponge until she had a thick lather and rubbed her chest and arms before moving down to her legs. Since she shaved yesterday, she only needed to wash up.

She quickly cleaned her feet and legs before working her way into her bare berry patch. She ran the sponge in between her legs…

"Wait…"

Clara looked down and found a golden, viscous fluid and rusty clots on the sponge, with more washing down into the drain. The sight of her blood caused her to freeze in place, while holding her breath.

The blood of angels and gods was gold in colour, but turned red when drawn from the body. *That's how they hide among the flock.*

She started breathing once her mind made the link between several disparate events. The twinging and pulling sensation from two weeks ago, the aches and pain, and Evelyn's fangs. *They made me barren.*

All hunters were sterile. Doing so prevented them from yearning for a family or having to deal with the complications of a pregnancy during extended missions.

"I haven't had a cycle since my thirteenth birthday…"

Being barren was empowering, and one of the reasons why the Roaring Twenties was so memorable for Clara. A single question remained in her mind. *How?*

In the back of her mind, there came a sound. It was rhythmic and reminded her of a purring cat…

"Horsefeathers!" Clara swore.

Before that word echoed off the bathroom walls, Evelyn was standing outside the shower with the door open. Those eyes were wild as though looking for a threat but finding none.

"What's—(*wrong*)?" Evelyn asked.

"…Fertility…"

"What?"

"…I killed… the goddess of fertility and absorbed her powers!"

Months ago, Clara ended up face-to-face with Bastet the Egyptian goddess of fertility. Bastet was beyond reason due to an earlier attack by Sparky forcing Clara to put down the catlike humanoid. Until now, there had been no adverse effects. *Those powers restored my fertility.*

Evelyn cocked a brow before looking at the sponge. Spots of red were forming among the golden liquid. At the sight of that golden blood, Evelyn's fangs dropped back into place.

"That explains the taste of copper last night…" Evelyn said.

"You knew?" Clara asked, her eyes flashed bright blue for a fraction of a second.

"*Ma chère*," Evelyn began, taking a deep breath to find the right choice of words. (*My dear.*) "We've made (*love*)—been intimate for a while now. You've never shown any signs before… Besides, *you* told me that they made you barren."

Those words and that soft voice were enough to snap Clara's emotional control back into place. The betrayal experienced was not brought on by Evelyn, but by the dramatic change in situation. It was Clara who killed a crazed goddess in self-defence and this was one of the repercussions.

"Look on the bright side," Evelyn said, to snap Clara back into reality.

"What's that?" Clara asked.

"I can't get you pregnant," Evelyn said, before stepping into the shower, getting onto the tips of her toes, and kissing Clara on the cheek.

"What—Oh—Right…"

Clara kissed Evelyn back and hugged her. She sensed that the vampire was wound tight and realised that the blood of a goddess might have been too potent even for Evelyn to handle. Vampires were vulnerable against the faithful and creatures of faith. *Odd that Evelyn appears to be immune to me.*

When a vampire bit her, the effect was like drinking concentrated acid straight from the bottle. *If she can't hold herself back and takes a bite…*

The angel pulled back, and Evelyn immediately relaxed. After a few minutes, those fangs retracted and she flashed her trademark smile.

"Sorry," Evelyn said.

"Why?" Clara asked. "It's not your fault."

She was not worried about Evelyn, because Clara could easily hold her at bay. Her sire, Marc, was another matter. The old soldier had great discipline but this development could appeal to his predator instincts. *Best I steer clear of him.*

Water welled up in Evelyn's eyes. Her heart stopped for what would have been three beats before regaining control and she backed away.

"I-I-I'll call the front desk and ask them to send up a supply of sanitary products."

There were advantages to Evelyn and Marc repurposing this hotel for their use. While these floors were exclusively theirs, the rest functioned as a high-end hotel. *With tons of surveillance equipment for blackmail.*

It also helped that they lived effectively on the thirteenth floor. People were accustomed to seeing that number missing from elevators. It also meant few questioned why there were no doors between the adjacent floors. *What's bad luck to a vampire?*

"Thank you," Clara said, but Evelyn was already gone.

CHAPTER 3

DINGLE DANGLER

Clara used the keycard to unlock the door. She walked inside and noticed the air had a bite to it, which sent a chill straight down her spine. A glance at the window at the far end of the room revealed that it was open.

The room was decidedly nondescript, suitable for a generic, hotel-room setting found in movies and television. Admittedly, she did like the bare, brick exterior walls, and the shower in the bathroom was spacious. *At least I can let my wings hang out.*

"It's not exactly the Ritz," Clara mumbled.

She could afford a suite at the most expensive hotel in the city, but Clara preferred to be practical. Women who walked in from off the street and asked for their best room got noticed. *Who needs that level of scrutiny? Being recognised as the Valkyrie is bad enough.*

The Valkyrie was the nickname the media had chosen for her. She had been caught on camera several times with her black wings in plain sight. The first time, she was stark naked, locked in a battle with a werewolf. It came as no surprise that the videos from that fight went viral… *and thus a legend was born.*

21

She closed the window, took a deep breath and smiled. There was no hint of cigarette and she was thankful for the hotel being non-smoking.

"At least the sheets were just changed," Clara said, after picking out the distinct scent of detergent.

Her stomach growled and she remembered there was no kitchenette. *At least there's a phone with a stack of flyers.*

"Everything a gal needs…"

Clara sighed, dropped her backpack on the bed along with her keycard on the desk. Next, she slipped out of her leather jacket and focused. Her plain-Jane persona was shed in favour of her true form, wings and all.

She stretched out her wings and sat backwards on one of the chairs by a small, round table. From this vantage point she had a great view of the street below. Even in the dead of winter, tourists braved the elements to find restaurants, bars, and entertainment.

"It was supposed to be date night…"

She let out all the air from her lungs and closed her eyes. None of this was Evelyn's fault, but she was disappointed nonetheless.

"*I've never reacted like this to someone's blood before,*" Evelyn protested.

"*I'm not afraid of you,*" Clara replied. "*I'm afraid for you…*"

The last time a vampire bit Clara, a failsafe kicked in. Dozens of vampires ended up dead in the process, so this angel was not about to take any chances. *I'd never be able to forgive myself.*

"So, in a hotel for tonight until—(*I figure this out*)."

Her phone rang and her head snapped towards the source. She got up from the chair and slipped the phone out of the pocket of her leather jacket. *Who actually calls?*

Clara looked at the screen and immediately recognized the number. This was one of the phones she gave to Julia, which sent the contents of her stomach to the tip of her toes.

The last time she got a call from Julia, it was a plea for help. The young werewolf in human form had been seconds away from being captured, and Clara heard every chilling detail of that scuffle.

Clara put her phone on speaker and kept quiet. If Julia was in danger, the angel had no wish to identify herself over an open line. *It may work for movies, but I don't want them to know that I'm coming for them.*

"I hear you're a *woman* now," Julia teased.

Clara smirked, because that smart-assed banter was the Julia she knew. The werewolf had a way of getting under someone's skin. *Very much like I do.*

"How did—(*you find out*)?" Clara blurted out.

The answer was obvious, Evelyn must have called Julia. The reason why was not immediately obvious, that is until the phone vibrated in her hand.

She unlocked her phone and saw the notification.

> **Evelyn:** I thought you could use the distraction. It's a good reason to chat with Julia. I know you've been worried about her.

"Evelyn…" Clara said.

"Fuck! Right out of the park," Julia responded. "I was going to string you along…"

"Sorry to disappoint."

"I can't believe you shacked up with that corpse," Julia began. "Still, she's clearly into you."

Clara put the phone down on the table and closed her eyes. Whatever Evelyn said to Julia, it must have been more than a courtesy call.

"She's wonderful," Clara said, while beating down her emotions to keep her breathing and heart rate under control.

"She is," Julia began. "When I met her in that restaurant with all that food, she treated me with respect. Like I was deserving of it and not to be beaten down… like a stray… dog…"

Clara's eyes welled with water. This was another instance of catching a glimpse of the woman behind the monster.

"She has a beautiful soul…" Clara said, while her lower lip trembled.

"Why do I get the feeling you're being literal?" Julia asked.

This was a reference to the angelic side of Clara Grey, who could look past the flesh and gaze upon the soul of any living creature. The sight was not enabled by default, and Clara preferred to rely on the skills she honed as a human over the years.

"You two have something in common," Julia added.

"What's that?"

"You both opened my eyes."

Clara was the one who killed Julia's father in self-defence. The death of the pack alpha led to a downward spiral. A year later, it was Clara who saved Julia's life and entrusted the werewolf to rescue someone near and dear to her. *I helped her see there was a life beyond the pack.*

It seemed that Evelyn taught the werewolf that *corpses did not all deserve* to be chew toys. Werewolves were the natural enemy of the vampire, which is why vampires rarely strayed from the cities. *Evelyn helped her to see that allies could be found even among her enemies.*

"You're going to make me cry," Clara confessed.

"Must be that time of the month," Julia teased.

Clara took in a sharp breath before her emotions and reason reached the same conclusion. She burst out laughing and slapped the table so hard that her phone flipped in midair before landing onto the mattress.

"Horsefeathers," Clara said. "I needed that."

"What was that?" Julia asked.

"I slapped the table," Clara said, while blood flushed through her cheeks. *Why am I feeling so warm?*

"You must have some werewolf in you," Julia said. "How do you feel about what happened?"

It appeared that Julia was done beating around the bush. In a way, Clara preferred the diversion over dealing with her endless well of feelings.

"Mortified," Clara confessed.

"That must be one for the record books," Julia began. "You're old enough to be my great-grandmother."

"…I'd add two or three greats to that."

"Damn! Are you older than Evelyn?"

"You'd have to add about a dozen greats to mine."

"So, she's robbing the cradle with a great-great-great-great-great-grandmother?"

It was the first time that Clara really considered their age difference. Evelyn was very much a creature of the now. Sure, she sometimes mentioned living in France before *La Révolution* and her time in *la Nouvelle France*, but it was more like someone spewing out random trivia.

If anything, Clara was the one anchored to an era long past. She had been uprooted from the nineteen-twenties and had yet to catch up entirely.

"I was never a mother," Clara said. "Although I can vouch for her considerable experience… I lost count of how many times I—(came)."

"Ewww," Julia said, "Too much information!"

"Never ask me about petting parties then."

Clara was smiling, enjoying the verbal riposte with the werewolf. There was a pause, the silence filled in by the sound of tapping against the phone.

"Oh my God!" Julia said.

"What?"

"I can't unsee what came up in the search results…"

"I did warn you," Clara reminded.

"That may as well have been a dare," Julia said, before taking a deep breath. "I'm sorry for losing my cool back in that forest."

"All good… no apology needed."

In the distance, a couple walked down the sidewalk towards a row of restaurants. It was beginning to get dark and the fog from their breath came out in long streams. The way they held their hands hinted they had been together a while. *I never had that in life, the mission always came first—*

"I'm… still not where I want to be," Julia said.

Clara only realised the werewolf was talking once the last few words were muttered. After a few breaths her mind cobbled together the message.

"Look… I—" Clara began, but cut herself off. *The phone is the last place to confess.*

"I owe you," Julia said. "You picked up that phone and made sure someone was there for me."

Hearing those words led to a sudden drop in blood pressure. The sounds of the city just outside the window sounded as though it was underwater. *You were at that dark place that long because I sent someone else.*

"Also, thanks for stopping me from making that kill…"

"Oh?" Clara asked, without trying to make it sound like a lead-in to '*I told you so.*'

"I don't need to be more fertile or whatever side effect that Katnip Evercry wannabe left you with…"

Clara had no idea what that reference was about. This effectively sent them back into their starting positions.

"Evelyn said there was a silver lining," Clara said.

"What's that?"

"She can't get me pregnant…"

Clara smirked while Julia giggled like a schoolgirl. The humour was all to avoid delving into their troubles. Bastet happened to be a convenient way of skirting the periphery of various topics.

"Fuck me," Julia said. "I'm in a lesbian version of the Munsters with me cast as the kooky, werewolf aunt."

Clara made a note to look into that reference, or just ask Evelyn about it later. The way Julia was laughing was a clue on how far out of date she was for popular culture references. *I need to catch up on ninety years…*

"Sounds like you needed a distraction," Clara said, once the laughter died down.

"You have no fucking idea," Julia said. "I'm going to stick around our campsite for a while. It's peaceful and I want to find myself."

"Do you need me to—(*help*)?"

"You've done plenty," Julia began. "When I feel ready, we'll meet up again."

"Feel free to embrace your inner dingle dangler."

Clara was about to explain that a '*dingle dangler*' was someone addicted to using the phone, but she never got the chance.

"I will—bye!"

And with that, the line went dead. It was hard to imagine, but Clara simultaneously felt better and worse.

"Purgatory, if such a place exists, must be somewhere on Earth…"

CHAPTER 4

MARCONI AND BELL

The next day, Clara found herself facing a nondescript shop. The man she came to see was Zachary, a technological wizard, one who worked in the shadows, and often on commission by Evelyn and her kind. *To think he once told me that vampires weren't real.*

The man wore large glasses with thick lenses that magnified his eyes. If not for his peepers this dark-haired and fair-skinned man would have no notable traits.

The room was filled with electronics and displays that nearly made Clara's head swirl. At the centre of this electromechanical monstrosity, there was a *throne* made up of old server chassis. She found him seated, those eyes locked onto a tablet, staring at lines of code.

"Sorry for being late," Clara said, before an errant question crossed her mind. "Do you ever leave?"

The man launched himself off the throne and plopped back on violently. The surprise of someone popping in from out of nowhere caused him to fumble his tablet, which sent it hurtling towards the floor.

Before it crashed to the floor, Clara had the tablet in hand. She read through the visible lines and decided her time would be better spent on deciphering a long-dead language instead.

"Here," Clara said, with a smirk. "You dropped this…"

"You could have knocked," Zachary said, while gasping for air between every word.

"Why ruin the fun?" Clara began. "You improved your security system… impressive."

"Thank you?" Zachary asked. "I see it didn't do much to slow you down."

She figured her first visit must have spooked him and this further confirmed her hunch. When she flashed her glowing electric-blue eyes, he realised there were threats far greater than disappointed clients and nosey cops. *I'm the least of his worries.*

"It's a compliment," Clara said. "I'd have trouble bypassing your measures had this been my first time here."

She leaned in closer, and he instinctively backed away. Once he was flush against the back of his throne.

"Make sure there's no way to get a visual of the interior," Clara whispered, before teleporting to a workbench.

In the background, Zachary yelped. Clara did not turn around to see if he was all right as his heart rate and breathing were within normal ranges. Instead, she focused on the antique radio, with a red, steel casing, two white Bakelite dials and a glowing panel.

While the volume was low, someone was dutifully reading out a sequence of numbers. When she was alive, the sequence always revealed a biblical reference that hunters used to infer orders. *The code is more complex now.*

"How did—(*you do that*)?" Zachary asked.

"You said that you wanted to see me?"

"We agreed that you'd drop by yesterday."

She was impressed that Zachary would challenge her. Even in her plain-Jane form, Clara was known to make the bravest soldiers cower.

"I apologise for that," Clara said, and turned to look him straight in the eyes. "Unexpected... developments... forced me to alter my plans."

The man grabbed his cane. With his feet firmly planted onto the floor, Zachary limped his way over. While it looked painful, she could see in his eyes that he considered it a win. *I wonder what happened to him.*

"I played with a lot of advanced communication and cryptographic systems when I was in the service."

Bingo! A soldier wounded in combat would certainly explain his bearing and limp.

"That device of yours that you *claim* is over a century old nearly stumped me."

Clara kept quiet, crossing her arms while waiting for him to finish. He needed to go over the details to highlight his genius... *all to earn himself a bonus...*

"The technology itself is only part of the problem. There were two unexpected challenges to reproducing the circuit to recover the algorithms used to generate a chaotic, spread-spectrum signal..."

"Time?" Clara guessed.

The Tower, the home for her order, was anchored to a specific point in space and time, while somehow remaining in sync with the world. It was their last line of defence, as no enemy would dare lay siege in the shadows of Mount Vesuvius' eruption. Since the Tower was now isolated, this feature turned into a major deterrent for finding her way back to the order.

"...yes..." Zachary confirmed.

The man looked at her as though expecting her to sprout a second head and wings. Clara smirked but had no desire to illuminate him on how she arrived at the answer.

"What's the other?" Clara asked.

She could spend the day guessing the missing element. Ultimately, the angel wanted an answer more than winning a game.

It was Zachary's turn to smile. *It'd help if he spent some time in the sun instead of surrounding himself with glowing monitors and displays.*

"Ever heard of the hiccup?" Zachary asked.

Clara was intimately familiar with the hiccup, an effect created by an experiment gone wrong. An enigmatic group known as only the Georgians attempted to nudge probability. Alter a single decision and one could shift an election, or reverse the tide of a war.

Something went wrong during one of these attempts. The experiment shattered space and time, causing alternate timelines to merge with their own. People who perished in fiery car crashes ended up face-to-face with their own graves. Housing developments that were saved from the wrecking ball ended up merged with the contentious, new constructions that replaced them. *I even remember a case where a serial killer was executed twice.*

Pockets of the hiccup lingered still throughout the world. It was said that one could hear echoes of events that might have been. Some of these bubbles became tourist attractions, while others were avoided entirely because of their inherent danger.

"Yes… I'm… familiar with it," Clara said.

Clara ended up on Earth specifically because of the Georgian meddling. *The damage they wrought will be with us for millennia.*

"Whatever the source, it's behind large distortions of space and time," Zachary said.

That did not necessarily mean it was related to the hiccup, the hunter gate hub, better known as the Terminus, could generate a similar effect.

"How did you come to that conclusion?" Clara asked.

"I'm glad you asked," Zachary said before moving over to a device laden with buttons and switches attached to a phosphorescent screen.

Clara was not trained in signal processing and display. However, she saw the outline of a wave propagating from right to left. There were spikes that corresponded with the speaker, which reminded her of the grooves on an old wax cylinder recording.

"That's the processed signal," Zachary explained. "You'd see this by playing any analogue recording."

"Okay," Clara said, surprised that she was following him so far.

He pressed on several toggles and dials until the visual changed entirely. The signal narrowed somehow, but spikes were frequent and random, none of which corresponded with the spoken voice.

"That's the signal we are picking up," Zachary said. "While it may appear to be random noise, that's by design."

"Hiding in plain sight?" Clara guessed, because it was tactically the smart thing to do.

"Precisely," Zachary said.

His features softened and his jaw went slack, leading to his lips parting by the thickness of a nail. She realised by a change in heart rate and breathing that he was getting aroused by her responses. *This better not be another side effect of absorbing the goddess of fertility.*

Clara tilted her head to the side and counted down from ten. When done, she cleared her throat to snap him back to reality.

"…right," Zachary said. "The background noise isn't entirely random. Certain elements can be mapped out and predicted to a high level of accuracy."

This was starting to be a bit much for her to follow.

"And?" Clara pressed.

"I've looked up research on the bubbles the hiccup left behind. Similar effects have been recorded at those sites."

While that explained his conclusion, Clara suspected there was something else left to bring up. *The piece de resistance.*

Clara decided to slow down time to take a better look at the signal. For her, it was little more than a bunch of random lines, but in slow motion, it appeared more like a heart rate monitor at a hospital.

She watched the phosphorus tip move from one end to the other in minute detail. He was right, the core signal was more manageable at this speed, and some of the spikes were predictably cropping up at specific points. *The spikes are predictable.*

That is until the signal was amplified and the sequence changed, creating a new pattern which in turn changed again. After five of these cycles the pattern repeated itself from the start.

"A pattern within a pattern," Clara said, in the accelerated state.

As such, those words came out sounding like a bird's chirp. Zachary's face began to distort, likely confused how someone could make such a peculiar sound. This forced Clara to return in sync with time.

"What was—(*that*)," Zachary said.

"A pattern within a pattern…"

The man cocked an eye and paused. The schoolboy's gaze locked onto his crush. Clara ignored it to save herself the trouble of dousing the flames of his fantasy… *and shutting him down.*

"Wait." Zachary said, once he stopped thinking with his secondary head. "You could see that? It took my signal processing software a week to find a definitive pattern in all that noise."

"Lucky guess…" Clara replied. "…did you find anything else?"

"You said the signal was available globally?"

Now that was interesting, since Clara never surrendered that particular detail. These radios did work globally as hunters were dispatched anywhere vampires were found. *He must have reached out for help.*

"I wouldn't know," Clara said. "My grandmother never spoke about that feature to me. To be fair, she rarely ventured beyond our neighbourhood."

Again, there was a pause, followed by raising a finger and opening his mouth. He must have realised the risk of pressing the matter. *That's the smartest thing you've done today.*

"Why would that matter?" Clara asked genuinely curious.

"There's clearly a source and it's stable."

Now that was interesting. The signal was once broadcast from several points to avoid detection. A single source could be traced, jammed, or destroyed. *After a century, the other stations might have gone offline.*

"So?"

"We are near the periphery of the signal," Zachary said. "In adverse weather, the signal fades to the point of losing it entirely."

"You managed to track down the source, didn't you?"

She had to smile at his resourcefulness. The man clearly knew far more about the radio than he was letting on. *I'm not the only one in this room who's keeping secrets.*

"Yes," Zachary said.

"*What you seek can be found where your past and reality diverge.*" This was the last piece of advice Ray gave her before another disappearing act.

Ray was the *man* whose features were perpetually marred by the sun. He appeared from out of nowhere, spouted off some riddle and vanished just as suddenly. *Everything Zachary says lines up with that clue.*

35

"Like the outskirts of a resort city on the Pacific coast of Mexico?" Clara asked.

"There's no way you could know that!"

"That's where my grandmother went for her honeymoon."

She could see his eyes darting from point to point as though searching for a reason to challenge her reply. A *ritual* that appeared to help him find his centre. *Whatever works.*

"Have you been able to replicate the functionality?"

She hoped to avoid any questions surrounding her fictional grandmother. *Eventually, he'll find a hole in my story and exploit it.*

"I did," Zachary said. "It's streaming as a live podcast on a couple of music apps."

Clara furrowed her brow before placing a finger over the centre of her chin and lips. She always included the broadcast while posting as the Valkyrie. *At this stage, millions know about the signal.*

This way, Clara could access it from anywhere while appearing as a random connection among many… *especially if I post a link to it in my next video.*

"That's ingenious," Clara said. "Hiding in plain sight."

The fact that Zachary was now avoiding eye contact indicated there might be a side deal. That explained why he asked about the global reach of the radios. *I'll let Evelyn know to keep an eye on him.*

"Thank you," Zachary managed to say.

Clara grinned but remained quiet. For effect, she faded into the ether, leaving nothing more than her toothy smile in place.

When Zachary's eyes bulged, Clara's disembodied laugh filled the room.

CHAPTER 5

A MEETING OF MINDS

Clara was walking through the hotel lobby as her phone vibrated. Based on the pattern, it was Evelyn reaching out. While comforting to know the vampire was keeping in touch, Clara was still bitter about their plans blowing up.

"You shouldn't take it out on her," Silver said.

"I can't help how I feel," Clara replied silently.

She was more in touch with her emotions these days, more so than at any other time in her life. Her motivations were simple as a hunter, as all she had to do was complete a mission and move on to the next. That trait made her a formidable hunter... *but a terrible friend.*

Those failings ruined several relationships, some of which could have led to skirting the edge of normality. *Instead, I ended up with a monster.*

"You can't choose who you love," Silver interjected.

Is that actually true? Clara certainly made choices that ensured love never developed before.

"I miss her," Clara said, while passing by the front desk.

The clerk did not look up from their phone nor acknowledge her existence. Clara found comfort in the fact that she did not need to apologise for talking to herself.

She walked up the stairs and used the opportunity to check her notifications. Evelyn sent a picture and knowing the vampire's proclivity to tease, it was likely racy. *I don't need to be further reminded of what I'm missing.*

What Clara needed was someone to talk to, to take her mind off this situation. Julia was otherwise unavailable, and Evelyn was at the centre of it all. *It's not her fault.*

That left few options, one of which she rarely availed herself of.

"I'm starting to get the feeling she doesn't like us very much," Sparky said.

"That's not true... this just doesn't jive with the parts of me yearning to be normal."

The keycard reader beeped, and she stepped inside her unit. It smelled of stale pizza from last night. She ignored the scent, grabbed something out of her night bag and sat at the table next to the window.

She opened the compact mirror and angled it to give her a view of the door. From her leather coat, she removed two, nine-millimetre pistols and placed them on either side of the table. *In case someone tries to storm through that door.*

"As easy as falling off a log," Clara said, before closing her eyes.

* * * *

Clara opened her eyes and found herself in an entirely different place. The blue, vaulted ceiling worked beautifully with the blue and gold carpet running down the length of the passageway. In turn, the cream marble flooring and dark oak walls made the brass fixtures pop.

Her black, leather, high-heeled shoes resonated throughout the hall with every step until they were muffled by the carpet. To her left, she spotted her reflection in the brass light fixtures.

She was dressed to the nines, wearing a black, low-cut flapper dress and a white, felt *cloche* hat with a black band and bow.

"This baby vamp is rocking it tonight," Clara said.

Her style and fashion changed with every visit. There was no rhyme or reason to the choices made, but today she had no complaints.

At the end of the hallway, there were two, large, oak-and-brass doors. They opened for her automatically and brought forth the bright, white light of the sun.

This room changed based on need. However, it generally contained a large table with eleven seats. The chairs were made of opulent leather, while the table itself was made of mahogany with banker's lights illuminating every place setting.

The style was decidedly art deco, including the bar at one end, and a stage big enough to accommodate a twenty-piece band. Opposite the doors there were two, eye-shaped windows that were arguably more at home in a greenhouse.

Beyond the eye-shaped windows, Clara saw what was going on in the street as well as the reflection of her room door.

"Good afternoon," Clara said.

Her steps echoed throughout the room until she stopped at the end of the table. Five *women* were already seated at the table.

The first three needed no introduction as this was Hecate in her three forms. Silver always sat on the right and Sparky on her left. Ethereal was always at Silver's side to prevent personal grievances from escalating. Each wore the same, electric-blue gown that would be right at home during the Roaring Twenties.

On the other side of Ethereal was Bastet, who wore the same black cocktail dress she died in. While the style was modern, the catlike features and fur of the wearer were decidedly more fitting in Egyptian hieroglyphics. Bastet rarely spoke and when she did it was in an ancient Egyptian dialect. *Sparky must have done a number on her mind before I had to put her down.*

Their newest member was Artemis, wearing a white toga, white and bronze chest armour and with a gold bracelet around her upper, left arm. She was impressive to look at, but those eyes burned with hatred… *it doesn't help that they gagged her.*

"Why the gag?" Clara asked.

Sparky's eyes glowed blue while nodding several times in rapid succession. *At least that answers who did it.*

"She's not… *adjusting* well," Silver confessed.

"I don't think you three did either," Clara replied.

"I was reasonable in comparison," Ethereal said.

The deadpan delivery normally leeched the warmth from the very air Clara breathed. In this case, it came across as an attempt at humour. Clara glanced at Ethereal and despite her translucency the smirk was clear as day. Doubting her eyes, she looked away towards the windows before checking again. *Is it real?*

"I didn't think it was possible for you to smile," Clara said, to tease.

When Silver and Sparky laughed, Ethereal scowled. Clara kept her focus on the translucent goddess, winked, and mouthed noiselessly, '*Thank you.*'

"Be it as it may, Artemis deserves respect."

Without anyone making a move, the gag disappeared. Artemis opened and closed her jaw several times before coughing. After taking a deep breath, those lips went white and the fire burning in those eyes became an inferno.

Clara maintained a smile and looked at everyone at the table. She did not expect to win over everyone early on. Hecate was also aware they were there to keep new arrivals in line.

"Artemis," Clara said. "If you ever want to talk one-on-one, let me know."

That was a misnomer since it was nigh impossible to keep secrets from oneself. But the other goddesses were not always tracking what Clara was up to. *Especially when I'm with Evelyn.*

Clara caught a flash in those eyes that highlighted her comprehension. Alas, like a prisoner of war, Artemis would not aid the enemy. *I may no longer be aligned with Heaven, but that doesn't necessarily make me the enemy.*

"Any thoughts on the lead to find my way back to the Tower?" Clara asked.

"Why?" Ethereal responded.

"Why what?"

"Why do you care about that place?" Ethereal asked.

Clara had grown accustomed to the killjoy that was Ethereal. However, the goddess of ghosts and necromancy often exposed the harsh reality of a subject. After a pause, Silver decided to interject to smooth out those words.

"I believe what my sister means to say is why would you wish to find your way back there?" Silver asked after raising a hand. "They took away your childhood, lied to you, turned you into a weapon, and even embedded a fail-safe into your mind."

Minus the childhood, Clara had every reason to take the war to them. A part of her still believed in what the Tower stood for and knew that the problem did not lie with the rank-and-file hunters and acolytes. Still, she took several breaths, her mind working through a reply while keeping her temper in check.

"There's the potential for allies?" Clara asked.

"Zealots who would just as likely kill you… and Evelyn…" Ethereal said.

Clara took in a sharp breath, her eyes flashing blue for a second. It hinted at her irritation, even if Ethereal had a point.

"Sister!" Silver said.

This led Clara to imagine Sparky with a big tub of popcorn in hand. The goddess of magic was practically salivating at the idea of Clara *addressing* Ethereal's poor behaviour.

"It's okay," Clara said. "Ethereal is right and I'll say this now. Either I find allies willing to join my cause to fight against the night, or I leave behind a tomb…"

A collective smile grew across the face of every goddess in the room. *Except for Artemis.*

"I thought you didn't kill humans?" Silver asked.

The difference in tone between Silver and Ethereal could not be adequately described. While those words alone implied defiance, especially from Ethereal, it was clear that Silver was confirming if Clara considered every aspect of their plan. *Silver seeks to guide, whereas Ethereal points out the flaws.*

"I never made a vow to save every life I come across," Clara said. "Besides, this is my opportunity to find closure."

"Perhaps if you moved forward instead of circling back to places from your past?" Ethereal asked.

That was a low blow and she was thankful that Ethereal rarely took such liberties. *Her sisters once sewed her lips shut to get some peace.*

"Anyone have a better idea?" Clara asked.

It was Hecate who explained that worship was a potent source of power to an old god, but it was Evelyn who made it possible. *Livestreaming my life and death battle at The Grand made me an international superstar.*

Every goddess avoided Clara's gaze, save for Artemis. *She's not going to cooperate.*

"Look," Clara began. "I get the frustration, I'm feeling it myself, but I'm stumbling around in the dark…"

Clara pointed a finger towards the windows that represented what her eyes saw. It served to remind them that only one of them could exist permanently within the physical realm… *unless I end up dead.*

"I also don't have a lot of allies," Clara added.

"None you can take with you…" Silver commented.

That was true, as the Tower's defences actively screened for vampires. Clara would likely be fine as there was nothing quite like her on record. *I'd be liable to lose my composure if Evelyn is wounded, and she'd kill me if Marc didn't make it back.*

She did have Julia, and as long as they avoided a full moon, she was physiologically human. It was a shame that Julia needed to heal, but Clara was not about to rush that process along to suit her needs.

"What about Eleanor?" Sparky asked.

Eleanor was the woman in white, the angel of death who guided souls to their final destinations. As a goddess, Ethereal once commanded the angel, but Clara now had supremacy over that power.

"You'd need to ask her," Silver said, before Ethereal could open her mouth.

Ethereal huffed, but remained quiet. Since the Goddess of Necromancy happened to be staring at Bastet, the cat goddess broke eye contact, focusing instead on her razor-sharp claws.

"Eleanor runs independently of us," Silver continued. "We don't know if she visited the Tower after the gates were closed."

Clara sensed the angel of death would prioritise her duties over an adventure. *I don't intend to alter that directive.*

"So, we wait?" Clara asked.

"Or go alone?" Ethereal asked.

Sparky jumped up and down in her chair while clapping her hands together.

"Time for an adventure?" Sparky asked, her voice so shrill she may as well have been yelling.

That excitement turned out to be infectious. It meant that Clara could crawl out of this rut and do what she was made to do. All this waiting made her antsy, and it risked her choosing to remain permanently with Evelyn. *Such a beautiful, gilded cage.*

There was nothing wrong with settling down, especially with such a prize waiting for her every night. *Is that really me?*

Clara remembered being bored in Heaven, all duty and no action. Deep down, the angel knew that she would never allow herself to be happy by giving up on trying to make a difference.

"I did promise you that I'd burn down the gates of Heaven," Clara said.

The room went quiet, even as energy filled the air. Perhaps she should have considered a rousing speech that kings made before sending their nation's armies to war, but Ethereal broke the silence.

"A thought occurs," Ethereal said. "Evelyn will kill you if you don't go over this with her…"

CHAPTER 6

COOKING WITH A VAMPIRE

Clara flipped the switch near the kitchen's entrance. The fluorescent lighting flashed throughout the room, causing the stainless-steel appliances to reflect the cool, white light.

"It makes me wish I had your eyesight," Clara said.

There came a giggle from behind Clara. Evelyn was just now making her way down the stairs towards the kitchen. The vampire had just returned from her studio and was, as per custom, was stark naked, save for flecks of paint covering her body. *I love helping her clean them off, and guess what she's working on based on the colours.*

"You lost your chance in the twenties," Evelyn said. "You and I as vampires? Drusilla would have never seen us coming."

That line was a reference to a chance encounter in this very city in the dead of winter. A feral vampire had been killing women of the night, and Clara cleaned up their mess.

As a way to *thank* Clara for her assistance, the vampire arranged to buy Clara a drink at a local restaurant. They then had a chat over a table full of food, and Evelyn made it clear that her life would be spared for dealing with their mess and passing on a message to her superiors to back off. *I never did that last part, I simply reported that activity dropped off sharply in the city and no longer warranted our attention.*

Despite being into men at the time, Clara felt an intense attraction to this vampiric flapper. Part of it was due to a vampire's ability to use their voice to disarm and seduce their prey. Clara also had to admit that she was naturally drawn to that bubbly personality and inherent thirst for life.

"As it stands, I can go after your enemies day or night," Clara said.

The floors that Evelyn and Marc used for their home were intended as a club. Hence, the kitchen was designed to feed hundreds. Before Clara arrived, it sat mostly unused, save for a toaster and kettle. *Which was all Evelyn needed.*

Clara kept the kitchen stocked when she was here, and used any opportunity to cook for them. Evelyn often claimed it was not worth the effort to create elaborate meals, but the fallen angel loved to cook. *Especially, if it's for someone else.*

"True, *ma chère*," Evelyn said. (*My dear.*) "Why have a vampire when you can keep an angel firmly on Earth?"

That was a tease, as were most things Evelyn said with that musical voice. Every syllable carried with it a note, and listening to her recite poetry was akin to listening to a musical concerto.

"You make it seem like I ended up being shortchanged…" Clara said, while looking over her shoulder and winked.

Clara pulled out a few items from the fridge. She then lit the flame on the gas stove, setting it to low. Next came the cast-iron pan and a couple of tablespoons of butter.

"I—*Merde*," Evelyn said. (*Shit.*)

Evelyn grabbed a stool and dragged it closer to the area while Clara was working. The space was immense, accommodating a crew of twenty. *It's just the two of us.*

Clara grabbed a large pot, filled it with water and set it atop the stove with the flame set to high.

"For the record," Clara clarified, while cutting open a package of thick-cut bacon, heavy on the fat. "I feel like I won the jackpot in a numbers game."

Evelyn's eyes twinkled, even in this god-awful light. Clara's heart nearly skipped a beat in response, but the rational part of her mind had to spoil the moment by reminding her of Evelyn's expert ability to hide her emotions. *Why couldn't I have this moment? Even if it's just an illusion.*

"Keep this up and that pot will boil down to nothing," Evelyn teased.

Clara grabbed a chef's knife from the block and began to dice the bacon. She had to admit that she enjoyed the butcher block tops. *You never have to look for a cutting board.*

"And ruin the meal I planned for us?" Clara countered.

"Speaking of which," Evelyn said. "What are we eating?"

"Why ruin the surprise?" Clara asked. "I learned to make this during my time in France."

"*Vraiment?*" (*Really?*)

"*Oui, ma belle.*" (*Yes, my pretty.*)

Clara placed the bacon in the pan after adding a bit of olive oil. While that was cooking, she picked up a handful of potatoes.

"You must thank the Tower for teaching you to speak like a native Parisian," Evelyn admitted.

Clara gulped upon hearing that name. The angel pitched her plan to Evelyn after returning from the hotel. Soon after, the vampire retreated to her studio for a couple of days. *The shock has worn off and she's had a chance to digest the idea.*

"How do you feel about—(*my plan*)?"

Evelyn raised her hand with fingers together and the palm facing Clara.

The angel tossed the potatoes into the boiling pot as they were diced, then chopped an onion along with three cloves of garlic.

"*Agree* would be a strong word," Evelyn began. "I *understand* your intent and, most importantly, *why* you wish to find your way back."

That had always been part of Clara's plan. Evelyn even signed up to assist the angel. *At the time, I may as well have been shooting for the moon.*

"I confess that I'd love nothing more if you stayed here with me."

While not much of a secret, hearing that caused Clara to take in a sharp breath. Still, the angel placed the onions and garlic in a small bowl, checked the bacon and found it was crispy along the edges. She drained the grease from the skillet and set it aside.

Another pan was brought forward and warmed up. More butter was added, permitting it to melt while the potatoes softened.

"I'm not blind," Evelyn said. "You need to spread your wings and fly. In your case, both literally and figuratively."

It was not every day that one's girlfriend had a set of wings. Clara wondered why Evelyn never asked her to go flying.

"It's not like you don't grant me a great deal of leeway," Evelyn went on. "You permit me to feed when you are near, and never complain when I retreat to my studio."

These were all valid points. Clara remained uncomfortable with Evelyn feeding in general. At least she fed from the willing and always left them standing with a smile on their faces. *As long as no one gets hurt.*

Clara used a strainer to drain the potatoes and refilled the pot with fresh water. She then added olive oil and *sautéed* the onions and garlic. Despite Evelyn having something to say, Clara noticed the vampire was very much focused on the cooking process. *It's slowing down the conversation.*

"I guess what I'm trying to say is that you seeking out hunters leaves me feeling as though my heart is in a vise," Evelyn said.

Clara tossed in the potatoes and bacon, stirring the contents until she had a consistent finish. All the while she added salt, pepper, and herbes de Provence to enhance the flavour.

"I don't like feeling like that," Evelyn admitted. "I spent the Great War wondering if Marc would make it back."

That was something about Evelyn that Clara knew nothing about. Those two were inseparable, never far from each other. The idea of them being apart for four years led Clara to forget what she was doing. *Oh, right!*

Clara opened a bottle of dry white wine and poured it freely into the pan, filling the kitchen with the aroma of wine and alcohol. The starch thickened the wine into a sauce.

"I'm a big girl," Evelyn said. "We've all made sacrifices for the common good…"

Clara sensed this was where Evelyn had been leading this conversation all along. She placed the chef's knife into the boiling pot of water to heat the blade.

Meanwhile, she used a peeler to remove the rind from a wheel of cheese that she stashed in the freezer when she took out the ingredients.

"You have made *more* than your fair share of sacrifices."

What did Evelyn mean by that? Clara tilted her head to the side, while cutting the cheese wheel lengthwise. With every cut the blade would cool causing the cheese to stick. She reheated the knife by dipping it back into the boiling water.

"What do—(*you mean*)?" Clara asked, after the pause felt too big to ignore.

"Just… promise me that this won't be a one-way trip?"

That lower lip trembled, and Evelyn had to turn around to wipe a tear from the corner of her eye. That emotional reaction caused Clara to hold her breath while her blood pressure dropped. As her heart raced to keep up, so did her mind, until everything fell into place. *I've earned a reputation for being a martyr.*

Clara sacrificed herself to destroy the most dangerous vampire ever known to the Tower. She later went after a pack of werewolves with no expectation of coming back alive. *I would have died if it wasn't for learning how to channel Hecate's powers.*

She then went back to The Grand to confront her sister. Clara knew full well that she could never kill her. *I knowingly walked into a trap with one hand tied behind my back.*

While Clara mulled over what Evelyn said, she layered the potatoes topped with thick cheese slices into a stoneware pot. With the four layers combined, she placed the dish into the oven.

"When I was alive," Clara said, in a whisper. "I lived for the mission and achieving my objectives was my only goal."

If not for good fortune and training, Clara would have died several times over. It was a miracle that she made it past thirty. *Most hunters are lucky to reach their mid-twenties.*

"I continued along the same path as an angel," Clara confessed. "A weapon of mass destruction that only needed to be pointed in the right direction."

Evelyn could no longer maintain eye contact with Clara. What the vampire was hoping for and where this conversation was headed did not appear to converge.

"I can't—(*do this*)!" Evelyn began.

"I've never had a reason to return from a mission before," Clara said. "It's not something I'm accustomed to."

Clara walked up to the counter and took Evelyn's hands. She intertwined those cool fingers with hers and kissed Evelyn on the forehead. The vampire looked up slowly, those eyes reflecting all her hopes and dreams. *All I'd have to say is that I love her, and all of this would be forgotten.*

There was plenty of emotion when it came to being with Evelyn, but using that four-letter word never felt right. The disconnect was between her emotional and rational selves, mixed with a strong fear that this was all a part of an elaborate con.

"I lived my life looking for my next opportunity to put my life on the line for another adventure," Clara said.

In exchange, the Tower gave her a high degree of autonomy and funded her lavish lifestyle. Clara loved being a financially independent woman in the Roaring Twenties. Evelyn gave her just as much and more. *Why can't I say it?*

Clara kissed Evelyn on the lips, it was light and tender. There was yearning in the vampire's response but also plenty of hesitation.

"I once said that I needed you, but didn't want you," Clara said.

At the time, that was her way of living with the fact she made a deal with the devil. All to justify returning to Evelyn in exchange for resources and assistance. *An attempt to make what we have is nothing more than a business transaction.*

"You did," Evelyn said, in a whisper. "I-I-I'm fine with that."

"I was wrong," Clara said. "I may need you, but being forced apart made me realise how much I *want* to be with you…"

Evelyn smiled, her face practically glowing with excitement. This time, they kissed until Clara's lungs begged for air. The salty tears from Evelyn's face flowed nonetheless, so much so that Clara could taste the salt.

"You're my reason for coming back," Clara said.

That lower lip trembled and for a moment, Clara wondered if the water works would open up again. It appeared that Evelyn peered into the angel's soul and found what she wanted and just like that her mask was back in place.

"*N'importe quoi pour vous, mon amour*," Evelyn said. (*Anything for you, my love.*)

Clara always prided herself on being able to fake every aspect of herself. In that moment, she realised that she was a neophyte when compared to the green-eyed beauty before her.

"It will take about twenty minutes for the meal to be ready," Clara said. "Why don't you get all dolled up? We can go out for a night on the town."

"That's a wonderful idea," Evelyn said. "I'll be quick as a flash."

Evelyn was gone in the blink of an eye as vampires were capable of moving at supernatural speeds. That's how hunters would notice them, as their faces would blur, leaving people to wonder if it was just a trick of the eye. *It almost never is.*

With some time on her hands, Clara decided to prepare the table.

"Look who's coming to dinner," Clara said.

CHAPTER 7

LOOK WHO'S COMING TO DINNER

Clara was not surprised when Evelyn walked down the stairs to the main floor wearing a tight-fitting, black dress, along with the makeup and hair befitting of a runway model. With every step, a bare leg poked out of the slits in the dress.

Clara realised that her mouth was half open and snapped it shut. The grin on Evelyn's face made it clear that she very much noticed. *She lives for it.*

Although the situation was soon on the other foot, once Evelyn realised there were seven chairs at the table. Even with Clara expecting a reaction, she was challenged to catch Evelyn's smile faltering momentarily.

To further confuse the vampire, Clara went to one end of the table and pulled back the chair. Holding out her hand, Evelyn grabbed it and hopped onto her seat.

"Since when are these a formal affair?" Evelyn asked.

"Dressed as you are?" Clara confirmed. "I should hire staff to cater to your every whim."

Evelyn giggled, but this time it was forced. In the shadows, she heard her sire lurking about. The confusion and discomfort from being caught unaware must have given him a reason to investigate.

She ignored him, as Marc would certainly know if anyone else was here. Evelyn and Clara maintained a regular heartbeat, whereas his was silenced since death. *Makes it easy to know where we are at all times.*

Clara was wearing a comparatively simpler dress. As an old flapper, she often went back to the styles and fashions of her era. Like Evelyn, her dress was black, but looser to give her a boyish look. It also featured a white belt and bow tied at the back.

Other than a cupid's bow done in carmine red, Clara had no other makeup on. *I didn't have the time.*

"One second," Clara said.

She walked into the kitchen and fetched a trolley. In addition to two bowls filled with the fresh bread she bought from a *boulangerie* this morning, there were six dishes all prepared and ready to serve.

"You'll have to forgive me," Clara said. "There's only one course tonight."

Evelyn giggled, before saying, "As long as you're dessert."

Without a word, she transferred the plates to the tables. There was one dish that was decidedly out of place. It looked to be a combination of *paté* and gravy, with a cookie crumble mixed in.

That dish really got Evelyn's attention, and she even wrinkled her nose until the scent from her own plate overpowered it.

"Okay. Who have you invited?" Evelyn asked, tiring of being kept in the dark.

Clara sat and adjusted herself. She focused on those emerald-green eyes and smiled.

"No one that's not already here."

"Then why—(*are there five other plates.*)"

Clara signalled to the goddesses and went from a single individual to six. It was as though the angel was a prism exposed to white light. The transition was as quick as lightning, resulting in every chair being filled.

Evelyn gasped, but quickly covered her mouth to conceal the slight. This was not something Evelyn expected, even if she witnessed something similar take place in the summer.

"You're already familiar with Hecate and her three personas," Clara began. "Silver, Sparky and Ethereal."

The vampire played the game well, acknowledging them without staring. Although there was a pause on Ethereal, a hint that her translucency and corpse-like appearance were off-putting.

"The one with feline features, and wearing the latest in ancient, Egyptian fashion is Bastet," Clara went on.

Evelyn quickly realised why the meal choice differed for Bastet. Clara caught her gaze and winked because the selection might prove entertaining.

Closest to Evelyn was Artemis, who adopted the demeanour of an impudent teen. *Down to the crossed arms and a scowl.*

"Last we have Artemis," Clara said, and left it at that.

"I love what you've done with your hair," Evelyn said. "What's your secret?"

"The blood of my enemies," Artemis replied bluntly.

Until that moment, Clara had been getting the silent treatment exclusively. Even Silver confessed that their newest addition had yet to utter a word.

Evelyn giggled, while maintaining her impeccable composure.

"Is that all?" Evelyn asked. "I have a long list myself, especially men."

Artemis did not reply, disappointed that her attempt to intimidate failed. The angel suspected that their newest member was done with the silent treatment. *Now for the hard part.*

"You are special to me," Clara said, to Evelyn. "Like most *older* couples, we come with a lot of baggage."

She had no desire to insult the goddesses. So far, there was a *détente*, but that could change if she got into the habit of alienating them.

"You don't happen to have Adonis in there?" Evelyn asked.

"He's already dead," Ethereal said.

Even Evelyn reacted visibly to hearing that voice. A cold stare from both her sisters caused the translucent goddess to sink deeper into her chair.

"Shame," Evelyn said. "Ah well, a girl can dream. Although, I could lose myself in Artemis's eyes. Is it true that you're considered one of the most beautiful goddesses of your time?"

Evelyn flashed her trademark smile, and Clara could have sworn that Artemis was blushing. After all, that particular deity was known to have virginal women travel with her. *There might be more to that lore.*

"Why don't we dig in," Clara said. "There's always more if anyone is hungry."

Everyone reached for their utensils. It was Bastet who showed some hesitation, cocking her head to the side.

Clara's lip curled to one side and Evelyn stifled a giggle.

"None of us speak ancient Egyptian, Bastet, so we couldn't ask," Clara said. "So, I looked up delicacies for cats."

The slits in Bastet's catlike eyes made her look all the more like a predator. Clara knew from experience that in feline form this one was deadly and fast. *Even Hecate keeps a wary eye on this feline.*

The dish was known as a kitty birthday cake. It was two layers of chicken *paté*, covered in a thick gravy. Cat treats were used as a middle layer and as a topping, then scattered around for effect.

Bastet extended one of her claws and sliced through the *paté*. She then licked the claw with that rough tongue and began to purr.

Clara and Hecate visibly relaxed. They knew that the cat goddess loved to play with her food, but this angel was not about to lure men to the table for the goddess to torment and kill.

Bastet's hands transformed back into a feminine form. She then grabbed a fork and dug in.

By then, everyone else had taken a bite or poured themselves a glass of wine. Clara let the melted cheese, wine and bacon tickle her palate. It had been a long time since she prepared this particular meal, and she nearly moaned as the flavours mingled with her tongue…. *So rich… so bad… so good!*

As a surprise, Marc exited from the shadows. His movements were so silent that Clara might have missed him entirely had he not been facing her. The elder vampire approached even as Evelyn wiped off a long string of melted cheese from her chin.

"You want a taste?" Evelyn offered.

Marc rarely spoke aloud, especially with Evelyn. From what Clara understood, those two were linked by blood, sharing their thoughts and emotions without outwardly appearing to do so. *Evelyn avoids it when I'm around because she thinks it's impolite to exclude others.*

Evelyn's sire was a beautiful man, with black hair, dark brown eyes, and sunburned skin. He was built like a strongman of old, but had the demeanour and bearing of an old soldier. He was only one inch taller than Evelyn, which meant he stuck out in the modern age where women were taller on average than he was.

Evelyn picked out a bite from her plate using her fork and held it out for him. Without a sound, Marc leaned forward and enveloped the food with his lips before pulling back.

The fork was clean when he was done. Chewing slowly, as most at the table were doing, he let the flavours mingle. However, instead of swallowing he walked silently into the kitchen to spit out the food before rinsing out his mouth. *Evelyn says he reacts poorly to eating food.*

In truth, many vampires did not handle solid foods well. While most could get away with wine and drink, fewer still could grab a bite at a local greasy spoon. The poor reaction was due to an atrophied digestive system, and ingesting food for most meant making a mess that rivalled a visit to a slaughterhouse.

"My sire cannot eat food," Evelyn clarified. "He did wish to thank tonight's *hostess* for giving him a taste of home."

While not planned, it seemed that Clara made Marc's day. *At least no one has drawn blood yet.*

CHAPTER 8

DESSERT

T houghts?" Clara asked.

They were walking along the quiet streets. It was past the witching hour on a weekday in an area of the city that was in deep slumber. On occasion, a car passed by as though they were not there. *Just how I like it.*

"That was wild!" Evelyn exclaimed, through a thin scarf.

The vampire pulled Clara in and interlocked their arms. They gazed into one another's eyes and both smiled.

While Clara could not see the result, the sound of fabric brushing against those cheeks was all she needed. Winter was a dangerous time for vampires as they left telltale signs in their wake.

With every breath, Clara pushed out a stream of fog, but Evelyn's body temperature quickly dropped to match the ambient temperature. Shortly after leaving the hotel, the fog disappeared entirely. *She uses a scarf to conceal that.*

"Which part?" Clara probed.

"Where do I begin?" Evelyn countered.

"Very true," Clara replied. "Thank you for getting Artemis to open up."

"*Ma chère*, it was a pleasure to see such a *delectable* specimen smile."

Clara took a half step, leading them to fall out of sync. Evelyn looked up, and saw those glassy eyes. She pulled down her scarf and, with a hop, kissed Clara on the cheek. The jolt of cold from those lips shocked her back to reality.

"I only have eyes for you," Evelyn said. "That being said, as an artist, I can still see the... *potential* in others."

"I'm sorry," Clara confessed. "I was being—(*selfish*)."

"Human?" Evelyn countered. "Yes, you were. I felt the same when you went hunting with Julia."

"Really? You?"

"Why would that surprise you?"

"...I just never saw her in that way..." Clara blurted out. "I-I owe her."

"It's all about perception," Evelyn said. "You've never taken me on a hunt, but you drag along a *psychotic shag carpet* the first opportunity you get..."

Clara chuckled and saw where this was going. They both had insecurities, because *this* was still new for the both of them. *We have yet to set our boundaries.*

"See," Evelyn said. "You get it now..."

"But?" Clara guessed from the way her voice faded off.

"*However*," Evelyn corrected. "Why introduce me to them at all?"

That was a great question, one Clara had yet to flesh out. She knew the choice was instinctual instead of being based on reason.

"I guess I wanted you to better understand what I'm dealing with," Clara said.

"Ethereal is a poison pill," Evelyn commented. "There's wisdom in those words, but the delivery..."

"...is lacking?" Clara replied. "That's been the source of several, long spats between the sisters."

"Wait," Evelyn said. "Can they hear us?"

"I can't shut them out entirely. They did make a point of telling me they would give us some time alone. Hecate appears to be grateful for the opportunity to interact with the world."

"We should all go for a night on the town!" Evelyn said. "Get a limousine, and hit a club or three."

The idea had merit, but it was just as likely to be fun or disastrous. Hecate would need to merge her three personas; otherwise, people would react poorly to Sparky and Ethereal. *Unless...*

"It would work well for Halloween."

"Yes!" Evelyn said. "We could just be ourselves."

"...and still end up losing the costume contest..."

"All fun aside," Evelyn brought things back on track. "Marc confessed that your *surprise* threw him for a loop."

"Really? Him? Why?"

"*We all have inner demons, but Clara can manifest them for the world to see,*" Evelyn said, while mimicking his disturbing cadence.

Marc tended to speak in a way that made even Ethereal appear warm and cuddly. The words rolled off like the steps of a marching soldier. His manner of speech was entirely devoid of inflection, warmth, and emotion further marking how far removed he was from his humanity.

Clara once took a look behind his flesh and found his soul was mostly gone. *Imagine spending eternity as a cold, calculating creature without any emotional counterbalance.*

"It's eerie that you can do that," Clara said. "He should try living with them."

They came to an intersection and caught sight of a couple of large flakes falling from the sky. While there was no traffic, they waited for the lights to cycle through.

"There's more to that meal than just meeting your …coworkers?" Evelyn said.

"Family is more like. They backed my plan to look for an active gate."

"Then why discuss it with me?"

"They realised how much you mean to me and reminded me that you'd be less than impressed if I just ran off on some adventure without going over the matter with you."

"That must have been Silver?"

The crossing sign lit up and they crossed in silence.

"Nope," Clara answered.

"Who?"

"Ethereal… for both…"

"…great wisdom, but lacks delivery…" they said, in unison.

Clara kissed Evelyn on the forehead. From out of the corner of her eye, she spotted three men looking their way. Their awkward and exaggerated movements were a clue they had way too much giggle water.

"Do you see them down the road?" Clara whispered.

She was accustomed to seeing vampires appear to be in two places at once. What made this experience unsettling was being in physical contact with one while that happened.

Evelyn grabbed both of Clara's hands to keep them in place as she turned around for a good look. Clara's mind registered the sensations and visualised Evelyn facing two directions at once. *That was off-putting...*

"It looks like fun," Evelyn sang.

A vampire's concept of *fun* diverged greatly from hers. While comfortable with Evelyn feeding from the willing, allowing a vampire to let loose meant bodies and drawing unnecessary attention.

"*Ma chère,*" Evelyn began. "You know I can be a *good girl...* when the situation calls for it. Trust me."

"Okay," Clara said. "Only if they deserve it."

Evelyn giggled and pecked Clara on the lips, before replying, "*Bien sûre!*" (*Of course!*)

They had at least a block to walk before they reached the point of no return. Both acted naturally to avoid escalating matters. In their case, even crossing the street might antagonise them. *In their state, they'd see it as a slight.*

"You'll have to thank Ethereal for passing on her wisdom," Evelyn said.

"I will."

"To be clear, you're going there alone based on little more than conjecture... at best a guess."

"So was accepting your offer to assist me," Clara countered. "It worked out well for both of us."

"*Mon Dieu, oui!*" (*My lord, yes!*)

One of the men disappeared entirely from sight.

"Do you suppose he's using the alleys to get behind us," Clara said, in Latin.

"Evidently," Evelyn responded, in rusty Latin. "These are drunks, not Rommel on manoeuvres."

They sometimes exchanged more discreet statements in Latin. However, the vampire clearly spent far less time in church than Clara did. She nodded to silently acknowledge Evelyn and went back to their subject.

"It's the only lead I have," Clara said.

"You also need closure," Evelyn said.

"I'd *love* closure."

"Wouldn't we all?" Evelyn asked. "The difference is that you have an opportunity to find it."

This area primarily housed small businesses which were long closed by this hour. However, there were too many steady heartbeats around to determine if someone was doubling back on a parallel line.

"Can you track the third?" Clara asked.

Evelyn shook her head before returning to the subject.

"I want you to go and we both know you can't take me... or any other vampire."

"So, you agree with the plan?"

"I think it's the best available given your allies," Evelyn said.

"I'll wait a week to see if Julia calls," Clara began. "I have my doubts that she'll be ready for another mission."

"You'd also put her at risk," Evelyn said. "Why don't you just admit it?"

"Admit what?"

"That you want to spend another week with me?"

That was a given, and she squeezed Evelyn's hand. By then, they were close enough to have a full view of the remaining two. The footsteps behind, and heavy breathing, also confirmed this was a trap. *They really underestimated who they're up against.*

"You might get your wish," Clara said, in Latin.

"What luck! It's not even my birthday," Evelyn replied.

As they neared, Clara led Evelyn off the sidewalk to get around them. If they valued their lives, they would not do anything to warrant a—

"You two look good enough to fuck," the lead drunk said.

Clara squeezed Evelyn's hand as though lending her some courage. They moved on without acknowledging them. *One step... two steps... three steps... four—*

"They think they can just ignore us, Cody," the lead drunk repeated.

"I would say so, Erik," said the man behind them.

"She does more for me than some limp-dick asshole like you ever could." Clara countered.

"Oh, I can get it up," Erik said, while pointing down the alley. "She's a testament to that..."

They spotted a pair of bare legs, with their pants scrunched around the feet. Those legs were covered in the filth of the street and blood. If not for a faint steam of fog, Clara would have assumed the worst.

As humans, Clara or Evelyn might not have had the time to signal for help. *A night of hard drinking stripped them of reason.*

"He's—(*all yours*)."

"Clara, Bastet requests permission to join," Silver said.

Clara hid her frustration from getting cut off. Now was not the time to waste coordinating the *entertainment.*

"Kitty wants to play," Clara said, in Latin.

Those words led the drunks to look at each other with furrowed brows. It was a dead language, so very few people ever heard it spoken aloud, especially in their age group.

"Bien sûr," Evelyn said, with a smile. (*Of course.*)

Separating a goddess from the whole could be done covertly. In this case, that turned out to be a wise move tactically.

"What are we waiting for?" Cody asked.

Emboldened by *getting away* with their first violation, every man converged on them. The lead drunk went right for Clara, and lunged at her. She moved out of the way, leaving a wide berth for Evelyn.

By then, the vampire's fingertips transformed into thick, black talons. Clara knew just how sharp they could be. Hunters who survived encounters with the likes of *them* often mentioned their light armour did nothing to slow vampires down.

If not for the scarf, they would have seen her pearly, white fangs drop in place along with a twisted smile. Clara even picked up a quickening heartbeat, a sign that Evelyn was beginning to enjoy herself.

Erik nearly tripped over his feet, but stumbled through the recovery relatively fast. He lost patience and threw a punch. There was power behind that attack, but Clara grabbed his fist and arrested the forward motion entirely. They stood like that for several heartbeats, the man utterly unable to grasp what just happened.

That left Clara exposed, but she was not worried. Instead, she gradually increased pressure around his fist.

Cody ran into the fray only to be intercepted by a lithe feline that happened to be the size of a black panther. The force of the impact drove the man into the wall.

Before moving away, Bastet slashed his forehead and neck. The first blurred his vision with blood, while the latter was done with surgical precision to destroy the muscles controlling his vocal cords.

Clara gulped, but continued applying pressure. At this point, even under the influence of alcohol, he could feel intense pain building up. Those glassy eyes widened, and he was about to let out what promised to be a blood-curdling scream. She covered his mouth with a firm grip, muffling the call for help. *That might have been loud enough to wake the dead.*

Instead, there was the sound of bones popping out of their joints and snapping. It did not take much more for the man to faint, which was exactly what Clara wanted. *I swore not to take a human life, including sadistic fucks like this one.*

"I'm going to check on the woman," Clara said.

"No worries!" Evelyn said. "I'll handle the cleanup!"

"Don't forget my coat," Clara said, and left it by the alley entrance.

Evelyn must have signalled to Marc to make sure the necessary arrangements were made. *Vampires don't exist for centuries without mastering the art of making people disappear.*

As she walked towards those legs, her wings grew out from her shoulders. She did not need to take on this form, but was certain to be caught on surveillance cameras soon. *I don't need them to know that I can adopt other forms.*

The angel knelt by the woman and made the only determination that mattered. Her breathing was laboured but steady, as was her heartbeat. The angel took her by the hand and smiled, even if she did not appear to be consciously aware of what was going on.

"Let's get you to a hospital," Clara said, and in the blink of an eye they both vanished.

CHAPTER 9

IN BETWEEN

Clara appeared near the emergency room's front desk. The shock of two people appearing from out of thin air caused many to gasp, yelp, and one even grasped their chest before their pacemaker interceded.

For effect, those black wings were unfurled, which left a shadow against the floor. People surrounding her naturally gave her room. One wing drooped slightly, as Clara's mind was focused on what Evelyn and Bastet were about to do instead of adopting a picture-perfect pose.

"It's her," someone said.

"The Valkyrie," another said.

She looked at the clerk, who eventually realised there was more than the fallen angel to gawk at. When he spotted the victim, his face went white.

"*Mon Dieu*," the clerk said, in a whisper. (*My god!*)

Clara vanished, leaving the woman in good hands. Small comfort that those responsible won't live to see the sun rise.

One individual who was recording the scene dropped her phone. The spectators were silent, shocked upon discovering that their realities were layered with lies.

* * * *

To clear her thoughts, Clara spent the rest of the evening out. She ended up at an all-night diner and settled at a booth that ran along a wall. From there, she watched the wave of customers ebb and flow until the sun was high in the sky.

No one took notice of her, even though she wore a formal gown that went out of fashion on Black Thursday. That suited her just fine, because the Valkyrie was trending on Twitcher, which only served to infuse her with a surge of power.

The servers changed over shortly before she left. Fatigue was etched on their faces, and as judged by their interactions with the regulars these two often worked nights. *They both look old enough to be in their golden years.*

While not hungry, she had to admit their coffee and sugar cream pie were quite good. Still, Clara left more than half of her slice behind along with a substantial tip that left the waitress with a tear in her eye.

"Thank you," the woman with '*Isabelle*' on her nametape said.

"Enjoy your day," Clara said, before getting up and walking out into the brutal morning wind without a jacket or care.

The cold hit her like a bucket of ice water on a hot, summer day, but it did clear her mind. The shock was enough to realise that had those drunks been something that went bump in the night she would have joined in. *They never took my oath, why should they be bound by it?*

With more spring in her step, Clara made her way back home using the relatively quiet back streets. Burning through the night meant that fatigue was settling into her bones. Physically she could go on, but her mind was desperate for sleep. *So much for being a morning person.*

She went straight to the kitchen for a quick snack, and a big glass of water. After counting down from ten, Clara headed for the stairs. The only other heartbeat in this home was slower, which tied with the deep breathing. To avoid waking Evelyn, Clara removed her high heels, and left them just outside the door.

Clara carefully opened the door and slipped inside. While asleep, that could change in a second. Predators were almost always on alert, especially when left, vulnerable.

In fact, she was tempted to say that sneaking up on Evelyn was one of the greatest tests of stealth. Without so much as a word, her dress puddled onto the floor and she slipped into the bed with her wings unfurled.

She opted to return to her regular form because it often silenced the voices in her head. Before she had the chance to cover herself with her wings, Evelyn rolled over and moved in for a cuddle.

"Thank you," Evelyn said.

That voice was slower and deeper in pitch than normal, as though she was still in a dream. Clara kissed Evelyn on the cheek and covered them both with her wings.

"No details," Clara said.

"*Oui, mon amour*," Evelyn said, before nuzzling into Clara's neck while her breathing further slowed. (*Yes, my love.*)

Clara was challenged to consolidate the thoughts and emotions swirling around in her head. The idea that someone so smart, funny, and creative could love an old hunter made her heart feel light as air.

Errant thoughts lingered that poisoned her thoughts to the point of inducing physical discomfort. She knew why, but her mind had yet to fully come to terms with the truth. *We're both monsters.*

Clara focused on Evelyn and saw beyond the flesh and bone to peer at her soul. On their first encounter Clara noted the soul had been beaten and flayed to the bone.

Now, it shined brightly and was nearly as radiant as the host's personality. Good and bad were far more subjective than Clara had been raised to believe.

The vampire before her did not stop killing, but did so only to those who *deserved* it. She knew of several child predators who met a grim end, along with violent pimps and rapists. Every victim served to satiate her bloodlust while benefiting the whole. *The difference is that I was never there for those.*

Clara took an oath not to take human lives, but she could not comprehend why society gave them enough leeway and understanding to continue unabated. *She's a splotch of colour on my black and white canvas.*

"Where's my dessert?" Evelyn asked, seemingly from out of the blue.

Those words tore through her mind forcing a reset. Meanwhile, Evelyn kissed Clara's neck tenderly, the passion building up with every breath.

"You just want to distract me from myself," Clara said.

"Oh… don't submit my name for canonization," Evelyn said. "I'm aiming to enjoy *our* sin."

There came no reply, but when Evelyn reached the angel's lips, their tongues greeted each other and danced…

* * * *

Spending the morning in the throes of passion with Evelyn did wonders to help her find her centre. It helped that the vampire sent her a link to an article stating that '*the Valkyrie*' was attributed for saving the life of a victim of sexual assault. It seemed the *alleged* suspects were already out on bail for similar crimes and stated the authorities were on the lookout for them. *I'll probably be blamed for their disappearance.*

The news boosted her morale, but that did not help Clara in finding a way ahead with Julia. The werewolf had been visibly shaken when Clara took the *life* of Artemis, which further indicated they were all monsters… *How many times will I have to repeat that line before I end up believing it?*

For now, it was enough for Clara to focus on her mission. *I'll have to deal with my demons later.*

For her last mission, Clara flew into another city to use their gate to reach The Grand. This time, she could simply teleport to a point near her destination and make her way there on foot.

That meant she only needed to bring a sturdy backpack, good boots, and her twin pistols. The biggest advantage of being able to hop, skip, and jump across vast distances was that neither customs nor a nation's security apparatus would ever know she was there.

After a week went by without hearing from Julia, it was time to get going. Evelyn kissed her softly in the morning and went straight to her studio without exchanging a word. That was where the vampire would spend her days until Clara sent word or returned home.

With the room to herself, Clara shouldered the backpack, and focused on the destination.

CHAPTER 10

A HOP, SKIP, AND A DROP

T ravelling in an instant over a short distance was a snap for the mind to process. After all, the weather conditions and the sky itself were essentially the same.

That changed as the distance increased. For this particular transition, she moved through four time zones and skipped over a country entirely.

Warm, tropical air and the scent of brine were the first differences noted. Clara smiled, taking in a breath of the briny air that reminded her of home.

The natural, ambient heat was also a welcome change. It was winter back home, which meant exposure to the bitter cold or confinement to an artificial, indoor climate.

Next, was the position of the sun, or more accurately, the lack thereof. The sky to the east was beginning to take on shades of purple and blue. *The sun won't peek over the horizon for another thirty minutes.*

Clara pulled out her phone, and as predicted, there was no signal. Phones tended to get confused when they lost track of towers along with their home network. She went through the menus, switched to a local SIM, and forced the phone to scan for available networks.

Within a minute, she had data and sent a secure message to Evelyn.

> **Clara**: Having the time of my life in Mexico.

She then took a selfie of herself with her backpack. Other than being in the crepuscular light, she was dressed like most backpackers travelling the back country as a tourist. Namely, a sturdy pair of hiking boots, black leggings that fit her like yoga pants, and a dark grey, sleeveless top. She had a light coat in her backpack in case the weather turned on her.

There was no response, which was expected. Evelyn would avoid dealing with the situation by focusing on her art. Some of her best pieces, now worth millions, were made under similar circumstances.

"If they only knew about her hoard," Clara said. "Or the other names she sold under..."

Clara rarely ventured into Evelyn's studio, because it was a maze. Not only could she get lost among the clutter of pieces, but she might also lose herself in the art. Clara was also not a fan of coming across nude statues of herself… *and she gets every detail.*

"You seem less than thrilled to be here, Clara," Eleanor said.

Clara was so accustomed to hearing that voice without any warning that she did not react. It seemed the angel of death decided to bless her with a visit.

She turned around to find the First Nation's woman with raven-black hair and black eyes staring at her. As usual, she wore a long, white gown that never interacted with the physical realm. There was a faint smile, a clue that the angel was trying to appear more *human* during their interactions.

"I want to go," Clara countered.

"Why would the goddess then message the one she left behind?"

Eleanor did not knowingly attack or manipulate, because she was a construct. An angel fashioned by Hecate to guide souls to their final destination. *That means she's simply being direct.*

"You're getting too good at reading me," Clara teased.

"I've been at this for over a millennium," Eleanor replied.

What was left unsaid was that Eleanor was also everywhere. Several versions of her were active at any given time, and Clara personally witnessed multiple incarnations of the angel at a single location. *I imagine that's useful after large battles or disasters.*

"We need to hang out more," Clara said.

"Evelyn might have something to say about that."

"True."

Since she had Eleanor here, Clara decided to ask some questions.

"Have you been there?" Clara asked while pointing towards the horizon.

"Not lately," Eleanor said.

"Meaning?"

"Time is fractured there."

That much was expected, given the distortions Zachary described.

"Not the first place—(*I've encountered hiccups*)."

"This is worse," Eleanor said bluntly. "They fenced off the area and posted guards to keep the adventurous hiker from disappearing."

"*We can help you see*," Silver said.

A memory from two years ago floated to the forefront of her mind. Hecate once said they could see if someone or something did not belong in this realm.

"*Lend me your eyes?*" Clara asked.

"*You only needed to ask*," Silver replied.

The change to her vision was more subtle than expected. Everything was blurred, or more precisely shimmered until she slowed down time slightly. Most of everything was vibrating in harmony with objects surrounding them. *Except for Eleanor.*

"Why are you vibrating at a different frequency?"

Eleanor did not react. It was odd to see the angel of death as an immovable object.

"*You're out of sync with time*," Silver reminded her.

"*Oh! Right…*"

"*Eleanor doesn't exist in this reality. She merely interacts with it as needed*," Ethereal said,

That did not explain the copies, but then again, there was plenty she did not understand.

Clara returned in sync with time just as Eleanor was about to speak.

"I'm not a part of this world," Eleanor replied.

"Silver just finished saying the same," Clara said.

"She can explain it better than I ever could."

Clara smiled and slipped the straps of her backpack onto her shoulders. She figured it would take a while for her to hike the distance, scout the site and find a way in… *wait.*

"Do you know what's waiting for me?" Clara asked.

"I only know that it's not natural," Eleanor replied.

The temptation was there to press for more, but she knew from experience there was no intent to deceive. Eleanor did not have time or the luxury to learn things beyond her duties… *and sometimes that comes across as ignorant.*

"Is it dangerous?" Clara asked.

"I escorted several souls away from that site that attest to that."

"Why away?"

"The distortions create *challenges.*"

It was telling that a construct who could be anywhere and everywhere had trouble with this locale. *I still need to know.*

"I'm going."

"As the goddess wishes," Eleanor said, after bowing.

This was new behaviour for Clara and she admittedly did not like it. While she was a *goddess*, the fallen angel preferred her allies to treat her as an equal.

"Stop that," Clara said.

Eleanor did not appear to be bothered by that order. Nevertheless, Clara smiled warmly before moving in to hug the angel.

Her choice at showing a measure of affection soon became awkward. Eleanor did not return the hug and she might as well have been carved from granite. When Clara pulled away, her smile was crooked, parted just enough to see a solid row of perfect teeth.

"I'm sorry," Clara said.

"For?"

"I didn't want to hurt your feelings."

"I have none, Clara."

Clara knew that was not entirely true. Eleanor did, in fact, have something that approached emotion. She had taken liberties on several occasions to help souls pass instead of remaining in this realm. Eventually, those trapped became shadows of themselves, twisted, shallow, and sadistic. *Like poltergeists...*

"Okay," Clara replied, with no intent to push matters. "I should get going."

"Be careful."

"I w—(*will*)."

Before Clara finished, the angel of death was gone. Eleanor could be summoned back, but they both had duties to attend to.

Clara looked out in the distance, as the sun broke over the horizon, she caught the silhouette of a high fence against the red sun. Just beyond were the ruins of an old church, destroyed during a conflict that slipped through the cracks of history.

"Right," Clara said. "Off we go."

* * * *

Clara last walked through these lands during the Roaring Twenties. She had been on her way here when the Terminus was attacked, resulting in a complete loss of the gate network. Like the Tower, this structure did not exist as part of the physical world and was only accessible by one of its many gates.

The memory of a ball of fire approaching her as she was shunted to an alternate exit point was seared in her mind. Just a flash of that memory was enough to force Clara to suppress a physical response.

"The flames scorched the back of my dress," Clara quipped.

With no other choice, Clara travelled overland by train and ended up walking along the same, dusty road. The difference a century made was significant. Back then, the scars from the conflict were fresh. *The scent of cordite lingered in the air.*

Now, the jungle had reclaimed most of it. Some patches of earth remained scorched, while others appeared as though the land was rendered to an arid desert. Her vision allowed her to see that these patches vibrated at different frequencies. *Alternate realities that blended in with our own.*

"*Be careful,*" Silver said. "*Interaction with pockets may have unexpected consequences.*"

"*Like?*"

Clara quickly learned how to internalise her replies to avoid appearing unhinged. *Hearing voices and replying back is not seen as a hallmark of sanity.*

"*From benign to lethal,*" Ethereal replied.

"Sounds like the side effects of medication… *So, avoid at all cost,*" Clara said.

There was no response, and Clara shifted her focus to the scene. This church must have been grand in its day, as even an artillery barrage could not strip away every intricate detail in the surviving mouldings and sculptures.

It occurred to Clara that she never reached the gate last time. A former mentor and friend of hers, Edith, laid out a trap which Clara fell for. Through their attempt at interrogation, Clara learned the church was destroyed by a powerful vampire named Drusilla.

"Public enemy number one for every hunter."

Drusilla was an ancient vampire who made it her life purpose to destroy the Tower and subjugate mankind. Clara and this vampire crossed paths on numerous occasions, with Clara surviving despite being utterly outmatched. *Luck had a big part to play in my making it out alive.*

After Clara was cut off from the Tower, she dedicated her time to hunting down the vampire. In the end, she was not hard to find, given the wild parties she held to celebrate her latest victory.

"We both died at The Grand a month later…" Clara said.

"*The good old days,*" Ethereal teased.

"You see a *lot* more action with me," Clara countered.

Hunter gates were normally concealed behind an existing doorway, with crypt doors being popular when located in a cemetery. *The idea was to select a door that people overlooked and rarely used.*

She remembered hearing the story of a couple living in a house for twenty years, only to *discover* a door that opened up into a room under their front lawn. It turned out the previous owner built a bunker there, replete with a pool of fresh water, supplies, and a sizable weapons cache. *People only notice what they wish to see.*

The church was in ruins, so the doorway could be anywhere. Given the passage of time, the scorch marks denoting ground zero had been erased by mother nature. *I have no idea where to start.*

Clara felt a tug, as though she were being drawn and quartered. It was a sign that one or more of the goddesses wanted to come out and play. She had seen Hecate deal with her sisters splitting from the whole. Clara swore that Silver had to physically hold back her sisters from breaking away.

"*Please,*" Silver said.

After a quick nod, the tugging sensation returned with a vengeance. In the span of a heartbeat, a copy of Clara stood a foot away, before taking on the visual traits of the goddess.

"I'll never get used to that," Clara said.

"I never did," Silver said, as her sisters groaned.

"Comforting…"

A thought crept into Clara's mind, "Wait… Why did I feel it this time?"

There was a brief pause, before Silver answered, "I initiated the process."

"How about this? Unless it's an emergency, I'll handle it…"

"That's a perfectly reasonable request."

Silver turned around in place several times before stopping. *I wonder if she's dizzy or there's something of note.*

Clara aligned herself to face that direction. At first, there was nothing, but there came a flash reminiscent of a lightning strike. Clara began to count.

One…

There was nothing. Not even the sound of insects or birds.

Two…

The silence weighed on her like a ton of bricks.

Three…

There came another flash. Clara started counting down from one again and on the count of three the flash returned.

"Like a beacon?" Clara asked.

"Very good, Clara," Silver said. "What else did you notice?"

She had to think about it and used this opportunity to further slow time. Six of every seven flashes had a different frequency than their reality. *Their timing is short.*

"Every seventh flash is of our reality," Clara said.

"Twenty-first," Silver corrected. "The seventh and fourteenth are closely aligned with our own, but nevertheless different."

"The difference a couple of millennia of experience can make." Clara said. "Do you think we can make it?"

"Yes," Silver confirmed.

They used the *beacon* to guide their way through the ruins until they came upon a collapsed floor. The fragments of the ceiling nearby indicated this had once been part of the attic.

At the centre of this piece of flooring, Clara spotted a hatch. It glowed, the colours and frequency changing with every flash before fading out of reality.

"Be careful," Silver said, before returning to the whole. "It might be easier if we do it as one."

Clara approached as much as she dared. Whatever this phenomenon was, there was no need to open the door. The doorway to the Terminus was damaged and effectively locked open.

Five…

Silver was counting, and Clara prepared for the countdown.

Four...

Clara tightened the straps on her backpack.

Three...

Clara slowed her heart and took a deep breath.

Two...

She exhaled, and calmed her heart.

Now!

Clara hopped onto the gateway. She expected to fall through, or transition from one point to the other. Instead, there came the sound of steel-toed boots slamming onto wood.

"What the—"

The flash of light enveloped her, leaving Clara to wonder if she was herself made up of light. But it was the sudden sensation of falling, shifting the contents of her stomach that got her attention.

With that, Clara fell through the solid hatch cover...

CHAPTER 11

FRACTURED REALM

H orsefeathers," Clara swore.

No sound left her lips, but the words echoed back at her from separate directions. Clara scanned those points to find a cause. *Nothing.*

"At least nothing the human eye can see," Clara said.

This appeared to be the Terminus she knew well, at least for some parts of it. Clara thought back to her first visit here, after having been told to go through a small door in a cemetery, finding herself within the hunter gate network.

The Terminus was first and foremost a long corridor that stretched on for so long that one barely noticed the curvature in the walls. The black onyx stones were seamless, and the source of light bled through a thin gap in the vaulted ceiling. Every door was identical, with seven grouped by section and identified by an arch denoted by a biblical reference.

Hunters could not rely on multiple-destination gates like the vampires did. There were risks associated with a system that rotated through destinations. Besides, some of their endpoints were clearly not meant for humans.

As a result, the Tower relied on obfuscation to confuse anyone who found their way inside.

"Some of the initiates lost their minds while trying to find their way through here."

Clara found herself surrounded by bubbles of reality. Some clearly aligned with her vision of the Terminus, but the more she looked, the more subtle nuances became apparent.

"There's no 1 Corinthians Chapter 17…" Clara said, in reference to the clue that served to find her way into the Tower.

Other bubbles diverged greatly from the reality she knew. One featured a hall fashioned from quartz, while another had stone walls that showed signs of melting due to exposure to intense heat. *Turned into glass.*

A smaller bubble crossed her path bringing with it screams of agony that made the hairs on the back of her neck stand straight. What bothered her was not that someone was screaming per se, because that was part and parcel with hunting. *Holy water tends to do that to vampires.*

"That's me…"

That was her voice screaming in agony, and as judged by other sounds filtering through the rift, she was being burned alive. That must have been an alternate exit point. It was sobering to learn firsthand just how lucky she was. *I missed being engulfed by flames by a fraction of a second.*

"*Clara,*" Silver said.

"Where the fuck am I?" Clara blurted out, her voice once more originating from seemingly out of the ether.

"*You said that aloud,*" Sparky chimed in.

That bubbly and energetic personality nearly defused the situation. However, Clara remained at risk. These bubbles were in motion and they might intersect with her at any time. *Given the unpredictable nature of what lies within.*

"I know," Clara said. "I'm not trying to be a mustard plaster, but this is clearly not what I expected."

"*We… miscalculated,*" Silver said.

Clara laughed maniacally while doing an all-around search to ensure there were no *surprises* on the horizon. *I'm not even sure that moving is wise.*

"*It's not,*" Silver replied.

"You do know that you can admit we fucked up?" Clara asked. "I doubt you'd put me and by extension yourselves at risk."

They never broached the subject of what would happen if Clara just dropped dead. While gods committing deicide brought about a transfer of powers and persona, Clara had no idea of the effects of a god or goddess succumbing to their wounds.

"*We've seen your wrathful side,*" Artemis snapped.

"True," Clara said, with a grin. "My point still stands, it's not like I can shoot myself with a bolt of magical energy just to spite you."

There were likely ways of getting at them individually, but Clara had no desire to discourage future discourses. *I got lucky the last time they tried a coup and there's no way to know if I'd come out on top again.*

There was chatter in the back of her mind, and Clara guessed the *council* was deliberating her words. Once the whispers died down, it was Silver who delivered the consensus.

"*We assumed the gate in our reality was functional.*"

"*Mean—(ing)?*"

To Clara's knowledge, none of the gates worked after the attack on the Terminus. When she dropped into position, Clara interacted with a solid object. *Until reality switched to one where this place was still active.*

"…Fuck me…"

"*Exactly,*" Silver said.

This wasn't their reality… *not by a long shot.* The most pressing question came with an obvious answer.

"*We don't know,*" Silver replied anyway.

"Just ducky," Clara said.

"*Our sentiments exactly,*" the three personas of Hecate said, in unison.

"Does Bastet or Artemis have anything to add?"

In hindsight, it might have been easier to escape into her mind and confer with them. However, Clara did not want to be caught unawares if a reality bubble crept up on her.

As a precaution, she slowed down time, but the attempt proved to be ineffective. The space inside this Terminus responded as expected, but the bubbles were immune. *I'm going to run out of swears.*

There came no response and that was sadly what she expected. The ability to see the sub-atomic vibrations was something Hecate possessed. *It would be a fluke to absorb anyone else with that particular skill set.*

"I'm going to start moving," Clara said.

"*How will that help?*" Silver asked.

A good question, to which she had no good answer. The truth was Clara had to do something and the idea of waiting for her doom did not sit well with her. *It's like sitting out in the middle of the woods, covered in barbecue sauce, naked during a full moon.*

"*Yesh*," Ethereal said, followed by the sound of her upchucking.

"*That was kind of hot*," Sparky said, to antagonise her sister.

"Like I need the image of Ethereal spewing chunks inside my mind…" Clara countered.

This exchange did have the advantage of relieving some of the anxiety concerning the immediate danger.

"Still… Evelyn is going to be pissed…"

* * * *

Clara walked on for what appeared to be an eternity. The Terminus was designed to influence people psychologically, with everything looking the same, rows upon rows of doors on both sides that looked to be no different from the ones prior.

"I don't have a suitcase with me this time," Clara said.

She ended up using the suitcase as a point of reference the first time she was here. In turn, Clara learned the hall was circular in nature.

"Not like Jack helped any…"

Jack was an acolyte a year ahead of her at the Tower. They would send acolytes into the Terminus posing as a new arrival to help initiates find their way to their new home. *Jack slowed me down.*

"I'd have beaten the record if not for him," Clara said with every word oozing with venom.

Clara never told a soul that she once had a crush on the older boy. An attraction that transcended the physical, which made the impact he had on her life more poignant.

Jack was like Clara in many ways, someone who sought to upset the apple cart and enjoy the ensuing chaos. The difference was that Clara was a good hunter who aimed to make the world a safer place. Whereas her crush went the other way and was expelled for reasons that were never made public. When they met years later, it did not take him much coaxing to get her into his bed naked and willing.

"Evelyn's not the only one of her kind who lures in prospects with little more than a smile."

Jack had been turned by the likes of *them*. Clara remembered how the chance encounter had been too convenient and how a tiny voice in the back of her head was screaming for Clara to wake up and run. *Instead, he modulated his voice, and I complied without resistance.*

Unbeknownst to her, the Tower placed a failsafe in her mind. She reacted violently and regained her faculties shortly after Jack's head rolled off the bed.

"I was drenched in blood," Clara said.

Coming back alive from that encounter earned her a place among an elite group of female acolytes. *I got to spend more time with Edith.*

Edith was a woman a couple of years ahead of her. As a young acolyte, Clara could not help but worship the older student who seemed to have the world at her fingertips. When they assigned Edith and Clara to the same hunting team, she felt as though the Lord himself sanctioned their friendship. *The best of times and the worst of times...*

"I had to fuck that one up too," Clara added.

"*You sure know how to make friends,*" Ethereal said.

"Too true..." Clara replied, while tasting the bitterness in her mouth.

Owning up to her own failures had a way of shutting up Ethereal. The goddess of death and ghosts was not accustomed to people agreeing with her.

"Nothing?" Sparky asked before whistling.

The sound cut through Clara's mind causing lightning bolts to fill her field of vision. She winced and closed her eyes until it subsided.

After taking a long breath, she opened her eyes, the world before her was marred by purple streaks. *This is something new.*

Without realising, Clara was back in sync with time. The world before her lacked detail as though pushing through a hard night of heavy drinking, causing the contents of her stomach to do somersaults. The burp that followed was vile, heavy with the taste of acid and bile. *If I didn't know better—*

Clara dropped to her knees and evacuated the contents of her stomach. She did so several times, even though there was nothing left. After wiping the bile from her lips, she tried to stand again and felt no better than before. *I don't get motion sickness!*

There came a snap of someone's fingers and a bubble of time enveloped them. Just like that everything within the bubble quit shimmering and her stomach settled. *I still have one hell of a headache.*

"Thank you," Clara managed to say, after turning her back to the mess she made.

"Apologies, Clara," Silver said. "We didn't realise that seeing the world through our eyes came with side effects."

"Probably made worse by being within the Terminus. Everything looks the same save for the odd bubble that moves counter to what the mind expects."

"What can we do to help?" Silver asked.

"Give me a minute," Clara said. "Will this bubble hold?"

The bubble itself could be held as long as needed, but Clara was worried about the interactions with other anomalies. The world beyond the shimmering wall kept on moving. *Putting us all at risk.*

"We don't—(*know*)."

"Give me a moment…"

She took several deep breaths, and after a quick nod, the bubble collapsed. Clara focused on slowing down time and realised it did not take much of an offset for the nausea to taper off.

"Well," Clara began. "At least I have a point of reference now."

Clara turned back towards her direction of travel and the unease increased substantially. She instinctively closed her eyes and swore like a sailor for putting herself through this.

When she opened her eyes, the feeling of nausea returned. The scent of partially digested toast and eggs from this morning did not improve her condition. *What the…*

"…fuck…" Clara said.

Unable to handle the nausea, she turned around and experienced immediate relief. She furrowed a brow and crinkled her lips on the same side, further distorting her face.

"What if?" Clara pondered.

She shifted her angle and realised the sense of nausea and relief worked a bit like a compass. *Where does the needle point to?*

"At least I have a reason to get away from that smell…" Clara said.

She pushed out a narrow jet of air from her lips to clear out a stray piece of hair in her field of vision. Clara kicked off and walked until she felt right as rain.

"*That's our reality!*" Silver exclaimed.

It was another roving bubble just like the others encountered so far. This reality was the biggest one yet.

Several roving bubbles of reality floated by, moving along the three axes. Sometimes one blocked her view and her interdimensional sea sickness returned with a vengeance…. *This area is far more fractured.*

"Have we gone full circle?"

That was too convenient an answer. Clara closed her eyes, took in several deep breaths and turned around to face the other way.

Her *mess* was nowhere to be found. Clara must not have walked long enough to lose track of it. *It's over the horizon.*

This version of the Terminus was also an enlarged circle, but how she moved throughout differed.

"I just walked around this world…"

A sobering thought to be sure, one that would further confuse acolytes and their foes.

"Well, going straight for our reality won't work…" Clara said.

Without thought, she eyed the point she wanted to reach and imagined herself there.

"Clara!" the collective voices of Hecate yelled.

The warning came too late. Clara faded out of existence on a path that intersected with one of the distortions. At that moment, six copies of Clara came into being. That changed as the individual personas took on their distinctive appearances and dress. They writhed in agony before shooting out in their own paths.

Clara never saw where she landed. The shock of being torn apart so violently rendered her unconscious before slamming into something hard.

CHAPTER 12

OLDEST PROFESSION

After regaining her senses, Clara did not know if she was supposed to be alarmed or aroused. Something was pushing in and out of her nethers, and the rhythmic motion was having a very real effect on the whole of her body. *What the fuck?*

A wave of pleasure built up with every thrust and she knew it would not be long before climax. The motions were practised and, most importantly, skilled. *Only she manages to consistently hit the right spot.*

"Evelyn," Clara whispered.

Her partner stopped cold, and she was too far away to sail on through to ecstasy. Instead, she felt something pulsate between her legs, shooting hot liquid into her. The worst was the accompanying grunt that was decidedly not feminine. *I haven't been with a man in months.*

Clara's eyes shot open, her vision momentarily blurred by the blinding light beaming through an open window. *The shape of that face is all wrong.*

"You're not—(*Evelyn*)," Clara said.

"Who's—(*Evelyn*)," Jack said.

The last time she heard that voice, that man went into detail on how painful her death would be. *It can't be.*

"Jack?" Clara asked.

While outwardly calm, Clara's mind struggled to deal with the flood of thoughts and emotions that hit her. Their last encounter ended in his death, so waking up with the man she beheaded forced her to question everything she knew.

As her eyes adjusted to the light, the man's features gained clarity. Several traits were straight out of her memory, such as his chiselled jaw, cleft chin, and piercing, blue eyes. Other traits diverged greatly, like the salt and pepper in his hair, and a crooked nose that came to those who got into one fight too many.

His face was also covered in coal dust. Even through all that sweat and grime, Clara noticed his five o'clock shadow. His face and the well-built body were signs of someone who worked hard for a living. Even through his union suit, with that iconic flap revealing his bare ass, Clara could see the muscles outlined. *I'd guess he's about a decade older.*

"Who else?" Jack asked. "Who's Evelyn?"

She felt Jack deflate from inside of her before slipping out. That missed orgasm tapered off before fading away like a dream, whereas her discomfort increased markedly. Before rolling off the bed, Jack wiped the head of his cock against her leg, smearing her skin with his seed.

The way he focused on her hinted that his motivations went beyond curiosity. What confused her was the obvious disconnect in the era. Evelyn was a modern-day development, and long underwear had not been in fashion for over a century.

She averted her gaze to have a better look at her surroundings. There was paint peeling from the ceiling and walls, along with cracks in the plaster, and she felt a breeze from the closed windows. If not for the floor creaking every time Jack shifted, Clara would have no idea where she was. *This is where Mama died...*

She was about to smile as memories from her youth resurfaced, but the strong scent of semen wafted her way. Far stronger than a single miner could manage.

"This is all wrong…" Clara whispered.

"What was that?" Jack asked, his smile fading as he tensed his jaw.

"…a girl I met in church," Clara said, after realising she could not avoid answering his question. "She mentioned that her father was looking to invest in the mine."

It was a plausible explanation for her uttering the name. *He wouldn't believe the truth either way.*

Jack laughed, as he slipped on his suspenders. *Didn't he just get off a shift?*

"What's so funny?" Clara asked.

"You're lying," Jack said. "I almost bought it too."

"But?"

"The Reverend doesn't allow whores in his church."

Was that why they stopped going to church after their father died? Clara was a child when her mother was forced to sell her body to provide for them. She had been so young back then that she only became aware of it years after the fact.

The church bells chimed in the distance, their sound brought on by the breeze. The scent of brine and low tide assaulted her senses and mercifully carried away the scent of his seed.

"Speaking of which," Jack began.

He searched through his pockets for some change. With all that racket, Clara expected to see a small fortune. Instead, he produced six, silver coins, which may as well have been a slap to the face. *I won't let him see how much this hurts.*

Clara closed her legs and pulled up a blanket, to cover herself. She was not wearing much, little more than a slip. For a woman who approached vampires stark naked, Clara never felt more exposed.

"I should get going," Jack said.

"Fine…" Clara said. "Evelyn is a sultry vampire who knows how to get me off every time."

At least this version had a flair for the fantastical which might keep him talking.

It was said that the eyes were the windows to the soul and his proved telling. Quick as a flash, Clara caught a mix of confusion and surprise reflected in those irises. However, Jack broke into a laugh, pushing out all remaining emotions from his eyes.

"Is that the one who killed Ada?" Jack asked.

Clara could not contain her surprise, leading to her mask faltering. Her mouth went agape, because that lined up with a potential fate for her eldest sister. *Why would Drusilla come here to kill my sister but leave me be?*

"Out of all the Grey women," Jack said. "You were always my favourite."

That might have been meant as a compliment, but it certainly did not come across as such. *It's certainly not a comment about my beauty or intelligence.*

"You always come up with the wildest stories. Was this inspired by Dracula? No… Carmilla?"

Before Clara could counter, Jack added, "Do you know what the merchant seamen at the pub say about women like you?"

It was out of character for her, but Clara felt as though her strength and resolve was being sapped from her bones. The more Jack's *gift* oozed out from her, the less she felt like herself.

Unable to utter a single word, Clara shook her head while using every trick she knew to keep from shedding a tear. *I won't let this bastard win.*

Jack leaned in close enough for his vile breath to nauseate her. She nearly recoiled, but a part of her somehow knew that he used his fists to cope with disappointment.

"The crazy ones are always wild in bed," Jack said.

He casually dropped the coins on her bedside table, which made a racket as they settled. The amount he left behind barely qualified as a pittance. *One thing that hasn't changed is his swagger.*

"What my wife lacks in bed..." Jack said. "...she makes up for in respectability."

It was one thing to suspect something, it was another matter entirely to have it confirmed. Before opening her eyes earlier, she had vivid memories of a life that now appeared impossible for her to have.

Doubt seeped into her mind, poisoning her soul. *Is my life nothing more than the delusions of a twisted psyche?*

* * * *

Shortly after Jack left, Clara secured the house. Some of the locks were too worn to be effective, so she got creative to ensure the doors were barred.

All the while, Jack's *best* half trickled out of her. She ignored it as best she could, but wanted nothing less than a hot shower. *That's not going to happen if all I have is a hand pump.*

Not five minutes after the house was *secured* did a john show up. He was wearing his Sunday best, looking to cash in on his penance for kneeling before God. *Wait... I remember him as a kid! He came knocking at our door asking for Mama...*

Clara ignored the knocking and even slipped behind a wall to avoid being seen as he circled the perimeter. The idea that she was basically always open for business made her skin crawl. *How desperate am I?*

There were three other men who followed this one. Some even exchanged polite words as they crossed paths, making up an excuse as to why they were in the neighbourhood.

"Is this real?" Clara whispered.

* * * *

Clara stood stark naked in front of a cracked mirror. The draught from the windows ran over her skin, turning it to gooseflesh. At least she was clean... *even if I don't feel it...*

"I have no memories of this life..." Clara said.

Those she had were more vivid than anything she experienced before. She never remembered selling her body to make ends meet in a mining town. *Where the company owns everything and everyone.*

That did not mean that this situation was imagined, since she looked to be about five years younger. While she had the advantage of youth, life had been hard on her.

She was thin enough for her ribs to peek through, and her bust smaller by about a cup size. She was pale, hairy, and her body was covered in bruises. Some of which appeared to be accidental. *Those around my wrists sure as hell aren't.*

Along with the weight loss, there was a distinct lack of musculature. Clara was not a bodybuilder, but her muscles were normally toned, showcasing a high level of fitness.

"The lack of wings is hard to miss."

The most damning feature was her face. The Tower modified Clara to appear more appealing to those she hunted. Evelyn once commented that the angel was nearly perfectly symmetrical.

There were flaws she did not remember. She had a mole near her nose on her right side, scars from what appeared to be acne. *Then there's the sunken cheeks and dark patches under my eyes.*

Clara remembered being a hunter for at least a decade by this point. She had served as a nurse in the Great War and by now was hunting on her own.

At this age, Clara had several kills under her belt and lost track of the number of times she nearly died. *Be it death from exposure, evisceration, immolation, or being tortured for information I never knew.*

"I never looked this rough," Clara said. "Even after hoofing the night away at some clip joint."

It was said that prostitution was the world's oldest profession. *It clearly doesn't pay enough to live a comfortable life.*

A quick search of the kitchen and pantry revealed the cupboards were nearly bare. The home was in such disrepair that Clara wondered if she would end up being whisked away to Oz if a nor'easter hit. Her clothes were little more than rags. *I doubt my clients really care about my attire.*

"This isn't life…"

Clara's normally iron grip on her emotions broke entirely. As tears streamed down her cheeks, she grabbed a shawl and huddled in the corner of her childhood home.

The room was bare, the contents likely sold off or burned to keep warm. While she had a bed, Clara could not fathom returning to it. *I'll never feel clean again.*

* * * *

Clara woke up the next morning freezing. Despite the urge to pee, she had no desire to run into a john while venturing to the outhouse. Instead, she used a chamber pot, while her thoughts lingered on the door with a crescent moon carved into it.

"That's where Papa died."

The memory of that night took centre stage. Clara remembered the blued lips and the black blood from coal dust all over his long johns. Clara had to pee then too, which explained why she tried to wake up her father. *He was already gone.*

"That ghoul is the reason I left this town. Wait a minute... the council has been quiet."

The depth of her emotional despair ought to have weakened the walls between the goddesses and her conscious mind. Hecate once exploited this vulnerability at a pivotal moment during an encounter with Ada to escape. *Which ironically saved the day.*

Her mind was silent, which was something she was decidedly no longer accustomed to. Clara hated hearing the sisters and their incessant bickering at first. Once she reached an understanding with them, the angel discovered they had much to offer.

"At least I have my own voice to keep me company..."

Those words did not comfort her at all. She imagined herself standing in a cavernous space, unable to see more than a foot or two ahead. Every time she yelled out to see if someone was there, only a variation of her voice echoed back... *twisted and taunting.*

"No," Clara said. "Enough is enough."

* * * *

Clara rummaged through *her* things until she found something passable to wear. This dress was decades out of style, and folded in with a cedar shingle.

She pressed the dress against her body, and realised that it was not hers. She remembered seeing it in an old picture of her parents on their wedding day.

"It's been here all this time?" Clara asked herself.

Without the emotional element to this dress, Clara might have left it in the trunk. However, there was something about making a connection to her past, to a bygone era before life went off the rails for the Grey family.

"It didn't last long," Clara mused.

She remembered her mother being so tall as a child. By the way the dress fit on Clara, her mother must have been at least a half a head shorter.

"I wonder if she was saving it for one of us?"

Instead, she died and took her *surprise* to her grave. The Grey sisters never saw each other again in life. *I still don't know what happened to Maria.*

"If I was at my regular weight, this dress would fit me like a glove," Clara said, while looking at her reflections in the broken mirror. "I don't mind showing off my knees."

It took more effort than expected to find a needle and thread. All the while, her *clients* continued making their rounds, hoping for more than a passing glimpse. The idea of living off the proceeds of sex caused her tummy to fill up with bile… *or is it just because of my empty stomach?*

Clara burped, the acid burning its way up through her oesophagus. It left a bitter taste in her mouth, which was happening all too often of late.

"It can't be easy living day-to-day without knowing if you'll eat."

That explained her reasons for resorting to prostitution. The difference was that her mother did so to keep her three daughters fed. *Even then, we had to do half the town's laundry to get by.*

"They already think I'm a whore," Clara said.

With that she sat on the floor, where the bed she shared with her sisters had been. More memories of her all too brief, childhood resurfaced and put a smile on her face. She channelled that positive energy to mend her mother's dress…

CHAPTER 13

HIGH STREET

Hunters received a broad education that went beyond combat. Male hunters picked up a trade as acolytes to help them settle within a community. *Being a smithy enables them to mend their weapons.*

Female hunters were more limited in their choices. Much of that had to do with society's view of women in the workplace when she grew up. Clara learned how to type, sew, dance, and play several musical instruments.

These were varied skills that enabled her to pose as a lady or a servant to one. If not for the Great War, Clara would have never learned nursing, which she loved doing when otherwise not busy hunting things that went bump in the night.

"So much death," Clara said, to herself, as she walked down the dusty road.

Nursing soldiers to health before the advent of antibiotics meant that many succumbed from their wounds. More so when chemical weapons were introduced to the battlefield. *I'll never forget seeing the men writhe in pain, covered in mustard gas blisters.*

To keep her mind from dwelling on her wartime life, Clara shifted her focus to the houses ahead. She remembered little of her life in town, but knew this road led to the mine, houses, and of course, the company store.

Like all corporation towns, all the homes were similar in style. There was no interest in promoting individuality as that cost money... *and encourages free thought.*

Most of the workers lived in cookie-cutter homes that were half the size of the one she occupied.

As judged by the kids running around, large families made do within these cramped homes. She imagined five or six children sharing a single bed, and in some cases doing so with their parents as well.

Everyone who crossed her path were confused, giving way to an ire or averting their gaze entirely. The worst offenders were presumably the spouses of her *clients*, while the children were by nature more inquisitive. *I doubt it's the dress.*

Clara bit the inside of her cheek to maintain a stoic appearance and went on her way. The houses thinned out as she neared the high street. *Not exactly a metropolis.*

Ahead, there were two churches on opposite sides of the street, a public house, hotel, and of course, the company store. While sparse, the latter served as the unofficial nerve centre of the community.

Clara was too young to remember the church they went to. They stopped going entirely once her father passed away. However, the crucifix atop the steeple and general style of the simple, wooden church implied that was the Catholic church.

"Only the Irish go there," Clara said.

She had forgotten how poorly the Irish were treated back *home.* Some who attended the Protestant church considered the Irish to be parasites. *Especially the bosses who own the mine and the situation worsened if you happened to be French.*

No Irishman would ever amount to more than a labourer at the mine. Which was not entirely true, because her father did climb the social ladder by marrying his way up. *Mama was a Protestant…*

In a way, that may have been the reason why her father had the support of the workers after he died. He never forgot his origins. *That's why we managed to keep the house.*

"Funny," Clara began. "They'd all give a Frenchman the time of day over me…"

That was a sobering realisation. For all Clara remembered, had seen and done, none of that meant a damn to the townspeople. *Even if I had gone into nursing during the war, my soiled past would have damned me either way.*

She reached the company store and stepped onto the boardwalk. A woman she did not recognise exited as Clara was about to enter, and her jaw dropped visibly.

Clara smiled politely, and said, "Hello…"

All the while, the woman acted as though her feet were nailed to the boardwalk, eyes wide, jaw agape, and barely breathing. Clara was tempted to make a smart-assed remark, but figured she was already on thin ice. *They'll not tolerate the local whore making a scene.*

* * * *

"Mama. What is she doing here?" a young child asked her mother upon seeing Clara.

The angel did her best not to react, only glancing at the mother and child. Neither were recognisable which was a recurring theme for the day. *You'd think at least one person would spark a memory.*

The mother went white as a sheet and those lips nearly disappeared from being pressed together. Clara was accustomed to blending into the background when in her human form. It was said that '*clothes maketh man*,' but she clearly needed to change more than her attire to rehabilitate her reputation.

She mostly remembered the handful of sweets her friends would get for a penny. While the candy was still by the till, everything else was unfamiliar to her.

Clara nodded politely to both the mother and child; while wondering why the one she crossed paths with was still at the threshold. Her question was soon answered when a fire lit in those eyes, and she went straight for the counter.

"Missus Bradbury," a young man said.

The man must have been in his early twenties, well-built, sandy blonde hair and tall. It did not take much for Clara to guess he was related to the older gentleman near the dry goods.

"Since when do you…(*allow that harlot in here*)?"

Clara only caught the first part. Despite speaking at a whisper, those pent-up emotions boiled over sounding like a hushed yell. After catching the reaction from both clerks, the woman soon realised her place and corrected her tone.

From the body language alone, Clara could see that everyone in the store reacted poorly to her presence. The young man looked in her direction before taking in a sharp breath.

"Father," the young man said.

That man's response was in line with the rest, wincing once he made the connection. *You'd think he'd just walked into a wild rose bush and got intimately familiar with a thorn.*

After the initial shock wore off, the father marched into the storeroom. As judged by repeated clicking and blowing of air, Clara concluded that the elder was on the blower. *This must be serious.*

She had two choices here. The first was to see how far this rabbit hole went. The second was to exercise the better part of valour and leave. *I think this explains quite nicely why my cupboards are bare.*

"Excuse me," Clara said, politely before doing an about-face.

With her mind entirely fixated on this Greek tragedy unfolding before her eyes, she missed the fact there was someone right behind her. Clara took a step back before catching her bearings and slammed into his chest.

"Sorry!" Clara exclaimed.

She grabbed the edge of a shelf to steady herself, causing it to shake. The idea of further making a scene led her heart rate to shoot up to the point of the pulsating blood vessels distorting her vision.

The man did not offer a hand or any assistance, but his musk, even through the coal dust, told her everything she needed to know. *That's Jack...*

"This is the company store," Jack said. "Employees and *their families only...*"

His voice was cold, dark, and entirely devoid of emotion. For a man who had no trouble finishing off in her, the disconnect sent a chill down her spine. *I remember why I freed Jack's head from his shoulders.*

"*Whores* aren't welcome," Jack said, under his breath.

Right beside him was the woman and child from earlier. The girl was out of breath as though she ran out to fetch her father.

A twisted smile crept over the mother's face. This scene must have been unfolding exactly as she predicted, a delicious bit of revenge served cold for all the world to see.

When Clara tried to walk past him, he moved to block her. That made her blood come to a boil. Ladies were known to slap anyone who offended them, but Clara had never been a lady.

She made a fist, with her thumb on the outside and followed through with a jab to his stomach. The motion was quick and fuelled by her temper.

Emaciated as she was, there was little power behind that punch. But the placement was enough to make him crumple up, exposing his vulnerable head. This time, she followed through with a knee to his nose and was rewarded by a satisfying *crack*.

"Bank's closed you fucking, drugstore cowboy!" Clara yelled.

The twisted smile on his wife's face transitioned to a wild-eyed stare. Clara walked on by, and it was her turn to mimic that same sadistic smile causing the girl to cower behind her mother's dress.

"I'd keep a closer eye on your husband, if I were you. You might find his proclivities… *catching*," Clara said, before stepping out of the general store.

CHAPTER 14

SANCTUM

After landing a blow to Jack's nose, Clara could barely hold herself together. The moment the door slammed behind her, she bolted around to the back of the general store. From there, she travelled between buildings for cover.

She knew the repercussions would be severe. Jack would not take such a humiliation lightly, and she witnessed his dark side firsthand as a vampire. *Whatever he does, it will be violent and final.*

Clara massaged her fist; sure, that it would be tender for a couple of days… *but it was worth it!*

It seemed that God wished to relieve her of the burden of having too many options. The first of which was to head home and await further judgment. *He'll be on guard next time.*

There was always the possibility of making a run for it. A viable option if she could hop on a train. *I can't afford the fare and won't make it far on foot.*

"*Sanctum*," Clara whispered.

That word resonated within the depths of her mind, and Clara smiled.

"It's the best option I have to work with…"

* * * *

While Clara had a way ahead, she was betting on assistance from a faith that she abandoned years ago. She had seen things that hinted that God and Heaven were not as advertised.

However, it was the Church that gave her a chance to prove herself. She earned it the night Father Michael died and never looked back. *My biggest strength and failure as a person.*

Hunters were expected to play games of misdirection, but Clara felt that speed led to salvation. Delays created by laying false trails and feints would give Jack and his allies time to find her. *I doubt anyone from town will help me.*

Before a crowd built up around the company store, Clara was already approaching the Catholic church from the rear. She suspected there was an entrance for the priest and was thankfully proven correct.

She chanced a peek down the street towards the store. Jack was there, hands and face covered in blood. While she was too far away to catch what was being said, the wind saw fit to carry along a few choice words. *He sounds pissed.*

Even as a hunter, being pursued by Jack or even a small group of men was problematic. Hunters could not kill their fellow man, but that did not preclude breaking noses and bones. *Still, that would slow me down.*

Clara might be able to hold her own, especially when armed with the tools of her trade. Her dual-shot derringer would make short work of one or two. *More if I have a chance to reload.*

The small blade attached to Father Michael's crucifix would have given her claws. Last had she been wearing her jewellery, Clara would also have access to a garrotte to render them unconscious. *Tricky that.*

"I'm not even sure that I can run for long before my legs give out," Clara whispered, before opening the door.

Her legs were already sore from all this walking. As a hunter, Clara could dance all night and still have enough left in her to kill and dispose of a vampire. *I've never felt so vulnerable around men.*

"I prefer breaking them," Clara whispered.

The thought brought a smile to her lips. She dipped her hand in a pool of holy water and made the sign of a cross. *At least my skin isn't burning.*

From the outside, the church was in bad shape, but the inside was a different matter. The pews were made of quality wood and oiled to a shine. The altar featured silver candlesticks and accoutrements... *The crucifix is a work of art all its own.*

It astonished her how the poorest members of a community poured so much of their time and income into their faith. *Many would give you the shirts off their back.*

Near the crucifix, Clara spotted a familiar symbol. It was a double helix, indicating there was a hunter cache on the premises. *That doesn't make sense.*

"...why have one in such a small centre?"

With the key in hand, Clara would have access to enough supplies and weapons to start a new life. The cache always held a predictable amount of weapons, food, supplies, silver, and a healthy balance of local currency.

"I could fund a small war with access to a hunter cache."

Clara was getting ahead of herself, as evidenced by her racing heart. She focused to steady herself, but her body resisted the attempt.

The place was deserted, which was to be expected between shifts at the mine. Nearer to the front entrance, there was the confessional. Larger churches had several lined up, but in this case, there was only one.

She spotted a candle burning between the two doors. One had a lock, so she knocked on the other, and took three deep breaths. Without hearing a response, Clara opened the door slowly and stepped inside. The interior featured a screen that rendered this exchange anonymous. *I doubt he'll forget what I have to say.*

"*In nomine Patris et Filii et Spiritus Sancti. Amen,*" the priest said. (*In the name of the Father and of the Son and of the Holy Spirit. Amen.*)

Clara stopped mid-breath; her heart even skipped a beat. As judged by her autonomous responses, there was something intimately familiar about that voice. *Where do I know him from?*

Confessing after nearly a century would be lengthy. She assumed that being with Evelyn alone warranted severe penance.

"Bless you, Father, for I have sinned. Ninety-three years have passed since my last confession and my sins are innumerable," Clara said in flawless Latin.

As he had yet to interrupt her for speaking in Latin, Clara went on to the next part.

"For these and all the sins of my past life, I ask forgiveness from God, repentance and absolution from you, Father."

"I can't remember the last time anyone confessed their sins in Latin," the father said. "Although, I suspect that would have been more common ninety-three years ago."

Those words were spoken in plain English which surprised her.

"I see that you were paying attention, Father," Clara replied once more in Latin.

"That's a peculiar dialect," the father replied in English. "Where did you learn to speak Latin?"

That was saying something. Priests were not always from the local area, but elements of his accent were forced. *At best, he's a mainlander.*

The question itself was more telling. Hunters did not use specific phrases or codes to identify themselves. Instead, they weaved in hints during their exchange. It turned out that blurting out the name of an organisation that did not officially have one tended to get noticed.

In this situation, generous amounts of patience and caution were called for. She took a deep breath to formulate her response, pursing her lips as though deep in thought. A grin crept across her face when the solution turned out to be easier than expected.

"I went to school in Pompeii," Clara replied in Latin, to maintain secrecy.

"The city buried by fire and ash?" The father asked in the same tongue.

"A portion of the Roman city remains. This structure features a peculiar set of winding staircases…" Clara replied.

"You can't possibly know that," the father began, before belatedly adding. "Cl—Child."

Clara often forgot to add the title at the end. She was infamous for tossing them in a second or two after it ought naturally to be used. She would often cut off staff who were about to chastise her for the slight.

Witnessing that mannerism in another and the familiarity of that voice permitted her mind to make a logical leap. The reason why she did not initially place the voice was due to his death at the dawn of the twentieth century.

"Father Michael?"

"Where do you remember meeting me?" Father Michael asked, without confirming it was him.

"In the courtyard, when an old farmer and Sister Maria brought me to the school," Clara said.

She remembered how furious the Mother Superior was for Father Michael taking an interest in her. The school was cloistered, even the chapel was located off the grounds to further reduce the chance of men being near their residences.

"What if I told you that was Ada?" Father Michael asked.

"For killing the ghoul?" Clara confirmed.

That *truth* had been revealed to her when she encountered her sister at The Grand. Ada was too old to get the training opportunity Clara got, which was later exploited by Drusilla, twisting the eldest sister until there was nothing left of the kind soul she knew.

"So, you do—(*remember*)?" Father Michael said.

"That cloistered school did not take students her age," Clara interrupted. "Ada was old enough to start her training at the Tower."

The screen prevented her from gaining insight on his facial tics. For all she knew, he was sticking his tongue out at her. *Like I used to do during confessions as a child.*

She did pick up on any changes in angle and distance. When his head got smaller and changed position, she concluded that Father Michael must have pushed his head back in shock. Her response was clearly not something he expected. *I doubt anything I've said so far has.*

"Did you ever catch up with Drusilla?" Clara asked.

The memory of that ancient vampire slicing open his neck and draining him dry came to mind. She was curious how much history had to change just to be once again in his presence. *I could certainly do without being a prostitute.*

"Who is that?" Father Michael asked.

"Ask Reverend Mother Augustine…"

He was either fishing for information or genuinely had no idea. In a way, Clara was curious to see how far this reality differed greatly from the one she remembered. Still, it was notable that this man was not interested in delving into the bombshells she dropped.

Even if what he said was true, any hunter worth their salt would ask where her knowledge of the Tower came from. *Not to mention my grasp of Latin.*

The limits of the human body were something that Clara was no longer accustomed to. She had been something other than human much longer than she lived as one.

Clara closed her eyes and let her jaw hang loosely. It was an old trick that hunters used to further focus their hearing. As an angel, she could pick up hearts beating and the whispers behind closed doors. *Nothing but silence now.*

W-h-o...

Time appeared to stretch on as he spoke. In between every letter, there was something else. *Wait. That's not a single sound.*

W-o-u-l-d...

The first part was heavier, as though striking the bass drum. Whereas the other was closer to tapping on a snare drum. At this speed, they were separate and distinct, but the cadence between these two sounds was brief, and the repetition just as defined.

T-h-a-t...

Her eyes widened upon realising that someone was headed for the confessional. Like the dutiful hunter he was, Father Michael was hunting with a partner. *He's the b(ait)*—

B-e...

"Clara?" Julia called out.

The voice may as well have been a gunshot in the night. Her mind came alight, focusing on a source, but it originated from every direction. *It may as well have been yelled down from Heaven.*

M-y...

Her eyes shot open, and nothing changed other than her awareness of the situation. If Clara was the other hunter, she would barge in as the father was speaking to catch her prey unaware.

Clara shifted until her back was against the door and her bent legs pressed against the back wall. *That's the doorknob being turned!*

As soon as the mechanism drove home, the door flew open and Clara was shot out.

"Child," Father Michael finished.

What she did not see was the door's edge slamming into the face of the other hunter. Her back met the floor but she was reasonably prepared and launched herself into a barrel roll. Given her health, her body resisted every movement leading to a poor landing.

"*Clara? Say something!*" Julia said.

The voice came from inside her head, which distracted her enough to nearly miss the pew to steady herself. Clara's heart was beating wildly. *Feels like I'm a hare running from the fox!*

Right by the door, Jack was holding onto his nose as crimson poured freely between his fingers. *Why didn't I question why he was even in this town?*

Clara had no way of knowing the entrance he used let alone if Jack by himself. So, she ran towards the main doors and used her shoulder to open them hard. The heavy oak doors slammed against the wall but no one was there to greet her.

With her third option expended, Clara ran towards the sea. *I might be able to sell myself in exchange for safe passage out of here.*

It was hardly a desirable option but having hunters after her was something she never dealt with before .

"Horse… fucking… feathers," Clara swore, in between breaths.

CHAPTER 15

ALWAYS AN OPTION

You had one task!" Father Michael yelled, his voice echoing through the wooden walls of the church.

"She caught me by surprise," came the laboured response of Jack.

That voice carried a great deal of pain and frustration. It was clear that Clara not only wounded him physically, but also his pride.

* * * *

To ensure they could not immediately determine where she went. Clara ran until she was over the crest of a hill. From here, it was mostly farmland, and the long grass would serve her well... *it hurts to breathe*!

It was a challenge to evade an opponent. That worsened when the pursuer had the same training... *or better.*

Male hunters were said to be superior. Given the time periods, it was easier to prepare men for combat than the women. Clara was expected to entice her prey, and that meant she could not achieve that aim while wearing a suit of armour.

She knew the train station would be monitored, and suspected that the coal jetties were as well. Therein lay the crux of her situation, to evade them, she needed to think outside the box and that further limited her options.

There was a sizable settlement farther east known for its production of steel. That meant docks for coal, iron ore, and smelted steel. If she was a well-fed soldier on the march, she could get there in four hours, half that at a run. *I can't manage anywhere near that.*

The last time she made the journey, Clara did so by bus. There were no highways, or road signs in this era, and she was unfamiliar with the terrain. She was sure to stumble through the countryside, including at night. *I hope there's a full moon out—*

In the distance, she caught sight of a young brunette wearing blue jeans, a leather jacket, and a red backpack slung on her left shoulder. The sight of a modern woman in this era was nearly enough to make her cry…

"Is she really here?" Clara asked.

Silently she altered course, heading towards the water. Since it led away from the town, it met one of her objectives. She kept her distance, looking over her shoulder periodically to ensure no one was following. *Good for now.*

"Too good…" Clara said.

Clara pinched herself and watched the skin recover at a snail's pace. That was a sign she was dehydrated or less than the picture of health… *or both.*

All the signs were there that she would crash. Her heart rate remained at a gallop, and that was while standing still. After several deep breaths, she followed on even as her lungs burned. Julia was not moving particularly fast, pausing every so often to read the terrain.

"*What's she doing out here?*" Julia asked.

A most pertinent question that was also at the forefront of Clara's mind. Why would Julia be here, let alone heading farther and farther away from the settlement?

Clara did not wish to give herself away by calling out. While their search area grew with every step, stray sounds would narrow their search.

Instead, she did her best to hide using the natural terrain. Clara did so by walking through the tall hay, skirting the occasional patch of woods, or walking along a stone fence.

This went on for at least twenty minutes before something disturbing reached her ear. The wind brought with it the sound of dogs baying. *Oh… shit!*

Clara didn't care if her body gave out. She transitioned from a walk to a run and pushed past Julia. The werewolf did not even react to Clara passing by. *How's that possible?*

Even at a run, the sounds of the hounds grew louder with every step. Clara went on until she ended up at the Atlantic's doorstep. *It may as well be a dead end.*

One more step and she would fall for several seconds into the frigid waters of the Atlantic. She found herself at the edge of a sheer cliff, and as judged by the water crashing against the shore Clara realised this went on for miles in both directions.

Sure enough, the first of the search party broke over the horizon. She did not know this man, nor did that matter.

Clara was out of options. Even if she survived the leap, she could not imagine herself swimming against those waves. *Even a frigate wouldn't stand a chance.*

A minute later, Jack and Father Michael appeared over the horizon. Now that she was effectively trapped, the lead man slowed to a walk.

The men spread out farther along the coasts to prevent escape. *Those dogs would run me down before I took a dozen steps.*

Defeat left a bitter taste in her mouth, how could it not? She had no idea why they were dedicating so many resources to finding her, let alone why they kept her confined to this town. Ultimately, that mattered little, as this could not be her life. *If one could call it that.*

The cruel grin upon Jack's face was visible, even from fifty paces. It might have made her heart sink if not for the bloodied clothing and swollen nose. *That bastard will remember the day he underestimated me.*

"There are always options!" Clara yelled.

The three who were nearby shot her a curious glance. Clara was not speaking to them, but to the hunters behind them.

When her words reached the duo, they both furrowed their brows. Clara was committed, blew them all a kiss, watching their smiles collectively fade away.

After taking one last laboured breath, Clara leaned back until gravity took hold of her. She had done this thousands of times as an angel, going into freefall before opening her wings to soar. Clara kept smiling, remaining calm, cool and collected, even as the wind pushed past her hair.

In that moment, she nearly felt like herself. Before the sea spray from the crashing waves reached her, there came a bright flash of pure, white light. Even from town, those staring in her direction were momentarily blinded.

After recovering, the hunting party reached the edge of the cliff, but there was no trace of her.

CHAPTER 16

OFF-TIME JIVE

The last time Clara died, she ended up in a room bathed in white light. *Had I been there much longer it might have driven me batty.*

Like that time, her senses recovered at different rates. The sound filtering through her ears was like being underwater with a concert playing on above. It was disorienting, and as her mind reconnected with her vision everything before her was blurry. *It's like I'm spiflicated while trapped in a gallery filled with Impressionist art.*

The disconnect between her senses and what her mind expected threw her for a loop. Clara slowed down, falling out of sync with the loud rhythmic thumping in the washed-out audio.

Just ahead, a black-haired blur got bigger for reasons she could not yet grasp. After two more *thumps*, Clara experienced the feeling of being in free fall while her heart tried to crawl out of her throat.

A pair of hands grabbed onto her arms, and whisked her away.

* * * *

Day is ending, birds are wending…

The lyrics from a song reached through the depths of her mind. With it came several memories of nights spent hoofing the hours away, while breaking the hearts of men who sought to make her their latest conquest.

Those memories set a dreamy smile on her face, appearing as though she imbibed in far too much giggle water. Without realising it, Clara was humming along to the music.

Back to the shelter of each little nest they love…

Clara had no idea what was going on, but she enjoyed being in this state. She was comfortably numb, free to dive into the memories of a time that was never more *apropos* for her. *The scent of vanilla makes me think of…*

Nightshades falling, love birds calling…

"*Mon amour?*" Evelyn asked. (*My love.*)

The effect that voice had on her psyche was the equivalent of dropping an anchor while underway. It arrested her momentum even as her body and mind actively fought against it. Clara found herself hating the speaker for tearing her away from this quiet place.

What makes the world go round?

"Nothing but love," Clara whispered, in sync with the music.

She opened her eyes in a flutter and focused on those emerald-green eyes. There was water welling at the edges of those eyelids, as though something was wrong. *Wait…*

Clara had the distinct impression these emotions were not hers. *You'd think the world was coming to an end.*

While peculiar, what concerned her more was a distinct lack of a heartbeat. Sure, there were plenty of hearts nearby, including the one beating dead ahead, but her chest was still.

"Exactly, *Mon Amour*," Evelyn said.

The vampire made no attempt to hide her emotions like she normally did. This time, Evelyn wiped her eyes dry even while that lower lip trembled. She then kissed Clara on the cheek tenderly. *She's not cool to the touch.*

"What's with the off-time jive?" Evelyn asked.

That was a distinct piece of slang. Unlike Clara, the vampire was always careful to use language that applied to the era. *I'm the only one who speaks like that.*

"…off-time jive?" Clara questioned, to give herself some time.

The background music fit in with the era, as was the acrid, blue smoke, so thick that she could taste tobacco in the air. She grimaced and tried to scrape her tongue using her teeth, but the flavour was not going anywhere. *Just ducky.*

"We were out hoofing it on the dance floor, and you started fading," Evelyn said.

Clara was sure that statement was not literal. The vampire wore a black, loose-fitting gown that managed to show plenty of legs. The headband, pearl accoutrements, and use of feathers were all tied to an era… *Wait, I'm wearing the same type of clothing…*

To confirm her conjecture, Clara quickly scanned the room. Men and women were having the time of their lives on the dance floor. There was even a twenty-man band complete with a sultry singer crooning into a microphone.

She was about to return her gaze to Evelyn but noticed that she could peer into the shadows. While Clara did not see colour or composition, the outlines of a couple were clear. *They're doing a lot more than petting.*

"Those two have been at it for a while," Evelyn said. "I'm not into men, but I admire his stamina."

"*That's creepy*," Clara thought, after realising that Evelyn had an uncanny ability to follow her thoughts. *Unless I'm so out of it that I don't remember mentioning it?*

That signature smile faded from Evelyn's face which in turn made Clara's heart sink. Clara reached out and intertwined her fingers with the vampire. *While it didn't make everything better, the sting subsided.*

They both stiffened visibly as a thought took root in their minds. Whether the idea came from Clara or not she had no way of knowing, but it was like an echo in reverse. What started as a soft whisper grew louder and louder until they were both faced with the answer.

"You're not…" they said, in unison.

"My Evelyn," Clara said.

"My Clara," Evelyn countered.

They said this at the same time, but neither were done just yet.

"No… an earlier version of her…"

"Something that never was…"

There came a long pause, and the world came to a halt. While nothing more than perception, when the world began to move again, Evelyn's hands were at her side. The chaos outside of their conversation did not help Clara to consolidate her thoughts.

"Viens," Evelyn said. (*Come.*) "Our… my room is nearby."

Clara tried to stand, but her body reacted as though it was not hers. For one, she moved quick as a flash, but without being mentally prepared, the world went out of focus and she lost her sense of balance.

"I got you," Evelyn said, those words echoing in her mind before the lights went out.

* * * *

Clara heard her feet dragging against the plush carpet. It was eerie how the associated sensations were entirely absent from the equation.

She opened her eyes, and through the blurry field of vision Clara spotted telltale details. The plush carpeting, the art deco style, and four-hundred series room numbers.

When she passed by room four-one-four, Clara knew exactly where she was. While it made sense considering that Evelyn was a vampire, the thought of being in the unlisted wing at The Grand, where she died, did not sit well with her.

"…southern wing…" Clara mumbled.

There came the squeeze of a soft hand. A part of her could not help it felt more like an absent friend than a partner.

"Shhhhh," Evelyn said. "I have you, *ma chère*. Now, close your eyes…"

The musical elements of that voice were soft, reminiscent of her mother singing a lullaby. Without even realising it, Clara complied without protest.

CHAPTER 17

OLD WOUNDS

Wakey, wakey, *ma chère*," Evelyn whispered.

Those words were barely louder than the sound of air pushing through Evelyn's lips. In Clara's mind, she might as well have been yelled at through a bullhorn a hair's width away.

That voice became her world, and despite her desire to resist, she did exactly as ordered. Clara's eyes shot open, finding herself surrounded by the luxuries only The Grand could offer… *to monsters.*

A four-poster bed, large draperies, and rare art was everywhere she looked. Just ahead her there were those piercing, green eyes and that patented smile. One that promised so much if one simply submitted to this dark-haired beauty. *How I've fallen for her.*

In the bed, there was a human-shaped lump. Her breathing was impossibly slow like her heart rate. Due to the low-light conditions, she could not make out who this was.

Clara smiled and tried to reach out for the vampire, but those thick, leather straps resisted any such attempt. A quick glance revealed that she was strapped to a wooden frame with her legs spread wide open, and her arms were strapped apart at about shoulder level.

The contraption was at an angle that enabled her to see Evelyn comfortably. Clara had a sinking suspicion that it was not the first time she was in this particular contraption.

"Correct," Evelyn said aloud. "You've used it on me too, from time to time."

That was a notable difference in the dynamics surrounding their relationship. They may have used toys, and strap-ons, but never something like this, let alone seek to dominate the other.

"Domination has its uses… and pleasures," Evelyn replied.

"That's really annoying."

Evelyn giggled, before moving in closer. She was wearing the same gown from earlier, and realised that was a good sign. *She's always naked when she plans to get creative.*

As though to prove her wrong, she flicked a talon across Clara's bare left breast. It cut through skin and fatty tissue creating a large split in her flesh. At first there was no pain, but as blood welled up through the wound a stinging sensation made itself known. *What a bitch!*

"Do I have your attention?" Evelyn asked.

"We could achieve the same by sitting on a comfortable couch and having a chat."

"This happened before," Evelyn stated. "That Clara entered a trance and tried to kill me."

Droplets of blood rolled down her bare chest and onto her thigh before dropping off. As one impacted the plush carpet, Clara had the distinct impression that someone was pounding their fists against an empty cistern.

After the third drop, Clara focused enough to put together what was said. It was entirely possible that other versions of her were trying to find their way back to the Tower.

Every decision was multiplied by millions of subsequent choices made from that moment onwards. The odds were good that Evelyn was being truthful, but there could be other reasons why an attempt on her life was made.

"You?" Clara asked. "Or anyone without a heartbeat?"

Evelyn pressed her index finger against her lips while rolling her eyes towards the ceiling. Meanwhile the sound of blood pooling on the floor continued. *Why is it so loud?*

"You're seriously not going to heal?" Evelyn asked, annoyed.

Clara cocked a brow, baffled that Evelyn would make such a statement. Even as a goddess, Clara could not just close up her wounds. The network of veins were vital for feeding her muscles and organs with oxygen and nutrients. *I could no more stem the bleeding than stop my—*

"You haven't caught on?" Evelyn asked.

Clara felt an urge to stem the bleeding, the timing of which was too coincidental. Just like that, the flow stopped, and the last few drops of blood fell to the floor.

"You turned me?" Clara asked.

In her mind, Clara knew it to be true, but parts of her remained conflicted. How could I willingly give up who I am and embrace my dark side? *She must be lying—she's just kidding—there's no way—*

Evelyn pressed an index finger against Clara's lips. This had an immediate effect on Clara, enabling her mind to simmer down. Whereas, those talons slid neatly over Clara's tummy. The motions were so light that the razor-sharp talons nearly tickled.

"They exiled you for *letting* me live," Evelyn said. "You confessed to me that they tortured you for weeks just to see what I told you."

The more she learned about the Tower, the less she wished to make contact. Sure, these were alternate realities, but such events could have easily happened in her reality. *I just needed to fail or say the wrong thing.*

Evelyn moved in closer still, but from the back. Being this close to the vampire was normally sensual, but that open wound on her breast certainly dulled the mood.

The vampire was clearly not bothered; she ran a lone finger down a line of curiously insensitive skin. There came another slash, followed by another, but there was little to no pain.

The true horror was revealed when Evelyn gave Clara a first-person view of what the vampire saw. Her back was riddled with white scars, many overlapping, a firsthand view of the damage wrought by a whip.

"You did so out of the goodness of your heart?" Clara asked.

"Don't let my beating heart fool you," Evelyn replied. "There is no goodness to be found here… I had every intention of fucking you, draining you of all your blood and leaving your corpse on display as a warning to others."

It dawned on her that Evelyn was not using her mask at all. Even in casual conversation, both Clara and Evelyn hid their emotions. Still, her heart could not imagine this vampire as being capable of such depravity… *horny… sure…*

"How did you know that… *the other*… Clara attacked other vampires?" Evelyn asked.

"It's a failsafe the Tower embedded into my mind meant to prevent hunters from defecting. Jack triggered it when he tried to torture me for information. I assumed that the same might apply to an alternate version of me."

Clara remembered the mass of bodies surrounding her. Some had been shot, others burned, beheaded, or torn limb from limb. Every recognisable face was etched into her mind, but she had no memory of the act itself.

"You had this… failsafe?" Evelyn asked.

"I did," Clara said.

"How were you freed of it?" Evelyn asked.

"It failed the last time it was triggered… Still, it's just a hunch… Why don't you bite me to find out?"

Evelyn moved in a blur and reappeared ten paces away. This time the stinging in her right breast was hard to ignore. Clara focused her thoughts, until the pain became a distant memory. *A little bit more and she would have cut it off entirely.*

"Cuddling is far more productive," Clara said.

"You're hiding something," Evelyn said. "I'm going to get it out of you, and I'll enjoy every minute of it."

"What the fuck did she do to you?" Clara asked. "I've never met a more tender and thoughtful lover."

"I told her the first day we met that she would wake up and realise that she was in bed with a monster."

Clara pieced together the rest. Those words left a mark on her own psyche and still haunted her to this day. The difference was that Clara was herself a monster. *Just one that led Evelyn towards the light.*

This version had been betrayed and abandoned by the very organisation that she loyally served. It did not take much to realise that they brought out something in Clara that was truly ugly. Their mutual attraction amplified every aspect of their relationship. *Just like ours.*

No matter, Clara's dilemma was that she could not attempt an escape without thinking about it first. That meant Evelyn would pick up on the thoughts and act to counter. *That's why I need my quiet place.*

"You proved your worth when a fledgling vampire called me a whore," Evelyn began. "You gutted him like a fish and left behind a scene that would make Jack the Ripper proud."

That line was meant to appeal to her darker impulses. Instead of reacting, Clara applied her mind fully to creating a musical abomination. It was like splicing a song together using incongruous sources and music.

At the base was a cryptic opera from Mozart. She then tossed in the lyrics from her favourite shower song, '*Ain't Misbehavin*', translated to Italian. *The concept alone makes my head hurt.*

No one to talk with.

"Tell me this," Clara began. "How'd you know that I wasn't yours?"

Evelyn smiled, as though measuring out the benefits of toying with her. *Or would she prefer that I beg?*

All by myself…

"Begging won't get you anywhere with me," Evelyn replied. "Your mind is more… disciplined… wise… and surprisingly… emotional. You?"

"You're careful, and would never slip out slang from a time period unless you were looking to blend in."

All the while, she focused on the space in her mind where she held her convocations. With any luck it would bring her there, even with the goddesses gone.

"So, that's what you're hiding…"

No one to walk with…

CHAPTER 18

ENDOTHERMIC REACTION

Clara pushed through the doors and walked into the council chambers. As expected, the space was vacant, which forced her to manage every aspect of her plan. *That's just ducky.*

While pure conjecture, Clara hoped that diving deeper into her mind would hinder Evelyn's ability to read her thoughts. Through the windows, the angel saw Evelyn's lips finishing the last syllable of the word 'hiding.'

For Clara, there was no harm in being truthful and straightforward. This was an alternate reality and changing a potential past would have no effect on her own timeline. However, time moved more slowly here than she expected. Clara was not sure as to the how let alone why. *I won't waste this opportunity.*

But I'm happy on the shelf…

Her composition was terrible, perhaps bad enough for God himself to come down here and drag her down to Hell. *At least Evelyn doesn't appear to mind.*

Her musical score played in the background like demented, elevator music.

Clara now knew that she was a vampire, which gave her options.

"I could distract Evelyn long enough to weaken my bindings."

The plan had merit. The question was could she make that happen from the depths of her mind?

Clara had to act as naturally as possible. Lying in this state would tax her focus, and she had no wish to give away her hand.

"You never asked," Clara visualised herself saying. "It's odd, you always excelled at foreplay."

Nothing happened at first, which made her wonder if she had any control at all. After counting to thirty-three, her voice echoed out throughout the hall. *Enough to make the room shake!*

She grabbed onto something and waited for things to settle. It did momentarily in between words, an effect she found irksome.

Clara found her *sea legs* and maintained balance while staring out through the windows. At this pace Evelyn's eyes were easy to follow. With all that was going on in her head, Clara was bleeding again.

A drop of blood ran down her tummy, with the sensation being replicated in her avatar. The vampire's eyes locked onto the blood, tracking every movement. *Like the predator she is.*

Clara changed her focus, and was surprisingly able to will an index finger to transform. With a quick swipe, she ran it down the band, and nearly sliced into her wrist. *It's not much, but it was a start.*

Ain't misbehavin'...

* * * *

"I missed that witty rapport," Evelyn replied, after a longing sigh.

For Clara, this was an obvious clue that being turned did more than grant her immortality. *She's a dark rendition of me, one with an obvious bloodlust.*

Evelyn appeared to be deep in thought, those green eyes narrowed as though reflecting on the depth of their sins. Clara enjoyed it when the vampire dropped her mask, giving her a glimpse of her vulnerability. Someone who fought daily to get past her origins... *whore...*

I'm savin' my love for you...

* * * *

"What I wouldn't give to wake up in bed with you," Clara replied.

Another drop rolled down her tummy, and given the passage of time, it felt more like a slimy tongue sliding down her skin. For now, the deception appeared to be working, with every drop wasted, Clara managed another swipe at the band at her wrist.

Once more, the room shook as she spoke. Clara steadied herself like an experienced ship's master holding course in stormy seas, even as the horizon shifted.

Clara wiped the sweat from her brow. *Wait...*

"Why is it so warm?"

There were no obvious heat sources in sight. That made sense considering these rooms were typically reserved for vampires. *So why do I want to peel a layer of skin to cool off.*

"Why am I sweating?"

I know for certain...

* * * *

"Really?" Evelyn asked before giggling.

The vampire adopted a smile reminiscent of the cat getting away with eating the canary. It was mischievous and simultaneously alluring.

"I could—(*give you a night to remember*)—How are you sweating?" Evelyn added.

Clara shrugged as best she could. With an opportunity at hand, she used the distraction to get in another swipe.

"*Clara?*" Julia yelled out.

The one I love...

* * * *

Like her own voice, Julia made the hall rumble. The difference was the effect was more like an aftershock when compared to the earthquakes her own voice caused.

She did an all-around scan, even looked out the *windows*, but found no hide or hair of the young werewolf. Evelyn did not react in any way to Julia, and Clara figured the voice originated from inside her head. *Am I going crazy?*

Julia looked real enough when Clara followed her down that field to the cliff. Still, hearing a voice was not proof of sanity. *More like an indication as to the depth of my delusions.*

Clara believed that the cuts in her restraint were deep enough to free herself. How much would a free hand count against an elder vampire was a different matter altogether. *I have no point of reference.*

"I don't know?" Clara asked.

A reply that was both truthful and furthered her agenda. If Evelyn did not know the why, or how her progeny was sweating, then this had to be new territory. "*I must have slept through that lecture at the Tower.*"

The sweat interacting with the open wounds caused a reaction quite unlike anything she ever experienced. The now familiar stinging became an excruciating experience.

She imagined her hand placed within a large hole punch. Pressure was applied gingerly, leading to a slow and deliberate increase in agony. Just as her nervous system was about to burst into flames, the contraption punched through skin, sinew, and bone to relieve the pressure.

This happened repeatedly, making this Evelyn's idea of foreplay appear like the gentle caress of a lover. *Why me?*

I'm through with flirtin'…

* * * *

"*What happened to you?*" Julia said.

This time, the auditory hallucination was followed by visual cues. The young werewolf kneeled right in front of Clara, as though looking over a crime scene.

Julia reached forward and passed right through Clara's leg. There was no accompanying stimulus, nothing like interacting with spectral beings. *Not a check in the sanity box.*

It's just you I'm thinkin' of…

The werewolf pulled away leaving her hand covered in chalk. *That's not right.*

The consistency and texture of the powder was all wrong. The way it behaved when Julia rubbed it against her thumb and forefinger reminded her of… *ash…*

Ain't misbehavin'…

"What do you mean you don't know?" Evelyn asked.

The furrowed brow and non-existent smile hinted this was not the first time Evelyn asked.

* * * *

Clara found it progressively difficult to manage every aspect of their interaction. Mercifully, Julia faded from existence leaving her free to butcher the song to distract Evelyn. *That should be a snap?*

Clara crinkled her lips at one side, while snapping her fingers. The sound echoed in her head, which deflated her ego. *There's enough space to rent out.*

"Why would I?" Clara asked. "I've no idea what it's like to be a vampire. Don't you?"

She counted the seconds before the world began to tremble. Without realising, Clara managed to soak through her gown, while her hair was dripping wet.

The faltering smile on Evelyn's face indicated her level of concern. It seemed that the vampire truly had no idea. Clara thought back to her times with Evelyn, trying to remember an instance of her sweating... *I've never seen her sweat... ever...*

The idea itself was beyond the realm of reasonable. It would be like a corpse sweating—*ash*!

Clara witnessed vampires come aflame. Exposure to the sun was the simplest way to light them up, but that was impossible within the confines of this room, deep within the rock face of a cliff.

The next best thing was holy water. It burned like vitriol; especially when they were fully submerged in water. *That leaves... faith.*

Clara realised that she was the source. Her true form was a creature of faith inhabiting the vessel of a vampire. The longer she remained the more the incongruity asserted itself.

Evelyn was nearly overtop Clara now. The angel's avatar smiled, formulating what would happen next.

* * * *

Clara broke through her binding using the raw strength of a vampire. Without a hint of concern, Evelyn grabbed the freed hand and arrested its momentum entirely. *I never had a chance as her progeny.*

When the vampire realised there were no talons nor was Clara resisting, those green eyes came aglow. Meanwhile, she wore a smile, curled on one end. *She sees this as me being cocky.*

"I'm savin' my love for you," Clara sang.

There was hesitation shining in those green eyes. Clara used the opportunity to open her hand and brush up against Evelyn's cheek. In turn, the vampire nuzzled into the touch.

With a bit of wrangling she moved her hand through Evelyn's silky, black hair tempting her to move closer. Their lips met and found the vampire to be unexpectedly hesitant. They teased one another until Clara parted her lips and Evelyn followed suit.

Their tongues met, and Evelyn appeared to melt into Clara. Without the music playing in the background, her internal monologue shattered the silence in her mind. *I'm sorry, Evelyn.*

Clara once again chose the path of a martyr. She let her fangs drop into place and sliced open her tongue. The blood quickly filled her mouth before pushing it past her lips.

Evelyn's eyes shot open wide highlighting her fear, but Clara held on to her sire's neck with everything she had. The vampire's lips discoloured from the heat transfer and would soon start smoking.

Meanwhile, Clara's skin darkened before blisters formed all over her body. She was engulfed before Evelyn could pull away and the flames spread quickly over both of them. Their screams were like an intolerable, tingling sweetness of water glasses when played by a cunning hand.

* * * *

"*I'm sorry, Evelyn,*" Clara repeated, as the flames licked her avatar's frame.

CHAPTER 19

HALF-LIFE

Happy Birthday!" Evelyn sang.

Clara's eyes shot open and she was once more faced by those piercing, green eyes. The vampire's smile was warm and honest, but there was something missing in those eyes. *They lost their shine.*

The angel smiled in return as her mind registered more of the scene. Evelyn held in her hands a chipped, white plate topped with a cream-filled roll, adorned by a single candle.

It was a pastry-based confection available at any corner store or gas station. Evelyn was known for her extravagance, especially if she deemed it important. *This is anything but.*

"It's my birthday?" Clara asked, to get an idea of the date.

Whereas the 'where' was more obvious. This was their room back *home*, and most of the details were there. It was the minute differences that gave her pause. *Even if they aren't physical differences.*

The air was stale, and the mechanical hum she associated with the building's ventilation system was non-existent. To make matters worse, there was little more than the sound of the wind blowing against the outer walls. *Where's the city?*

"You don't remember?" Evelyn asked faintly.

The vampire's lower lip trembled, and water welled up in those beautiful eyes. Clara had no wish to hurt her feelings, so she smiled meekly before struggling to take a breath deep enough to blow out the candle.

Evelyn placed the plate neatly on Clara's nightstand and hugged her. There was a twinge of pain, and the angel tried to shift her wings out of the way. The agony that followed nearly blinded her, forcing her mind to focus on from the sound of bone scraping against wood. *What was that?*

"*Oh non!*" Evelyn exclaimed, and backed away so fast that Clara saw two of her.

Clara cocked her head enough to look over her bare shoulders and realised there was little left of her wings. All that remained were blackened stubs, as though burned away over an open flame... *or a blow torch!*

The reaction was delayed and disconnected, as it took a while for the angel to realise her legs did not respond. If Evelyn had not taken Clara's hand and squeezed it as a sign of support, the angel might have remained in a state of shock for a while.

"How did—(*this happen*)?" Clara asked.

"You were at ground zero during the attack," Evelyn replied.

The way those words rolled off Evelyn's tongue implied this was not the first time they were used in that order. It came as no surprise that Clara knew nothing of an attack, certainly not one that scorched her wings to the bone. *The Roaring Twenties' Evelyn did say that I wasn't her first visitor.*

"When—(*did this happen*)?" Clara asked.

Evelyn brought Clara's hand to her cheek and caressed it.

"What's the last thing you remember?"

The motion was so tender, so loving, that her mind had trouble accepting it. An image of the sadistic variant came into the spotlight, leading Clara to tear away her hand. *To think our relationship was going so well.*

Evelyn's jaw dropped, and her normally impregnable social mask shattered. Clara had seen her cry before, but this was different, raw, with no hint of this being for show. These tears were due to the culmination of trauma that could no longer be ignored.

Clara hesitated, her breathing erratic from anxiety. With a lot of effort, she managed to reach out to Evelyn for a hug. The vampire melted into her, while tears ran down her chest and onto the blankets of their bed.

"I'm sorry," Clara said. "I'm not at all myself."

At this stage, the truth appeared to be the best approach. *At least a couple of spoonfuls at a time.*

"I was just trying to cheer you up…" Evelyn tearfully replied.

It was hard to hear what was being said. Unleashing a deluge of tears left Evelyn's airways congested, muffling the words. There was also an underlying wail. *She's never been this vulnerable.*

"The last thing I remember is catching fire in your arms… before that, I jumped off a cliff back home."

"Wait…" Evelyn said, as she backed away. "What?"

The vampire's eye darted from point to point before she located a box of tissues to blow her nose with. Even then, it was clear that all those emotions were merely contained. *Waiting for an outlet.*

"Before that," Clara began. "I promised you that I'd come back alive from my attempt to find the Tower."

"You don't remember the attack?"

"No."

"…"

It was Evelyn's turn to come to terms with the truth. This must have happened before, but Clara must have had some memory up until the attack.

"You're a hiccup?"

This was the term people applied to the event which merged alternate realities with their own. Given the locale, and the use of that name, Clara was confident they were skirting her own reality. *End of the line?*

"I'm certainly travelling between bubbles," Clara said. "No idea how… or why…"

"We're together in your… reality?" Evelyn asked.

"You're the love of my life," Clara admitted, seeing no point in lying.

Evelyn swooped in and kissed Clara on the cheek. The angel could see the conflict in those eyes. She was elated from hearing the L word but torn that it was not *her* Clara.

"She never told me that."

"I'm not your Clara," she began. "If I were to guess, she loves you more than anything. She just can't get past her own fears and anxieties."

"Oh…"

Another torrent of tears followed. Clara cursed herself for the off-time jive... *I just wanted to reassure her...*

Evelyn managed to surprise her. The vampire hugged Clara through the waterworks and giggled... *I must've missed a cue?*

"I... am... sorry..." Evelyn said, between breaths. "I'm... all... over... the... place."

Clara gave Evelyn a moment to settle. This time, there was a mound of tissues by their bed. Those puffy, red eyes could not deter from the beauty of those green eyes.

"Okay..." Evelyn said.

The vampire let out the rest of the air from her lungs. She closed her eyes, took in a deep breath and the mask slammed back into place.

"So, you don't remember the dirty-bomb strike against seventeen cities aligned with us?"

If this Evelyn was anything like hers, *us* meant those from her society who believed that survival hinged on remaining hidden. Whereas Drusilla and, later on, Ada believed they were the masters of humanity and acted accordingly. Her Evelyn rarely mentioned the conflict, but it was clear it was far more than a clash of words.

The vampire went into detail about how a single container ship made deliveries to each city. Each site received a container rigged to explode and release a cloud of radioactive material. To avoid detection, they were landed at a small port and trucked in. From there, they were delivered to construction sites and hoisted into an elevated position. They were detonated at nearly the same time, spewing radioactive poison throughout the cities.

Hospitals and police were quickly overwhelmed, and the government response was bungled. What came next was not a surprise, looting, violence, and an abundance of death.

Clara listened to all of it, aghast that anyone would willingly do this. She immediately wanted to jump to the end and get to the bottom of this, but realised Evelyn needed to get through this. *Cut off from the world, tending to the needs of a lover who nearly died in the blast.*

"That puts us a few months after I came back from The Grand..." Clara whispered.

That would put her roughly in sync with her timeline. However, she had no memories of attacks of this scale happening back home.

"You... you never went to The Grand..."

"I never met my sister?"

"*Non...*" Evelyn confirmed. (*No.*) "You tore away in a rental... hell-bent on saving Julia..."

CHAPTER 20

DIVERGENCE

This was one of the few times when Clara was thankful for her instincts being proven wrong. Her version of Evelyn convinced her to focus on the mission and send Grace instead. *A part of me still hates her for making me see reason.*

While the other Clara got the same speech, she instead drove off, intent on rescuing Julia herself, but was caught on several surveillance feeds. That shattered their original plan to create a false trail to The Grand while Clara used an alternate route. *With our hang-ups for taking human lives, several witnesses remained to corroborate her presence.*

If there was a clear point where their realities diverged, this was it. Going to The Grand allowed Clara to make peace with Hecate and her sister. *The humiliation Ada endured on livestream caused those allied with her to sever ties.*

"Change a couple of variables and the world comes to an end," Evelyn mused.

Clara noticed that Evelyn's dress was grimy. It was odd to see the vampire, always dressed in the latest fashion, with some dirt and grease on her dress. Clara swore that Evelyn had some grey in her hair, along with crow's feet by her eyes. *It makes her look more human.*

"Or end up getting lost, jumping from one version of yourself into another," Clara said.

"That… would be unpleasant."

She wondered how her version of Evelyn was doing. Was the vampire worried sick, avoiding reality by hiding within her studio? Had Evelyn noticed that Clara had yet to report in? *I've been gone for longer periods without contact before.*

"I'm doubtful this qualifies as paradise," Clara said.

The longer she was in this body, the more she became aware of its limitations. A dull pain was constant, as was the itching. She took the latter as a sign that new skin was growing back. *Clearly, more than my wings were scorched.*

She also noticed *something* skittering in the distance. It was much larger than a rat, and yet she could not pick up its heartbeat. The most disturbing element was the sound of it sniffing the air. *As though searching for prey.*

It conjured up the imagery of a dark shadow stalking women in the night. *Like something straight out of Nosferatu.*

The fact that Evelyn appeared unbothered by it despite her superior hearing was worrisome. *She has to know it's here.*

"It's funny how two versions of you don't seem all that surprised that I'm a different Clara."

"*Ma chère,*" Evelyn began. "I have centuries of life experiences on you. One either learns to be adaptable or ends up with a stake through their heart."

Clara furrowed a brow, because the last line did not entirely make sense.

"That's not an effective weapon on you. At best, it would—(*slow you down*)."

"Why do you think we continue to perpetuate that myth?" Evelyn said, before winking.

Evelyn's mask once more faded away revealing her level of fatigue.

"I miss this," Evelyn whispered, before forcing her mask back into place as though nothing happened.

"Yes."

That single answer led Evelyn to cock her head and press her index finger against her chin.

"*Pardon?*"

"Yes," Clara repeated.

Evelyn's head moved back by about a hand's width.

"What do you mean?"

"Yes," Clara pushed.

"*Vas donc te faire foutre,*" Evelyn yelled. (*Go fuck yourself.*)

While the words were menacing, that smirk on her lips implied it was all for show.

"Answers," Clara taunted.

"Ans(*swer*)—What were the questions?"

Those razor-sharp talons were out, but an impish grin remained firmly in place. Clara figured the vampire was playing her part... *and enjoying it.*

"Yes, that I miss this too," Clara said. "Yes, I'd love to... and yes, that it would be cheating."

Evelyn made it clear long ago that she was fine with Clara taking others to bed. It came with the lifestyle, but taking another Evelyn to bed would be like drinking gasoline and lighting up a cigarette. *Neither could forgive themselves, the other, or me.*

Evelyn giggled before appearing right before her. Clara only saw a blur, but she felt the cool peck against her cheek, which put a smile on her face.

"*Merci*," Evelyn said. "It's just… been… me…"

"I can't imagine what you went through," Clara said. "A question remains…"

"How do you get back to your love?"

"I'm more curious to see how I can get her to skip laundry day…"

Evelyn's jaw dropped and she froze in place. The vampire's heart kept beating strong and true, and did not waver even as a pillow *whizzed* by Clara's head.

"*Putain!*" Evelyn swore. (*Whore!*)

The vampire covered her mouth the moment those words registered on Clara's face. She may have been a whore in her distant past, but Clara's experience was still fresh in her mind.

"*Oh, non—*" Evelyn said, her eyes wide open and round.

"It's fine," Clara said. "You were just reacting and that's okay. It wasn't really me… Entirely."

"It doesn't mean I can't be sorry," Evelyn countered. "It seems we both experienced firsthand the sting of that word."

"Too true…"

This led to an awkward pause. They both stared at the other, smiled meekly and said the only thing that could not offend.

"So, what now?" they asked, in unison, before laughing.

"I'm not sure if it's relevant," Clara began. "But I saw a modern version of Julia in both reality bubbles."

"Julia? You saw her in both versions?"

"Yeah… why?"

"…she went out for supplies an hour or so before you woke up…"

"You didn't think to tell me?" Clara asked.

"I'm not the Oracle of Delphi! How would I guess that you'd wish to know that?" Evelyn said. "You brought her here the day after you rescued her. Marc—(*was not pleased that you risked exposing us*)."

There was no obvious reason for the vampire to know that such a detail might have been important. *At least she's not reading my mind.*

Evelyn's inability to finish her statement after mentioning '*Marc*' was certainly noticed. *If I wasn't bedridden, Evelyn would probably be in her studio.*

"Does she head out often?" Clara asked, to take some weight from Evelyn's shoulders.

"Every couple of days," Evelyn said. "She's not big on confinement."

Werewolves rarely were. Those captured by the Tower ended up wasting away to nothing. Most died without divulging any information. *They can barely be contained during a full moon.*

"I'm surprised she stuck around," Clara said.

Evelyn's smile faded for a fraction of a second. That was followed by a *glitch*, where the vampire appeared to be facing in two directions at once.

"Julia felt—feels that she owes you her life," Evelyn said.

In Clara's mind, it was she who owed the werewolf something. Even if this reality *proved* that her choice to follow through with Evelyn's plan was the right one, her guilt would not subside. *You'd think this would help.*

"She never owed me," Clara said.

"Cl(*ara*)—My… Clara said that as well," Evelyn replied. "If anything, werewolves are surprisingly stubborn. Either way, she's been an absolute gem. She even risked her life to recover your—you after the attack."

In the background, the sounds of the lurking creature became more pronounced. Claws were now running along the walls, as though actively seeking a way out.

"Do you know what happened to the goddesses?" Clara asked, while doing her best to ignore the horror building up in the background.

"Clara made no mention of them after the rescue… You?"

"It's hard to describe," Clara said. "I felt as though we got separated when I missed my mark… not a peep since."

"Huh," Evelyn said, while keeping her eyes fixed on a point to Clara's left. "You sound like you miss them."

"We…" Clara began. "…reached an understanding. You even flirted with Artemis."

Evelyn giggled to the point of tearing up. When the vampire recovered, she dabbed the corner of her eyes before speaking.

"There are more of them now?" Evelyn asked.

"One is the *Virgin Goddess of The Hunt*, and according to you, the most beautiful. Funny how she was known for having young women with her while on the hunt…"

There was a loose smile on Evelyn's lips, and the glow in her eyes was back. *As though waking up from a rather vivid dream.*

"Are you looking for another notch on your bedpost?"

"I only have eyes for you," Evelyn countered.

There came three, long *thuds* resonating from deep within the building. Evelyn turned to face the source. Those lips moved as though she was counting.

When another two came after the count reached four, Evelyn returned to face Clara.

"You'll need to excuse me, I have to prepare…"

The angel could guess what that entailed. Power might be out in the city, but Marc would make sure there were alternate sources. *Ever prepared for the apocalypse.*

"Please," Clara said.

Clara yawned, as a wave of fatigue hit her unexpectedly. She had no idea why, but some rest would do her a world of good.

"Get some rest, *ma chère.*"

"I will," Clara said, as her eyes grew heavy enough that they could no longer be kept open.

CHAPTER 21

SHE HAS RISEN

S ounds from beyond were integrated into Clara's dream. The speakers called from out of the cover of a heavily wooded forest covered in fog. She stood in the middle of a clearing, her wings back to their original splendour, but she had no desire to fly.

Above her, wings flapped by the hundreds, and the cackling, old women from above made it clear there was something otherworldly waiting where the light dared not reach.

Out in the fog, the sounds of that dark, skittering creature were clear as day. One moment it was just ahead of her, in another directly abaft. Clara turned quick as lightning, but was never able to spot the creature.

"*Are you sure it's her?*" Julia asked.

The voice echoed throughout these lands. Clara was too focused on the threats surrounding her to decipher those words.

"I'm telling you it's her," Evelyn said. "Your details line up with her recollections."

"Including?"

"*Absolument.*" (*Absolutely.*)

The words changed to whispers, which in turn added to the dread filling Clara's soul. The winged women above were still beyond reach, but every so often she caught the sight of a talon, or the dark outline of something big skirting the light.

Meanwhile, the creature behind the treeline was even louder, reminding her of a man who fell off the precipice of sanity. Since vampires occasionally ended up in asylums, Clara was very familiar with those who stared into the void and ended up losing themselves.

"*How are you handling it?*" Julia asked.

"*How do you think?*" Evelyn said, in a hushed tone. "*I watched her—*"

"*Not here,*" Julia said. "*I'm sorry—*"

A heavy wind picked up, blowing away the fog and everything in sight. Clara tucked in her wings and leaned into the wind, but it was not enough.

"*…what would you do for five more minutes?*" One of the voices asked.

Clara grabbed onto a root from a tree. The wind did not subside and she was soon parallel to the ground.

"*…anything…*"

Her nails tore clean off, and she was pulled into the abyss before she could even scream.

* * * *

Clara shot up in bed, the dream was far too visceral for her taste. The act of sitting up so quickly led to a sharp drop in blood pressure, and she nearly lost consciousness.

The world swirled before her, with the outer edges growing dark. *Hang in there.*

It took her a good minute, with her heart pounding hard against her chest, before her vision returned. More than enough to realise that not every element of that dream was imagined.

In addition to the skittering creature, something was pounding against the steel and concrete. The way those sounds propagated throughout the structure came across surprisingly like wings in flight. *Enough to give me nightmares.*

In the other room, there were two, solid heartbeats. The second was female, young and in shape based on the resting heart rate. The other was Evelyn, but both were quiet. *Evelyn heard me wake up.*

Clara was tired of being relegated to a spectator in her own play. She scooted to the side of the bed and slipped her feet off the edge. Even that left her short of breath, but *her* body would not limit her.

After several deep breaths, she grabbed onto one of the bedposts and forced herself to stand. On the other side of the door, there came a sharp gasp. *The young one's heart rate just shot up.*

Clara wobbled, and her blood pressure dropped. Still, she forced herself to take a step, followed by another and another. Eventually, she reached the door and leaned against it.

"You can do this," Clara whispered, those words sounding hollow even to her.

Using an arm, she held herself in place while turning the knob. The door squeaked open, making a long, woeful noise that sounded like a bird's chirp slowed down significantly…

Clara took in a sharp breath and bit down hard enough to strain her teeth. While she had no wish to be stealthy… *That sound could wake the dead.*

With the door open, Clara found herself staring into the main living area. The monitors that normally provided a view of the outside world were dormant. That meant there was no *natural* source of light, making it impossible to pick up any details. Just ahead, by the stairs, there were two silhouettes.

"How?" Evelyn asked, which turned out to be the shorter of the two.

Clara was exhausted from getting this far. She held onto the door handle as though her life depended on it. Her wobbling knees indeed confirmed that might be true.

"That makes our plan easier," Julia mused.

"Hush," Evelyn said. "Good things are rarely easy."

"You should post that on a—(*motivational card*)?" Julia countered.

"Wh-Why... are you... two surprised?" Clara managed to ask. *Why is this so exhausting?*

Evelyn did not hesitate. Before Clara could collapse, the vampire was at her side and steadied the angel.

"She has risen!" Julia said, in a way that parodied televangelists.

"I don't—(*get that reference*)..." Clara said.

Her lungs could not keep up with demand and she had to stop speaking to take in deep breaths. All the while Clara licked her lips because she was parched. *My mouth tasted better after a night of hard drinking, bad food, and cum.*

"What Julia is trying to say," Evelyn began, in a soothing voice that verged on singing a lullaby. "Until a few weeks ago... you were dead."

"D—(*ead*)?" Clara asked.

The pieces of the puzzle fell into place. Her scorched wings, tingling sensations throughout her body, and the overall feeling as though she was an unwanted guest in her own body. *Not to mention Evelyn's odd behaviour.*

"I managed to pull your remains from the rubble," Julia said.

That statement left Clara with as many questions as it answered. Most of which could wait for an opportune time, but there was one that needed an answer.

"Are y—(*ou my Julia*)?" Clara asked.

"I'm pretty fucking sure that I am," Julia replied.

There came a large blast that caused the multi-story hotel to shake. What followed was the sound of rushing water, evoking memories of that dam bursting. *That brings back memories.*

"They blew the doors to the elevator," Evelyn said. "…and triggered the deluge system in the parking garage."

That was one of Marc's security measures. Large pipes were installed in the lowest level of the parking area, designed to prevent incursion. The idea was to prevent ingress by submerging their primary point of entry in water.

"Who invited the in-laws?" Julia asked sardonically. "That moves our timeline forward."

"I have her," Evelyn said.

Julia came up the stairs and slipped off her backpack. From within, she pulled out two, nine-millimetre pistols along with their holsters. Clara recognised these as being from one of Marc's weapons caches.

Next, Evelyn zipped away and returned with Clara's preferred daily wear. Jeans, combat boots, light shirt, blouse, and a leather jacket.

"*Tiens,*" Evelyn said. (*Here.*)

"Help her get dressed," Julia said.

"Why?" Clara asked.

The angel was surprisingly pleased that she managed to get a whole word in one breath. *I'll likely pay for it soon.*

"A lot of desperate people are storming this hotel," Julia said. "They mistakenly believe there's electricity, food and water up here being hoarded by the government."

"Huh?" Clara asked, her head drooping from the strain.

Evelyn adjusted herself so she could better support the angel. There came a quick peck to the cheek, followed by the soft caress of a hand.

Once steady, the vampire helped Clara to get dressed, followed by the holsters. These were not the type she was accustomed to, but at least they were functional.

"I rigged up a generator and the outer screens came to life," Evelyn said softly.

There were no windows on this floor, just screens in both directions to create the illusion of windows. Clara was not comfortable with Evelyn luring people to their deaths, but she was too tired to do much more than clench her jaw.

"It's time to take the war to my enemies," Evelyn said. "For that, I need Marc, and he hasn't fed in weeks."

That explained the sounds she associated with a slithering creature. A vampire starved to that point existed solely to feed. When unleashed on unsuspecting humans, Marc would tear through them without slowing down.

"No…" Clara whispered.

"You died, and I mourned your loss…" Evelyn said. "I need someone to get us through this and that's Marc."

The vampire was making the hard choices. That was the difference between them; Clara could never put human lives at risk. Then again, she never had to deal with an enemy that rendered several, major cities uninhabitable. *I'd tear out my sister's spine with my bare hands to prevent that.*

"Marc is the distraction…" Julia said. "We didn't plan on there being demolition experts among them."

"Ada probably left people behind to hunt us down," Evelyn said.

"Shit. That means the subway is out," Julia said.

"Our egress points never accounted for evacuees having to breathe..." Evelyn confirmed.

Neither Julia nor Clara could blame a vampire for implementing a system that stopped the living from pursuing them. Still, there was a look of shock on both their faces.

Julia rolled her eyes, because she realised where this was going.

"Fuck me..."

Evelyn had a sheepish grin that bordered on a maniacal genius.

"The roof?"

Whereas Clara mostly looked dead tired and confused.

"I can't fly..."

"Neither can we, *ma chère*!"

CHAPTER 22

FLYING TRUE

It figures the elevators are down," Clara whispered.

Evelyn had a private elevator that led directly to the roof. Of course, having reliable power would have taken the challenge out of this journey. *As if recovering from death wasn't enough.*

Julia was armed with a shotgun, wearing the same red backpack that Clara gave her when freed from prison. It showed signs of fraying and the red had faded from exposure to the elements. *At least she got some use out of it.*

Evelyn was harder to see, and that was by design. The vampire was holding Clara over her left shoulder while making her way up the stairs. It was humiliating in a way to be lifted so easily by someone who more appropriately belonged on the runway during the Paris fashion week.

Clara felt helpless, bouncing up and down as Evelyn moved. She was facing aft, giving her a great view of those bare legs and ass. *Lucky for me that I'm not prone to motion sickness.*

There was activity all around them, several heartbeats converging on their former home, while others fanned throughout the hotel. What they lacked was coordination, which was a good sign. *A mob is a lot less likely to strategize.*

They made it up seven floors before the sound of boots registered from below. Evelyn and Julia hastened their pace, but their pursuers were determined.

When one appeared from the stairwell a flight down, Clara took aim and fired. While aiming for the shoulder, the shot pierced the right eye and splattered brain matter all over the stairwell.

"Horsefeathers!" Clara yelled. "I didn't mean to kill—him."

"Fuck!" Julia said, at the same time. "My fucking ears!"

Neither heard the other, but they saw signs of return fire. The bullets scarred the white paint over the concrete, but a couple tore out chunks as they impacted. *That's not regular ammunition!*

"*Putain!*" Evelyn said. (*Whore!*) "I hate it when I'm right… Take this door."

Julia blew through that door and found herself staring at three, armed men. While they wore torn and dirty clothing, they had the bearing of soldiers. *Those combat boots are a dead giveaway.*

"I need one alive," Evelyn said.

The werewolf did not hesitate. While their kind were not as formidable in human form, they did have tweaked reflexes. Her shotgun roared to life three times, leaving two bloodied and dying from being struck by buckshot to the chest…

The third was bleeding from the leg, but had no time to make a sound. Clara found herself transferred to the werewolf, just as a room door blew out.

"What the?" they said, in unison, but pushed on.

At the threshold, they saw Evelyn draining the man dry. He looked to be having the time of his life, even as his heart faltered. *I'll never get used to that.*

Evelyn looked up from her victim, who left the world with a smile on his face. In a single feeding, she regained her youthful appearance and was utterly refreshed. *Ready to take on an army.*

In the background, the sky had a dark, orange tinge. At first, Clara thought it was the curtains, but it behaved like a fog would. *I've never seen fog take on that colour.*

"Pardon?" Evelyn asked. (*Pardon?*)

"Nothing…" the others said, in unison.

"I haven't fed in weeks," Evelyn said, with a grin.

"Remarkable restraint," Clara said.

They did not linger for long. Clara found herself once more upon Evelyn's shoulder as they ran to the opposite staircase. The crew from behind broke through the stairwell door as they were about to clear the hallway.

Clara shot half her magazine to distract them, but somehow managed to drop another two. *At this range, I should have missed every shot.*

Through the ventilation shafts, there came blood-curdling screams along with sustained gunfire. It did not take much for Clara to realise that several intruded on the confined Marc. *They unleashed the bloodthirsty creature.*

Clara's heart sank, but the level of activity around them was far too coordinated to be a mob. Teams were converging on them from multiple vectors, many of them running in lockstep.

As a precaution, Clara inserted a fresh magazine while keeping her backup weapon holstered. She did not feel particularly well, and had no wish to fumble both weapons at a critical time. *Sliding across a long, marble hallway with a wax finish.*

They went up another three flights. Clara realised that more were waiting for them above. *Enough to slow us down.*

"Through here," Evelyn said.

Julia complied and found this floor was empty. Evelyn left Clara by the werewolf, followed closely by several doors splintering in sequence. The angel had seen the footage of controlled detonations of buildings and it looked very much like this. *Evelyn's not fucking around.*

"Over here!" Evelyn said.

Clara managed to get on her feet, tired, but otherwise able to stand on her own. Julia helped her to walk inside.

Four, long cables were hanging on the other side of the window. One did not need to be Doctor Frankenstein to realise what Evelyn had in mind. *One small step.*

"You're not fuck—(*ing serious*)?" Julia asked.

"It's two stories down," Evelyn said. "We're out of time."

The grim truth hardened all their faces. Clara turned a shade paler as her heart rate kicked up a notch, but her body fought back the attempt. She clenched her chest, and Evelyn's jaw dropped.

"I'm coming with—" Evelyn said.

"It's daytime!" Julia protested.

"Do you see the—(*sun*)?" Evelyn countered.

Clara fired six shots at the window. Four struck near a corner, while the other two went through the centre of the pane. Cracks propagated throughout before shattering entirely after a seventh shot.

"Go!" Clara ordered.

Evelyn did not hesitate; she grabbed a chair and cleared out most of the remaining shards along the frame, permitting her to grip the edge. From there, she grabbed Clara's hand, while steadying herself against the frame.

The fog was thick enough that Clara barely made out the window cleaners' platform.

"Fuck me," Julia said, before hopping off the edge.

There came a *thump* and the cables wobbled.

"I'm okay," Julia said.

Evelyn grabbed Clara and dropped as well. The impact of both women hitting the platform caused everything to shake violently. It was enough for Julia's eyes to widen while her fingers went white from holding onto the railing so tight.

If not for the vampire's strength and balance, they might have fallen off entirely. But Evelyn managed to keep Clara steady, even as the angel's legs wobbled.

"Steady, *ma chère*," Evelyn said. "I got you."

Julia caught Evelyn giving her a look and nodded in response. The werewolf grabbed Clara, while Evelyn unholstered the angel's backup weapon.

Several shots were fired into the adjacent window, the echoes muffled by the fog. Clara watched in awe, not entirely sure of what was going on.

"You two need a distraction," Evelyn said. "Good luck!"

Evelyn grabbed onto the window's edge. The vampire then fired several rounds into the gearbox, causing the platform to plummet into the orange fog.

"I have a war to win!" Evelyn said.

She flashed a wicked smile when someone opened the door leading into the room. "Good timing, I needed a snack…"

* * * *

"Hold on!" Julia said.

There was the sound of Clara's shoes dragging against the ground as they moved away from the hotel. Shortly thereafter, bullets *whizzed* past them. In turn, Julia responded with a volley of her own.

"Almost there…"

There came a pause.

"Clara?"

Another pause long enough to insert a fresh magazine.

"Fuck!" Julia swore. "Just hold the fuck on!"

CHAPTER 23

RELEASE VALVE

A chill ran down Clara's spine. The discomfort made her aware that the other side of her was toasty warm and she tried to move towards the source.

A soft hand grabbed her by the shoulder, jolting her awake.

"I'd avoid cuddling with the fire," Julia said, before chuckling.

Clara stopped cold; her eyes wide open and focused clearly on yellow and red flames licking the logs with zeal.

Meanwhile, Clara shifted into a sitting position and adjusted her wings. Those black feathers were a sight for sore eyes. *I'll be able to keep warm with those.*

"I'm getting tired of waking up in a new place…" Clara muttered.

"That… was my life before we met," Julia said. "Crash at a friend's or my latest hookup from the bar…"

"I lived a similar life in the twenties," Clara said, with a twinkle in her eye. "The difference was I knew who I was waking up as."

"I guessed as much," Julia said. "I was looking to throw you off balance. Besides, if you're *my* Clara, we should be thinking about how to get the *fuck* out of here."

That was the first bit of good news in a while. The idea of jumping into another self chilled the blood in her veins. While initially hell-bent on finding the Tower, Clara was now all in favour of leaving her past buried under the sands of time.

"How would you know?"

"Good question," Julia replied. "It's a bit of a mind fuck, especially when stumbling into the aftermath of your misadventures…"

"I saw you there," Clara said. "I even followed you to those cliffs back home."

Julia froze in place as though trying to wrap her mind around that tidbit. After a moment, she furrowed her brow and hunched her shoulders.

"I figured I missed you by about an hour," Julia said. "I followed your trail until I came across some scorched rocks and several, blinded men."

"That… that certainly aligns with how the situation unfolded…" Clara said. "Save for the aftermath."

"By then, you were gone," Julia confirmed.

The blaze was losing its pep, so Julia tossed in a couple of logs before adjusting them to improve airflow. The ambient light dimmed for a minute, but the fire soon spread over the logs. *She's no stranger to campfires.*

Above the fire, there was a cast-iron pan, with something sizzling inside. The wind was blowing away from her, but that did little to deter the scent of garlic and herbs.

"Gone?" Clara asked after her mind regained focus.

"There was no body to find," Julia said. "Believe me, they were thorough. You'd think their lives depended on it."

"Did they say—(*why*)?" Clara asked.

"Something about you being bait for a powerful corpse... wait... oh yeah— Drusilla."

"Drusilla..." Clara said, at the same time.

"Yeah," Julia said, without missing a beat.

"She sounded like a real bitch."

"That would be one hell of an understatement..."

The update certainly revealed more pieces of the puzzle. While Clara was not a hunter in that reality, she still found a way to piss off Drusilla. The Tower must have hoped their foe would show up to exact revenge. *I'd never use an innocent as bait.*

"You had me worried there," Julia added.

The werewolf grabbed the pan with her bare hand and shook up the contents. Despite being tolerant of the heat, she was forced to let go. It was fortunate for them that the pan dropped back in place.

"Fuck," Julia swore.

"Everything okay?"

"Yeah," Julia said. "It'll heal."

That feat was nevertheless impressive. Clara could not handle anything that hot, especially for a prolonged period. For all her strengths and powers, fire resistance was not one of them.

"I owe you for this," Clara said.

"You owe me nothing," Julia countered. "Evelyn, on the other hand..." *What does Evelyn have to do with this?*

Clara could not have been gone for more than a week... *She knew full well we'd probably lose contact once I entered the anomaly.*

"She sent you?"

"Yeah," Julia replied. "She's hard to say no to, especially when she's in tears, and offers to take me anywhere I want using her private jet."

"Why would she be in tears?" Clara asked. "I haven't been—(*gone long*)."

"How long do you figure?" Julia asked, after cocking a brow.

That question was proof enough that unexpected variables were at play. Getting in contact with Julia must not have been easy, getting the werewolf into the city to chat more so. *Not to mention Julia's inherent distrust of vampires.*

Clara cleared her throat, before answering, "Clearly not four to seven days."

"She called after two weeks, and it took me three days to reach a viable airport. I found this *terminus* seven days after that."

"...horsefeathers," Clara swore.

"I used more... *colourful* language when I realised what you got caught up in..."

"We could have been in here for months..."

"Or longer..." Julia said. "You didn't make it easy for me to find you."

"And I don't owe you?" Clara confirmed.

Their relationship was complicated. According to Julia, the *Harpy* was both the start of her downfall and the beginning of a long journey towards salvation. Sure, Clara saved her life when Julia was at her lowest, but the angel could not prevent the werewolf from being arrested.

"You've done more than enough for me," Julia said.

One thing that did not sit well with Clara was the appearance of glorification. Shame took hold from the depths of her mind and it made her empty stomach do somersaults.

"You don't know—(*everything*)..."

"I know..."

Clara's blood pressure dropped, because she did not want to hurt Julia if things escalated too far.

"How?"

The werewolf instead checked the pan, and pulled it off using the same hand as before. She placed it atop a large, flat rock to let it cool.

The odour of seared meat, butter, garlic, and herbs put a smile on Clara's face. She took in a deep breath and momentarily forgot that she still had no clue where they were or how to get back home.

"It's a bit gamey," Julia said. "Sorry, I didn't bring more than a week's worth of rations."

"It's a feast," Clara said. "Thank you."

"Don't mind the shot," Julia said. "This place is a natural hollow. There's a stream farther north, an abandoned farm on the other side of the bank. There's game everywhere."

"Sounds lovely," Clara said.

Clara wondered how she managed to miss this little gem while looking for a way into the Tower.

"I caught the scent through the door after losing you the first time."

"So, what's for dinner? Was it a challenging hunt?"

"Sabretooth... She tried to stalk me."

To prove her point, Julia reached into her bag and pulled out one of the elongated fangs. Clara had seen a lot of shit in her lifetime, ranging from vampires to a pack of werewolves, but this surprised her.

"I doubt there are too many of those lying around on people's fireplace mantels," Clara said.

Julia smirked before leaning in to say something.

"I intend to bring these to a palaeontologist and watch them freak out once they realise these aren't fossilised."

Clara laughed, enjoying this bit of levity. This was also a prime example of someone looking to avoid a topic.

"You haven't—(*answered my question*)." Clara said.

"Fuck off!" Julia warned.

The werewolf's face went red and the large veins in her forehead bulged. Clara did not react as doing so would only escalate matters.

"Didn't you clue in that I didn't want to have this discussion? That I'd rather not get emotional with you... or anyone else."

Clara had seen this kind of reaction before. Emotion built up over time, and bottled up in a fragile vessel. *I just triggered the release valve.*

"Evelyn called me in tears, and quickly confessed that she was the one who urged you to let me rot. She also made it EXPLICITLY clear that you were itching to get in a truck and come to my rescue."

Clara wanted to be the one to reveal the truth, but her disappearance forced Evelyn to act. Hindsight proved the choice was the right one... *I still feel guilty about it.*

"That FUCKING hurt, and I nearly hung up on that corpse..." Julia said, before taking in several breaths. "Then it occurred to me that other than my mother, you're the only one who actually gave a damn about me."

There was the source of all that pain and conflict. Clara knew that Julia's life as a werewolf was less than ideal, more so after her father died. *I never guessed it would be that bad.*

"You saved my life," Julia began. "Even when I broke into your home with the intent of slitting your throat."

That situation ended with a naked Clara fighting a half-turned werewolf.

"You trusted me to save your friend."

In turn, Julia ended up shot and arrested for her trouble.

"You paid fuckloads of cash to get me a lawyer, which I fought tooth and nail against. The same lawyer who pulled enough strings to get me out of prison."

An act which ironically led to Julia's capture by human traffickers. *Why don't I feel guilty about that?*

"You left me with a backpack full of cash, credit cards, fake passports, and burner phones. I could have started a whole new life…"

Now came the hard part. No matter how hard Julia's life had been, no one deserved what happened next.

"You know the rest…" Julia said. "It was my fault that they captured me. THAT'S ON ME!"

Julia needed another break, and Clara saw that distant stare. The same she observed in hunters who had seen too much horror and would never hunt again. The angel had seen that look in her own eyes when situations escalated well beyond the point of mortal comprehension… *How am I still standing?*

"Look…" Julia began, after taking a deep breath. "I'm no angel, none—*most* of us aren't."

Clara wiggled her wings and grinned, but did not add anything. Deep inside, they both knew that she was not a model angel.

"Did my father help me when I started failing my classes and wanted to drop out of school? No."

Clara had a feeling there was a lot more to it than that.

"Did my brother say a word in my defence when the pack wanted to shun me for our father picking a fight with the wrong person? Fuck no."

She knew from Evelyn's reports that her brother was killed by a rival pack months after the incident at the dam. Clara had been the catalyst that led to the downfall of the pack.

"The pack? Not even those who hated Adrienne with a passion lifted a finger to help me get off of the streets."

Clara was effectively shunned, barred from returning to heaven. One would think that would have been a heart-wrenching fate for an angel, but instead, she found her *punishment* freeing.

In many ways, leaving the pack could have had the same effect. The difference was that Julia was not prepared to sever ties and walk away at the time. *I think she's coming to terms with that now.*

"I used to hate you with EVERY fibre of my being," Julia admitted. "Even dreamed about delivering your head on a silver platter and eating your eyes as a trophy."

Clara did not even flinch, no matter how much that visual filled her with the urge to shudder. Werewolves may appear human, but many of them viewed people as being on a lower link in the food chain. *I've done things that made Julia's blood curdle.*

"Yet you answered that call and gave me everything I needed to deal with it myself."

There was something more to this.

"The fact that I saw what happens when you risked everything to save me did a lot to alter my perspective…"

Tears welled along the edges of the werewolf's eyes, and her voice was fading. Little of this had anything to do with Clara and guessed that she was more a target of convenience. *She knows I won't strike back.*

"So, when that corpse came begging for me to save you…" Julia said, as a tear ran down her cheek. "I told myself that you were one of the two who cared if I lived or died."

Clara took in a sharp breath, her own eyes beginning to cloud over with tears. It was hard not to react to such an emotional display from Julia.

"My mom cared, but I never had a chance to save her from my dad…" Julia said. "Instead of opposing them, going to the cops, or just running away, I *embraced* my nature as a werewolf and joined them."

It was easy to judge Julia for making that choice, but several details were omitted. Julia was not looking for absolution, and purposefully left a dark cloud hanging over them. *She's giving me a way out.*

Clara chose wisely to not condemn the werewolf. When Julia realised there would be no scorn, she managed a brief smile, but her face was soon flush with blood.

"FUCK YOU!" Julia yelled, to the point of her voice cracking. "Only a fucking CUNT would make me work through that!"

Even through that burst of rage, tears ran down those red cheeks. By the time those words passed her lips, Julia sounded like she was recovering from a cold.

The werewolf went quiet, bracing for the wave of emotions that overwhelmed her entirely. She even had trouble taking in enough air through all that snot and tears to do much more than let it all out.

This time, Clara moved in close and pressed a hand gently against Julia's thigh. Before she knew it, the werewolf had her arms wrapped around the angel. *She needs a shoulder to cry on.*

"Thank you for coming after me…" Clara whispered. "Remember that I'm here for you."

CHAPTER 24

FROM OUT OF THE SHADOWS

This is delicious," Clara said, while chewing on the sabretooth bits.

Julia smiled, a big improvement over the blathering mess from an hour ago. She must have cried for a solid hour and Clara was there for all of it. *I'd gladly do it all over again.*

Werewolves healed quickly, which meant Julia looked like nothing happened. Even Clara needed a while to recover after a good cry, but she would never switch places. *I think being a werewolf is more of a curse than a boon.*

"Thanks," Julia said, before reaching for another piece. "I was worried the meat had gone bad."

Clara cocked a brow, before asking, "Oh?"

"Time moves differently here…" Julia said. "I'd been here before and wrapped the carcass in plastic before submerging it in the river."

On the surface of it, the idea had merit. The water would cut down on the scent, and keep the meat cool. *A poor man's refrigerator.*

"An unnecessary precaution, as I didn't see or smell predators or scavengers in the area even after tracing the outer edges…"

Clara's head snapped back. She already knew about pocket realities, but never realised there might be a visible edge to them.

"Describe them?" Clara asked.

"Hmmmm," Julia said, while biting down on another piping-hot piece.

They were too *busy* to eat their dinner earlier. To make up for it, Julia put the pan on the embers. *Just enough to make them hot again.*

"Almost… like…" Julia struggled. "Ah! Like looking up at the surface while submerged in water."

That described Clara's time bubbles. Eleanor could do them without the effect, but Clara lacked the experience and power. That implied the world beyond these bubbles carried on, oblivious to what happened within.

"The meat was fine the first two times, this time it… decayed."

Clara chuckled. She guessed that a werewolf preferred to eat meat from, off the bone.

"That's what aged meat is," Clara explained.

"Oh?" Julia asked. "Well, I cut away the bad parts and cooked what was left."

So, the Terminus was also connected to pocket worlds in addition to being littered with bubbles from alternate realities. It was a shame that the goddesses were silent, as their advice could be their ticket out of here.

"Wait…" Clara said, as her mind moved tangentially to a subject they never delved into.

"Why could I see you moving through those first two realities as though you were there?"

Julia made a circle using her index and thumb and moved the tip of her nose in and out several times.

"Fuck knows," Julia said. "Part of me wants to say it had something to do with my not existing."

"Huh?" Clara asked, trying to wrap her mind around that statement. "So, there was no version of you there?"

"Yeah," Julia said. "I could walk around, see, and hear what was going on."

It sounded like she was an observer in the world. That did not explain why Clara could also see and hear the werewolf.

"People were oblivious to my presence," Julia said. "I yelled in their ears, licked the face of one, and flashed another."

She imagined Julia exposing herself to some random miner and getting no response. *That might turn into a running gag.*

"I even tried knocking down the priest with my backpack and it just went through him," Julia said. "I've lived on the streets and was used to being ignored... but this was something else..."

"Screaming into the void," Clara mused.

"The void just takes it," Julia said.

That was precisely the point. There was no instance of Julia there to *snap* into that reality. While it did not explain why Clara could see her, that might have been on account of Clara not belonging either.

"How did you find me the second time?" Clara asked.

Clara eyed the last piece, but decided the cook should have the honours. However, Julia shook her head, freeing the angel to indulge in her gluttony. *I would have never thought the meat would cook white.*

"The same as always," Julia said.

Julia set the pan atop the fire to burn off the remaining bits and grease. The river was far off while soap was in short supply. *A rock will scrape off what remains.*

"You tracked me?"

"Yep," Julia said. "Like I said before, your scent is camouflaged. I just followed any smell that made me think of home... with mom..."

Clara went to reach out, but the werewolf raised her hand to stop her. Julia took several breaths and went on.

"After The Grand," Julia began. "I tracked you down to three, potential locations."

That statement made no sense until she realised that any modern version of Clara would be an angel as well... *two doppelgangers...*

"In these, I awoke in my body," Julia said. "In two cases, it took me days to reach..."

"Evelyn," Clara finished.

"Yeah," Julia said. "I hedged my bets, moving from one reality to another every couple of days... Until I realised that I could stand just outside a bubble to make a call...."

That explained why Evelyn said that Julia was out for errands. The werewolf had been out doing her rounds, hoping for an update.

"Our hopes grew when your... vessel? Whatever—its heart started up again..."

"I have no memory of that," Clara said.

"I'd count your fucking, lucky stars," Julia said. "There was not much left of you. It may have taken Jesus three days to rise from the dead, but it took you three weeks just to start breathing again."

Clara gasped, as that immediately made her realise how hard it would have been on Evelyn.

"It must have been hell for you two," Clara said.

"I have to hand it to that corpse—Evelyn," Julia began. "The love of her life was dead, possibly coming back from the dead, due to an alternate self, her sire had to be locked up, and she still carried on as though it was a regular affair."

Looks could be deceiving, and Evelyn, with her short, slender frame, feminine features, soft skin, and penchant for designer clothing, certainly disarmed many. However, that vampire had figuratively been through hell and lived a life that few would envy.

"Adding to that, people were actively trying to kill her and end the world," Julia added. "I'm pretty sure I'd crack under that much pressure."

Instead, the vampire enabled their escape and promised to take the war to her enemies. Evelyn might be the natural enemy of hunters, but she was also the most steadfast and powerful ally Clara ever had.

"Speaking of going off script," Julia said. "You haven't mentioned the voices."

"I felt myself being separated from them before waking up in the first reality," Clara said.

"Miss them?" Julia asked.

Clara went to say something and paused, leaving her mouth agape. Her eyes rolled towards the sky while her teeth were slowly reunited.

"Complicated?" Julia confirmed.

"Yeah," Clara said. "I've learned to get along with Hecate, but it's nice to feel more like myself."

"It's okay to say you miss someone," Julia said. "Mom would say that whenever I went off for a school trip or camp."

"The difference is," Clara said. "If I keep absorbing old gods, will I be able to remain a distinct and dominant personality?"

The flames were done licking the pan. Julia pulled it out of the fire. She did not delay long before letting it drop on the wet grass nearby, which began sizzling.

"I can't imagine it," Julia said. "Entirely distinct personalities, with thousands of years of rivalries and baggage."

"Nailed it," Clara said. "In a way, I'm afraid that I'll eventually lose myself among the voices."

A branch snapped In the distance. Both women turned towards the sound, but Julia growled. It sounded surprisingly like a wolf, even though she was in human form.

"You said something about there being an abandoned farm?"

"Yeah," Julia said.

"Did you notice a verse on the arch for this section?"

"Yeah… uh… Genesis… Nine…"

Clara's eyes widened.

"Three?" Clara confirmed.

"How did you know?"

Clara thought back to her studies in her youth. Knowledge of the Bible was the reason she found her way through the Terminus, and this was a clue.

> *Everything that lives and moves about will be food for you. Just as I gave you the green plants, I now give you everything.* Genesis 9:3

The abandoned farm, and the passage of time different from that of the Terminus. This pocket reality must have served as a food store… *in case of a siege…*

"We're being hunted," Clara whispered, as she opened her wings.

Julia nodded after reaching the same conclusion. From out of the red backpack came a nine-millimetre pistol, which she tossed to Clara. The angel smiled, and noted the werewolf armed herself with a shotgun.

All around them, there were several heartbeats. These were steady, controlled, and disciplined… *only hunters can manage that feat…*

There came a *twang*, and one of Clara's wings reacted on instinct. It opened and blocked the projectile, the weave and density of her feathers were enough to stop the bolt… *that would have missed us both…*

"Stay close," Clara said.

The sight of her wings must have had a psychological effect on their foe. Another three, crossbow bolts flew at her and these were aimed to kill.

Her wings handled them with ease, and she fired two rounds in the air. The gunshots rang out like thunder given the surrounding trees.

Several bolts were sent her way, her wings doing what they were designed to do. This game was beginning to bore her, so Clara focused until the passage of time slowed down. *I'm lucky that ability is integral to angels.*

At this point, she was able to focus on twelve, distinct heartbeats. Their tactics were sound, they kept their spacing, and ensured they could bring fire to bear from any direction.

These were clearly hunters and not soldiers. There would have been orders to fire, and further direction on how to proceed. This group remained silent and coordinated themselves using stealthier means. An impressive feat, considering that few at the Tower were capable of this level of coordination.

Namely, the elites of *Les Filles de Jeanne d'Arc*, were the only group she knew of personally. As judged by the heart rates, this hinted the boys must have an equivalent. *It's funny how we never talked about the boys having a club of their own when I was there.*

Julia showed signs of irritation, her face slowly hinting that she was on the verge of taking action. This posed a problem, because Clara was the obvious target, and they had no reason to suspect Julia.

Clara *blipped* for a second. She appeared right by Julia and whispered into her ear, "Stop. They think you're human."

Before Julia had the opportunity to realise what was said, Clara was back in place. Bolts continued to be fired at her, and her wings deflected them with ease. *I can't keep this up forever.*

On occasion, she grabbed one out of the air and snapped it in half. Clara thought that anyone approaching a winged woman who moved fast enough to accomplish such a feat would give them a reason to reconsider. *Not when dealing with fanatics.*

This would go on until they either ran out of bolts or their numbers increased in their favour. This far out of sync with time, Clara's reaction times were faster than their eyes could see. *That leaves me some options.*

Clara winked at Julia, long enough to ensure the werewolf caught it. When another bolt was fired, she grabbed it as the razor-sharp tip drove towards her chest.

Under control, she led the bolt in closer, crumpled in conjunction with an *impact*. Her wings covered most of her, preventing them from taking potshots. Sure enough, and an additional two struck her in the back, but the thick layer of feathers meant she felt little more than a prick. *They aren't taking chances.*

With their target *down*, they moved out from cover and approached in a deliberate manner. Julia remained where she was with her shotgun in hand, but they never took a shot at her. Clara was running at such a speed that she could intervene. *Julia can't take them on herself.*

At this rate their movements were slow and laborious, like watching snails *run* the thousand-metre dash in slow motion. Clara used the time to track the motions of the group, paying heed to where they were and how they behaved.

Their discipline was unreal, with barely any variance in their heart rate and breathing. What differed were their strides, which varied based on height and size.

The bigger and presumably stronger men were leading, whereas the smaller and younger ones hung back. If this were to devolve into hand-to-hand combat, those in the back would maintain their distance and engage with their crossbows. *I'd have problems engaging multiple threats at two ranges.*

They collectively stopped, once the lead group was within fifteen paces. The man who lined up with the direction from where she was shot made a sign to halt.

"What are you doing here?" Asked a man, who stood to the left of the presumed leader.

His voice was smooth as silk, and Clara heard the modulation in his voice. She was not sure how, but he somehow learned to use his voice like vampires did. *I'll call him Silky.*

"We got trapped in a fucking endless corridor and found this place," Julia said.

The best lies were those based on truth, but her already high heart rate went up a tick. It was not much, but someone like Clara would pick up on the deception.

"You're telling me that you just stumbled onto this place?" Silky asked, the modulation was more overt now, which would have been hard for humans to ignore. *I'll need to ask Evelyn to show me how to do it.*

Clara created the illusion of her heart racing to account for the blood loss while showing signs of faltering. She knew Julia might pick up on it and hoped she would ignore the realism or play it up.

"Next time, don't fucking use Bible verses that hint to their purpose," Julia said.

More truth to deflect. By pointing out that it was painfully obvious *vis-à-vis* her superhuman sense of scent, Julia could avoid making unnecessary lies.

The men surrounding Silky chuckled, save the presumptive leader. That forced the hunter to switch up his tactics. *I know what I would do.*

"Isaiah 43:4," Silky said without context.

Julia took a deep breath, gulped, and said, "Since you are precious and honoured in my sight, and because I love you, I will give people in exchange for you, nations in exchange for your life."

There came more chuckling. Which forced Silky to up the ante.

"1 Peter 3:3," Silky added.

"Your beauty should not come from outward adornment, such as elaborate hairstyles and the wearing of gold jewellery or fine clothes."

Julia was getting cocky, and her slowing heart rate was a testament to that. By this point, Clara's heart rate was so low that a physician would declare her dead.

There were more chuckles and even a few howls of laughter. Silky's heart rate blipped in the span of a single breath. Clara imagined that the man was not about to be shown up by a girl. *They may be as old as those who fought in the Great War, it doesn't make them wise.*

"Ecclesiastes 4:10," Silky said, without any modulation, instead, aggression filled in that void.

Clara knew the answer:

> *If either of them falls down, one can help the other up. But pity anyone who falls and has no one to help them up.* Ecclesiastes 4:10

It was a jab at having taken down Clara, leaving Julia to stand on her own. The werewolf was not so quick to respond this time. Her heart rate went sky-high and she gulped loud enough for everyone to hear.

"Fuck... You fucking got me," Julia said, but before anyone could react. "I'm more of a fan of Proverbs 17:28. Even a fucking fool who keeps silent is considered wise; when he closes his lips, he doesn't come across as an idiot."

There came howls of laughter, and Silky stepped out of formation. Julia echoed his movements, which left Clara curious as to who would win.

The presumed leader cleared his throat and Silky stopped cold.

"Ever heard of a vampire or ghoul who can quote scripture?" the leader asked.

Clara imagined Evelyn quoting the Bible word for word while shoving the *good book* up their asses. Vampires were once human, and many were well-read to avoid silly tests such as these. *There are rumours that some were once Cardinals and another even made it to Pope.*

"No, Sir," Silky said.

No one else dared make a sound, confirming that this was the authority among the group. Silky was sent to probe, while the leader observed. *Marc would call that poor leadership.*

"What's your name, my dear?" the leader asked.

There was sincerity behind that voice which made it hard to ignore. Clara assumed the leader was a hit with the ladies.

"Julia Black," she replied.

"A beautiful and strong name," the leader said. "I'm Adam."

The leader moved his arms, and Clara could do little more than guess what he did.

"What about that?"

Julia was not going to make it easy for them.

"You mean who?" Julia countered.

The leader balanced himself on his heels while smacking his lips. He may have had a way with the ladies, but Julia was out of his league. *She isn't falling for his charm.*

"Apologies," Adam said. "Does… *she* have a name?"

"You mean, did?" Julia said, as a jab. "Clara Grey."

It was as though the group collectively held their breath, but everyone recovered by the third heartbeat. Clara imagined that Julia was smiling, as her heart rate hovered near the resting point.

"Should that name have meaning to us?" Adam asked. *He's hiding something.*

"You've never heard of the Valkyrie? The infamous, fallen angel, vampire fu(*cker*)—hunter, slayer of werewolves, ghouls and gods?"

"Angels don't exist," Adam said flatly.

"The same goes for the sabretooth tigers, but I had thirds tonight…"

The angel wanted very much to burst out laughing at Julia's slip of the tongue. Clara realised the werewolf was fucking with them, feeding them just enough truth to keep them from seeing the omissions.

"That animal was sacred!" Silky exclaimed.

"And fucking delicious," Julia said, to further taunt them.

Their exchange was having an effect and most of the hunters had lowered their crossbows. They were paying attention to the discourse, their eyes off the feathered lump on the ground. *Smart girl!*

"Why would such… a powerful… woman need to use such… colourful language?" Adam asked.

A high-class insult like that was sure to land flat with Julia. The werewolf knew perfectly well this was an attempt to slander her intellect and persona, but Julia had been tempered by werewolves. *It would be easier to make a sailor blush.*

"You might want to dial up your insults," Julia said. "I've heard worse in grade school… As for your question. I'm—was her chronicler."

"Chronicler?" Adam asked.

"Do you have any idea how much of an ego a hunter elevated by GOD himself has?" Julia asked. "Day in and day out another miracle. Even the corpses knew to avoid the sewers whenever she took a shit."

A few laughed, but they were quickly silenced. Clara suspected what Julia was saying went over their heads, forcing them to challenge the Tower's dogma. *She's a breath of fresh air in their sterile world.*

"Corpse?" Adam asked. "How *wonderfully* colloquial of you."

Julia's heart rate shot up, a sign that she slipped out a clue about her true nature. Hunters never used the term *corpse*, instead, they used *them*, and neither group cared what vampires called themselves. *They spent enough time around werewolves to learn their slang?*

"Now, boys," Julia said. "Be nice, I promise you that this will be my best chapter yet!"

There was a pause before the reply. Clara kept herself in an accelerated pace, pushing her ability to the limits. The words took forever to say now, but that way, she could react to this ever-evolving plan.

"What feats have you written?"

"I was there when she fell from heaven and killed an alpha werewolf in the buff," Julia said.

That was the first time they met. Although Julia was less than impressed when Clara left with her clothes.

"I was there when she took out a pack of werewolves single-handedly."

The time when Clara enlisted Julia's help to save her friend's life.

"I was there when she used herself as bait to hunt down Artemis," Julia added.

"Gods do not exist," Silky said.

"Goddess... the tits are a dead giveaway on which word to use. You know, for someone who claims to know corpses, you have a narrow mind."

That was a line Clara used on Julia when the werewolf insisted that ghosts did not exist.

"She's lying," Silky said, turning around to face the leader.

This allowed Clara to further finalise her plan. *All I need is a sign.*

"Her greatest feat?" Julia teased.

"What was her greatest feat?" Adam asked, that tone hinting that he was nearly done humouring her.

"Her heart stopped for a fortnight, and three days after she walked once more among us."

That was her cue to get ready.

"Like..."

The single syllable sounded like an opera singer holding a note. What Clara really wanted was to act, but was also enjoying Julia's flair for theatrics.

"N..."

Clara jumped to her feet using a powerful flip of her wings. She then spun in place while the other wing knocked down several hunters.

"O..."

Her feet hit the ground, and Clara raced around the hollow. She accounted for every heartbeat while freeing every hunter of their bolts and cut the strings to their crossbows. At this pace, the bow limbs would not *snap* until she was done.

"*W...*"

She dropped the bolts into the fire and returned mostly in sync with time. *I left just enough to react if someone gets smart.*

There came the distinct sound of a dozen crossbow arms splintering after losing tension. While several dropped their weapons, everyone had wide eyes and gaping mouths.

"I'm back..." Clara said, in a cocky tone.

"You're a myth," Silky managed to say.

"They say that all myths are grounded in truth..." Clara said.

The angel opened her wings to their full size creating a shadow that blocked the light of the fire.

CHAPTER 25

INTO THE LIGHT

It was the eyes that sold these hunters that this was, in fact, *the* Clara Grey. The angel had never taken the time to consider that her steel-grey eyes were not all that common.

That did not stop them from forcing both Clara and Julia to confirm they were no vampires. The werewolf had trouble containing her laughter, and only Clara was privy to the details of that particular joke.

"You'd think the wings were enough of a clue," Clara whispered, to the werewolf.

That elicited a howl of laughter, which made several of the hunters nervous. Clara suspected two factors were in play. The first being that she was by far the biggest threat they encountered. The second was the simple fact that they were not in on the joke. *They are used to being the ones who say things that no one else gets.*

Clara guessed their plan when the hunters hung back as both women were sent through a doorway within the Terminus. As soon as the door behind them slammed shut, there came a blinding source of white light.

"Motherfucker!" Julia yelled, while shielding her eyes with her hands.

Clara closed her eyes gently while bathing in the radiant energy, seemingly immune to the intense light… *as though I were in Heaven*. Angels were creatures of light and this source proved to be invigorating… *which charges my batteries*.

This was a trap that targeted vampires, and now Clara guessed it was applied to anything that was not human. She slowed time a bit more, suspecting that whoever was here had not been briefed.

"Halt!" A female voice ordered.

"Abomination!" Another yelled.

The second yell came with the distinct *twang* of a bow string driving a bolt forward. The projectile flew fast and high.

Since Clara was immune to the blinding light, she grabbed the bolt with her bare hands. Just ahead, there stood three, older acolytes in uniform, all wearing the equivalent of welding goggles. The two who did not fire were dividing their attention between the approaching angel and the one who loosed the projectile.

"I believe this is yours?" Clara asked.

Right behind the acolytes, there was a doorway and another set of goggles. Clara left the bolt with its rightful owner before grabbing a set for Julia.

"Thank you," the acolyte said, in a shaky voice.

"Read up on your Bible," Clara said dryly. "I trust you two will assist?"

The others nodded, and Clara grinned. Had she been able to use her goddess powers, she would have interacted with them as her plain-Jane self. Alas, Clara had to get accustomed to people gawking at those black, feathered wings.

"Stand still," Clara told Julia.

It did not take long for the werewolf to realise what Clara was doing. Julia adjusted the goggles and tightened the straps to make sure they were snug.

"Been here before?" Julia asked.

"On both ends of similar transactions," Clara said. "Vampires would just burst into flames."

Julia made a silent '*Oh*' with her mouth. She must have suspected the Tower was hostile to vampires, but never assumed there were traps designed to eliminate them entirely. *At least she didn't give away Evelyn.*

"Thank you," Clara said.

"You're welcome?" Julia said, before realising why it was said.

"Through here, ladies?" Clara asked.

Again a nod, and Clara was beginning to wonder if these three would end up permanently traumatised by this... *Say...*

"It might look bad for you three if someone doesn't escort me inside," Clara reminded them.

Even with some prompting, none roused themselves from their stupor. Clara realised that she would need to defuse the situation.

"You know," Clara began. "I remember spending hours at this very post."

"You-you did?" One asked.

This was presumably the one who called out halt, since the one who fired a bolt was barely breathing.

"Is it still a duty bestowed to those who follow a maiden who hails from *Orléans*?"

The girls furrowed their brows, an indication that Clara further threw them for a loop. Such details were not shared with anyone outside their group.

Like the Tower, Les Filles de Jeanne d'Arc had no official name outside of their group. *That doesn't stop the rumours from spreading.*

"What's your name?" Clara said, asking the only one who appeared to be able to speak.

"Agnes," the girl replied.

"A distinguished name," Clara said.

The name was old and uncommon today. Since the Tower was isolated in the twenties, Clara wondered if most here bore the old names.

"I'm Clara Grey," the angel said. "My chronicler is Julia Black."

"Clara Grey!" Agnes yelled. "Like the hunter of legend?"

Clara smirked, and thanked her lucky stars for not living long enough to see herself turn into a legend. *It's hard to live up to the expectations of those who place you on a mantel.*

"Live fast, die hard, and leave a good-looking corpse," Clara said. *I certainly failed that last part.*

Julia chuckled, but the hunters did not react. She realised that paraphrasing a quote from the late forties would not resonate with them. Clara let out all the air from her lungs, before a disarming smile fell upon her lips.

"How'd you think I got these wings?" Clara asked. "It wasn't by living into my golden years."

Now it was the girls' turn to say, "Oh," in unison. *They really need to get out more.*

"Agnes," Clara said lightly. "Be a dear and escort us out of this room, please…"

CHAPTER 26

DOUBLE HELIX

Clara guessed there would be additional defences once she entered the Grand Hall. The moment she opened that door, Clara heard several weapons being drawn.

Julia, who was right behind Clara, responded to the sound by stiffening up. By Clara's count, they were surrounded by sixty hunters, full-fledged and presumably more experienced than the acolytes they dealt with before. The angel maintained a smile even as Agnes slammed into the back of the werewolf.

"Sorr…(*y*)," Agnes said.

A statement that was swallowed whole by this expansive space. Few outsiders had ever seen the heart of the Tower, but the double-helix staircase that weaved its way to the upper levels at the heart of this structure was well-known to hunters.

The walls were white marble, which contrasted with the onyx used for the Terminus perfectly. She often wondered if the choice of materials served to remind hunters they were stepping away from the light… *and into danger.*

There were bridges that crossed the wide expanse every couple of levels. Clara never before considered how much this architecture resembled a DNA chain. *That means the designer had a visual concept of genetics thousands of years ago.*

"Halt!" A man ordered.

At the hunter's side there was Adam and, surprisingly Silky.

Being this far out of sync with time meant that the single word played out longer than any opera singer could ever hope to hold. To avoid giving away her hand, Clara had to avoid showing signs of irritation. *It'll make me look like a vampire.*

While they no longer suspected that she was a vampire, they were sure to react if she *blurred* like one. So, Clara played her part and took a long pause before responding in her own operatic voice.

"Or what?" Clara asked, while moving forward.

Even Julia had her hands up by this point. Their opponents were not about to take any chances. With good reason, since Clara handily disarmed the smaller group. *I could do the same here, but I bet they have a fallback.*

There were a few reasons to worry for Julia. No matter the form, because werewolves were creatures of strength and dexterity, not speed. *Those ballistas pack one hell of a punch.*

That meant the angel needed to bluff, play her hand and hope they chose to stand down. However, that assumed a rational mind, which was the antithesis of zealotry. It might have taken her a century to realise it, but Evelyn did help her to accept that she was, in fact, a martyr. *One who was taught that angels, ghosts, and old gods did not exist.*

The man hesitated. Every one of his heartbeats resounded in her mind, as though a machine was pounding steel rods into the ground.

"Uh," the man said, denoting a rather inauspicious start.

This man might have been older than Adam, but he clearly lacked field experience. Some hunters froze as this was likely their first time thrust into the breach, but that was either resolved by death or by surviving the experience.

Clara let her black wings unfurl to their full size. She spotted several instances of her wings' shadow, and they even darkened the faces of the lead men.

There was a collective gasp, which confirmed how inexperienced this group was. *I don't think they've ever been outside the Tower.*

"See these?" Clara asked. "What creature has wings?"

There came another pause, which meant Clara was closing the space between them too fast. To give them a chance to *adjust* to her presence, she slowed down.

"Harpy?"

In the background, Julia chuckled, but Clara maintained a razor-sharp focus. This man must have been briefed, which meant he was playing with her. *They are sussing out other potential reasons for my existence.*

"A creature that is more bird than woman, renowned for being unbelievably ugly? You might want to get your eyes checked."

The men facing her gulped, and she was pretty sure that several women in the audience snickered. *That might play in my favour.*

"Valkyrie?"

"Do I look like a creature of Norse myth to you?" Clara asked. "Brown hair? Grey eyes?"

That did not preclude her from being a valkyrie, but she hoped it might be enough to throw him off. *He's not going to stop there.*

"Demon!" The man exclaimed.

That may as well have been a call to arms, as it roused a few mesmerised by this exchange. To be honest, she was surprised that the name even came up. *Demons were never mentioned at all at the Tower.*

Clara laughed, one so boisterous that even a few of the hunters joined in.

"I thrive in the light," Clara said. "I hunt things that go bump in the night."

No matter how much she slowed her progress, these delays meant this gap would soon close. Instead of fighting it any longer, Clara stopped ten paces away from the men. Took a stiff bow and looked up at them with a smirk on her face.

"I am Clara Grey," she began. "Hunter, flapper, and the one who sacrificed her life to end Drusilla's reign of terror."

Clara opted for a dramatic pause, which gave her time to confirm she had their undivided attention. The lead hunter's heart rate dipped a bit, as did several of the others. *The Reverend Mother would have our hides for such a poor demonstration of self-control.*

"For my sacrifice, I was permitted to join the ranks of Heaven's soldiers and did so dutifully for ninety years."

It dawned on her that this situation might have hinged on her being the attacker. Hunters were known to fight to the last. *At least for my generation.*

"I was sent back to Earth and remain to this day," Clara said, while making no mention as to why. "Today, I came home."

There came another pause, long enough that it became awkward. However, in the background, hidden from sight, there came a clap. It was soon joined by others until it built up to a thunderous applause.

Clara smiled and bowed once more, while ensuring her wings remained in view the entire time. *Sometimes you need to add a bit of flair.*

When the lead man breathed a sigh of relief, Clara confirmed this generation of hunters had not lost their predilection for being martyrs.

"They were expecting you to attack?" Julia whispered.

Clara could only nod while maintaining a warm smile. The applause had been going on for a solid three minutes and showed no signs of waning. Although, she suspected there was more to their praise than a simple reaction to a rousing introduction. *If I can get in, they can get out.*

Julia was correct, this group was here to delay her. The next step would have been to blow the Tower and entomb her under tonnes of stone and debris. *If it worked for Dorothy, it might work on me.*

The werewolf chose not to add anything to her earlier question, which was wise. The walls had ears and Clara was effectively a curiosity to staff and students alike. *Some would like nothing better than to dissect me to prove angels don't exist.*

"I never caught your name," Clara said, to the man who led the defence.

By then, the applause had died down enough to start a dialogue. One she hoped would yield answers.

"Walter," the man said, after a slight pause.

"Pleasure," Clara said.

"How did you find your way here?" Adam asked.

Walter's eyes locked onto the acolyte. Adam sucked in air through his teeth before blowing away a stray lock of hair on his forehead.

"The Terminus," Clara said, to keep things vague for now. "It's been a long road getting here."

"I apologise for—(*his outburst*)." Walter said.

Clara smirked before replying, "It takes a lot more than that to bother me. Besides, I'm chomping at the bit to find a way out too."

That appeared to soothe both their minds. Still, Clara had no desire to be holed up here for much longer... *interrogation in the form of small talk.*

"Would you care to join us for the evening meal?" Walter asked.

The idea was tempting, but that would simply keep her tied up in a different setting. What she wanted was a nice quiet spot to speak with Julia and freshen up. *I'd be willing to bet they will post sentries nearby, but beggars can't be choosers.*

"We would love to," Clara began, and immediately felt the eyes of the werewolf burning a hole through the back of her skull. "It's been a long trip, and I could stand to freshen up."

It was fortunate that Adam did not appear to view this as a slight. Clara made sure to maintain an emotional mask that would make Evelyn proud. Her smile appeared to be genuine, and those steel-grey eyes shined as though excited.

Like almost everyone here, her heart rate was steady. Julia was the exception, leading her to suspect the younger acolytes were elsewhere within the Tower.

"We can accommodate your request," Walter said. "We had our guest quarters readied."

"Readied?" Julia confirmed.

"They are prepared every day," Clara answered, to help defuse the situation. "Sheets washed, the rooms cleaned and dusted."

Since hunters never knew when someone might return to the Tower, a wing of guest accommodations was always kept ready.

"Precisely," Walter replied. "Agnes—(*will you please escort them*)?"

"I know the way," Clara said. "I spent more than my fair share of time preparing those rooms."

A statement that confirmed Clara was once a troublemaker. Walter smiled, while Adam remained oblivious. *I'm not the only one who got into trouble while here.*

There was an awkward pause, meaning that Clara was not fully trusted. The man was unwilling to broach that subject. *Afraid of challenging the legend in public?*

Clara turned around to find Agnes standing there with a crossbow in hand. While silent, those eyes showed she was cognizant of the discussion. *I'm starting to like this one.*

"Would you like to lead the way?" Clara asked.

Agnes did not hesitate, and responded with a single, curt nod. In Clara's mind, Agnes was excited, but knew enough not to give herself away.

"That settles that," Clara said. "How long until the meal hour?"

"The meal will be served in a little over forty-five minutes," Walter replied.

"Excellent," Clara said. "Will the Reverend Mother be there?"

She tossed in that question casually to hide its importance. Given her company, no one was fooled… *and yet we play these games regardless.*

There came another pause, followed by a dip in the heart rates of several within earshot. That detail was telling but by itself was not an answer.

"She… passed away recently," Walter said.

Adam started breathing again the moment that reply was uttered. Given the excuse, Clara only expected such a reaction from Agnes or another one of the girls. *The boys in my day rarely interacted with the Reverend Mother.*

"That's a shame…" Clara said. "We always made sure to pay our respects to our superiors."

"That remains true today," Walter said. "We have yet to appoint a replacement."

"I'm sure they'll have big shoes to fill… Agnes, if you please?"

Clara made eye contact with Julia before turning towards their escort. It was clear the werewolf noticed that something was off as well, but they had to wait for a debrief. *We need to be careful.*

CHAPTER 27

BUTTONS AND THREAD

I'll wait in the hall," Agnes said.

The young acolyte closed the door behind her, leaving Clara and Julia alone in this spartan bedroom. The pervasive smell of ammonia burned the inside of her nose... *Nearly a century without guests and they clean it every day.*

By modern norms there was one small bed. Both would end up sleeping with their feet over the edge. At least the mattress was comfortable, and Clara suspected it was made of down.

"What the actual fuck?" Julia asked.

Clara pressed her finger against her lips, followed by pointing to her ears and the surrounding environment. While there was no guarantee there was listening equipment, there was no harm in being cautious.

She wanted something from her bag, but remembered it was gone. *Did Julia pack an extra set of clothes for me?*

"Do you have one of my phones with a charge?" Clara whispered.

199

Julia nodded and dropped her own backpack onto the bed. After rifling through the contents, she found one that turned on with an indication of a fifty-two percent charge.

"That was standard operating procedure," Clara said aloud. "Were you expecting a brass band?"

Julia cocked a brow before the reason for the disparate dialogue hit her. The werewolf handed over the phone while considering her reply.

"Honestly, I'd prefer a wreath of tropical flowers and a kiss on the cheek," Julia replied.

Clara opened a secure storage app and put in her password. The dialogue gave her an idea, so she scrolled down to the right entry.

"Would a kiss make it all better?" Clara asked.

She showed the screen to Julia, above and below were pre-recorded conversations. Julia recognised a couple of the entries as being sourced from movies.

However, when those brown eyes focused on the entry Clara selected, her head snapped back. She took several breaths to think over, shrugged and nodded.

"You have no idea," Julia said.

Clara double-tapped on the file and the sound of two women kissing filled the silence. To further ensure they had some privacy, Clara cranked the volume to make sure the sounds carried beyond the room.

"You had porn on those phones all this time?" Julia asked.

Other visible entries listed various types of sex, all to distract eavesdroppers. *At the very least, it might keep Agnes entertained.*

"Again… what the actual fuck?" Julia asked.

"Which part?" Clara asked.

"Well… all of it," Julia said. "Mostly the standoff."

Clara summarised her thoughts related to that situation. They were either ready to martyr themselves, or planned to slow the angel down long enough to implement their end game… *matters little now…*

"That's fucked up," Julia said. "Well… that explains—you."

"Me," Clara said, in unison.

"Doesn't that bother you?"

"I'm… working on it."

By now, the women on the audio were well past passionate kissing. There came the rustling of clothing, their breathing heavy.

"Do you have a change of clothes?" Clara asked.

"A few clean shirts and jeans," Julia said.

Without being prompted, the werewolf went back into the bag and pulled out a few items rolled into logs. They were sure to be wrinkled, a better option than showing up to supper with dirty clothes.

As expected, there was a sink, with soap and clean towels. They would need to wait until *they* were done before making unrelated sounds to *their* activity. *I wonder if they installed a shower.*

"Thanks," Clara said. "Did you learn anything?"

"They were lying about the Reverend Mother," Julia replied.

Clara suspected, and the blip in heart rate certainly implied they were lying. She found it interesting that Julia also reached the same conclusion.

"How do you know?" Clara pressed.

"I followed my nose," Julia said.

Clara remembered how some liars would sweat while struggling to get out of trouble. The scent reminded her of curdled milk, but she attributed it to stress.

In the background, one of the performers moaned loudly. Whatever they were up to, someone clearly knew what they were doing... *or how to fake it.*

The women looked at each other, and realised they were thinking the same thing. It took all they had to stifle a giggle.

"You can smell out liars?" Clara asked.

"Yep," Julia said. "People lie a lot."

"All too true," Clara said.

"I can't tell with you, or a corpse," Julia admitted.

Since vampires did not sweat or breathe that certainly made sense. Of course, vampires had a distinctive scent that caught the attention of any werewolf downwind. *We had to leave a nightclub because they caught Evelyn's scent.*

The moans had progressed to screams with a great deal of urgency in them. It would not be long before the woman came, which gave them the opportunity to move on.

"I don't want to stay here," Clara said.

"You?" Julia asked. "Why?"

"Be careful what you wish for."

"They caught us before you could tell me?"

"Yep," Clara admitted. "I guess we redouble our efforts on finding a way out."

The angel reached for the phone as the performer sighed. While she could move faster than the eye could see, the phone was designed to accommodate humans. Fortunately, she was able to stop it at just the right time.

"Oh my," Clara said. "I needed that."

"Anytime," Julia said, not quite enjoying this aspect of her role as *chronicler*.

"We should get ready," Clara said, before walking towards the sink and turning the taps. "Wash up."

"Should I add this to our official records?" Julia asked.

There came a giggle from outside the door. The women smiled, but remained focused on the task at hand.

* * * *

Clara took one look at those wrinkled clothes and her heart sank. With her wings a permanent fixture, she would need to tear through the shirt. *That sort of defeats the purpose.*

She gave the shirt back to Julia, who hunched her shoulders while voicelessly asking, "What?"

Clara pointed to her shoulder and checked the dresser in the room. It was filled with clothing appropriate for a full-fledged hunter of both genders. She sifted through the contents until she found pants, shirt and coat. *That doesn't really solve the problem.*

"Wait," Clara whispered.

In the last drawer, there was an assortment of corsets. At least her shoulders would remain bare while covering the rest. *No one was wearing these in my day.*

The corset was a combination of steel and leather with a silk liner. Since women could not wear armour, these provided a measure of protection.

"That's pretty sweet!" Julia said.

"I was raised in a time when corsets were the standard," Clara said. "Married women of means and ladies were—(*expected to wear them*)."

"You were neither," Julia teased.

"…and proud of it," Clara said to avoid turning this into a verbal fusillade.

"Fuck… I'd be too."

The angel opened the door and faced Agnes with her crossbow at the ready… *to make sure we don't try anything.*

"I need something sewn," Clara said. "Know anyone who can help?"

"There's a sewing machine and supplies down the hall," Agnes replied.

"I'd have to leave this room…"

"*You* are permitted to…" Agnes began. "…besides, this wing is empty."

Clara could confirm that last detail herself. There were only three heartbeats nearby, and the fourth was nearly out of range. So, the acolyte was telling the truth, which highlighted how much that first part was telling.

The order must have been for Agnes to keep an eye on Julia. *It's not like anyone is old enough to remember who I was.*

That part was concerning. There was something else afoot, and Clara could not put her finger on it. It worried her and reinforced the growing desire to find a way out. *I need options.*

"I'll be right back," Clara said, while holding up a finger.

She grabbed the uniform, which had a faint scent of cedar, and went where the acolyte pointed. When the acolyte took up position to block the door, Julia simply swore up a storm and went back inside to clean up.

Meanwhile, Clara dug deep to remember her training as a seamstress. She loosened the seams around the shoulder and cut a perpendicular line to where her wings would protrude from.

On a counter, there was an old sewing machine complete with a foot pedal. Her heart sank, because the mechanism would not tolerate being pushed beyond its mechanical limits.

Clara abandoned her project with the shirt and moved on to the jacket. She repeated the steps, ensuring there was enough give at the top. Using pins, she bent in an edge and created the overall pattern.

She sewed the seams to ensure they would not tear. Next, she added buttonholes and buttons, so the top would close properly. Those she did by hand, with the needle moving quicker than the eye could see. Clara knew they were nearing supper time and left the shirt where it was.

"A hunter needs to know when to make sacrifices."

She grabbed the coat and ran back to the door, dragging in Agnes at the same time.

"Do you have experience with corsets?"

The young acolyte smiled, and Clara realised by those dreamy eyes that the show they put on might have found an audience. *Edith would be happy to know the Tower did has not done away with the practice of using pairs with differing sexual appetites.*

"Of course," Agnes replied.

"In or out of?" Clara teased.

"Both."

"Atta girl!"

Had they known that Clara could go either way, she would have never been paired with a sapphic friend. *I'm thankful they taught us to lie so well.*

CHAPTER 28

BITTER PILL

The room went silent when Clara was escorted into the main dining hall. In her time, there would be no more than sixty people on site, including a handful of hunters back from a mission.

Tonight, every table was filled with students and hunters. The room was hot and humid, even with the massive hearths at both ends of the vaulted chamber containing nothing more than ash.

"They were waiting for us," Clara whispered, low enough that only Julia would hear.

No one was eating, which was by itself unusual. Acolytes had chaotic schedules that forced them to be creative and adaptable. She remembered grabbing bread on the way to class, or skipping a meal entirely to make a schedule. *Some had nervous breakdowns while trying to adjust.*

Next, came a chorus of gasps followed by a wave of whispers. That ceased when Walter cleared his throat, which highlighted his authority and the hold he had on the rank and file.

In her day, the Reverend Mother wore the same uniform as acolytes. It was a symbolic gesture to ensure hunters were not overshadowed by her authority. *The men didn't feel the same way.*

The head of men wore the garb of a cardinal, which also highlighted that *they* had their place in the church. *We usually kept to ourselves.*

Clara was more aptly dressed like a nun, with notable exceptions. Even though her feathers were black, as was the uniform, those wings were hard to ignore.

However, the jacket was never meant to serve as a complete second layer. It was meant to be worn with the shirt. Instead, she just had a corset, which left a lot less to the imagination.

Clara had forgotten that detail because she had not worn the uniform in over a century. *Otherwise, I would have prioritised that shirt.*

While showing off skin, she was covered where it mattered. That did not stop many of the male acolytes from focusing on the two mounds of flesh pressed against her chest. *Corsets do wonders for the bust.*

They led her to an elevated platform, which was a new addition from her point of view. From there, she was met by Walter, noting the absence of a senior, female representative. She smiled as he took her hand, but a glance at those steel-grey eyes made her displeasure clear.

"Apologies," Walter whispered. *Too little and too late…*

Clara was tempted to let her *inner goddess* take over but thought better of it. At least they never bothered making an easily dismissible excuse. *Such as there wasn't enough time.*

Their steps echoed through the platform as individual planks squeaked from the change in weight. The sound made them focus all the more on her, which led to a momentary loss of blood pressure. *Why am I nervous?*

He slid back her seat, one off from the centre, and Julia sat next to her. She noted that Walter had Adam at his side, a sign they elevated male acolytes over all others. *The Reverend Mother Augustine would have torn them a new one.*

"Thank you," Clara said, as she sat down.

Fortunately, she was spared the torment of sitting through a formal dinner. There were no awards, notices, nor the expectation of a speech. *Verbal diatribes that people invariably forget after taking their first bite.*

Instead, their dishes were brought in from the kitchen. The Tower had never been known for its culinary delights. *Some things are constants.*

Their roots within the Church meant they ate more like monks. There was a sizable piece of bread, a soup composed primarily of broth, and a small plate of steamed meat and vegetables.

In contrast to formal dining events, there was one fork, knife, and spoon. She glanced quickly at Julia who did not appear to be bothered by the simple meal. Whereas this singular event reminded her just how often she had seen this on the menu. *They said that hunters rushed through their training just to expand their palate.*

"Just mumble along," Clara whispered.

The other tables must have picked up a silent cue from the head table. They all closed their eyes, completed the sign of a cross, and recited grace in Latin.

"Benedic, Domine, nos et haec tua dona quae de tua largitate sumus sumpturi, per Christum Dominum nostrum. Amen." (*Bless us, O Lord, and these thy gifts which we are about to receive from thy bounty, through Christ our Lord. Amen.*)

It may as well have been sung by a choir. Clara was taken aback by the level of coordination required. *That's not something we ever did.*

While hunters said grace, they did so on their own and mostly in silence. There were risks to announcing their religious nature when the likes of *them* were around.

Instead of mumbling, Julia recited Grace in English, with the cadence of someone who learned it from sheer repetition.

Julia turned to Clara and smiled, as though the werewolf was sharing something deeply personal. Clara returned the gesture, but did not immediately dive into her meal.

Instead, she scanned the dining hall. Almost everyone was eating the same dish in an identical manner. *If synchronised eating was an Olympic sport, they would handily win gold.*

Julia was dipping her bread in the broth before realising that Clara was observing the diners.

"What the fuck?" Julia whispered, after realising the eerie pattern.

"My thoughts exactly," Clara said.

Ever the shit disturber, Clara decided to follow Julia's lead. While messy, it was a tasty way to enjoy dry bread without butter.

Clara came to realise that this generation of hunters differed from her own. In the early twentieth century, hunters were trained to be independent thinkers capable of taking action on their own. In contrast, this group appeared to reward conformity. *You can't hunt effectively as an army.*

There were times when Clara would have loved having an army at her back. Admittedly, she imagined herself leading these troops out of here, which cemented her opinion of them.

In the far corner, on a distant table, Clara noticed that Agnes and a small group of girls were also bucking the trend. *I'm really starting to like her.*

CHAPTER 29

FIRE AND ASH

After supper, Clara politely excused herself. Most of the eyes were locked on her as she walked out of the hall. The most surprising aspect was the utter silence that filled the space until she crossed the threshold. Within seconds, a cloud of whispers spilled out into the passageway. *They expect me to snap my fingers and reconnect them with the world.*

Her greatest successes as a hunter were all accomplished on her own. *I'm not accustomed to leading much more than me, myself, and I.*

This was something Evelyn brought up during their chats. The same woman who had to push Clara to delegate instead of saving Julia herself.

She might have been a *provocateuse*, but she dreaded being in the spotlight. *You have to get out of the light to find the things that go bump in the night.*

"Feel like a walk?" Clara asked Julia.

The werewolf nodded vigorously. While initially impressed by the grandeur and design of the Tower, Clara suspected that the young werewolf was beginning to pick up on the predominant vibe at the Tower. *Stifling and oppressive, because there's no escape.*

"Where?" Julia asked.

"It's a surprise," Clara said, before turning around. "Can I escort Julia around the Tower?"

There was another young, female acolyte. It appeared that Agnes was given a reprieve from guard duty. This new girl was more stoic and appeared to be perpetually bored. *You'd think angels crossed her path daily.*

"You can't take her to restricted areas," the girl said.

"What's your name?" Clara asked, to avoid baptising this with a nickname that might stick for life.

"Dorothy," she replied.

"Ever ridden a tornado before?" Julia said, offhand.

The acolyte tilted her head to the side. It seemed that this one had never read any books related to Oz.

"Never mind her," Clara said. "Have these spaces changed since the twenties?"

"No.

"Good answer," Clara said. "I'll be sure she doesn't leave my sight."

There was hesitation in those eyes. Clara was effectively exploiting a loophole to get some time alone. The direction was that Julia had to be escorted, but Clara also outranked any acolyte. *I'm more than capable of watching a single woman.*

"Where should I wait?" Dorothy asked.

"Isn't there a lounge near my quarters?" Clara asked.

"There is."

"Go there," Clara directed. "You'll be able to resume your post once we return."

That hinged on Clara and Julia returning at all. Given that the poor girl may get in trouble for complying too loosely with her orders, Clara would not push that boundary. *I may need to rely on her discretion again.*

As soon as the girl broke ranks, Clara turned to get a feel of her surroundings. There was a pause, then she *clicked* her tongue before pointing to her left.

"This way!"

* * * *

There was nothing about the Tower that was intuitive or obvious. Classrooms were spread throughout; bedrooms did not follow any discernible pattern in placement or numbering. Armouries and kitchens were the only things that made sense. *The storerooms are another matter.*

That meant restricted areas were never strictly communicated. Students cautioned others about using certain routes, especially if they happened to get disciplined for using them. Other spaces were restricted by convention, or simply because it chilled the blood of those who ventured near.

Finding a way out of the Tower required someone willing to enter these restricted areas. That directive was waived after Clara was commended for finding her way into an abandoned wing of the school. It was the only wing, that she knew of, that opened to the outside world.

Clara achieved this task by squeezing through an opening in the walls designed to accommodate the plumbing. She was a lot smaller back then. *Not to mention these wings.*

She opted for one of the three other routes she found later. Her choice permitted them to avoid soiling their clothes. *I don't want to hire a seamstress full-time.*

As they approached the entrance, Clara noted there were two acolytes posted on either side of the door. *Not to mention the steady stream of traffic moving through.*

While they stuck out, Clara and Julia followed a hunter twenty paces ahead of them. Those posted at the door eyed them the entire way, but did not say a word. *They might not know how to react.*

These acolytes were older, which surprised her. While guarding the exit likely meant a degree of prestige, Clara could not imagine there being a more boring assignment. *Unless something has changed.*

They went through the door and walked into the corridor once covered with dust and bones, complete with curtains of spider webs. Now, it was pristine, down to waxed floors. Clara used her hand to conceal an involuntary gasp while Julia went on as though all of this was normal. *That's probably the closest to 'normal' she's seen yet.*

The classrooms, once full of broken furniture and shelves sparsely filled with banned books, were now offices and a lounge. There were dozens of people making use of these spaces now.

Clara pressed past the caponier, through the arrow-slit covered walls and through another set of doors. She half expected to end up in another instance of herself; instead, the angel was greeted by the cool bright light of the sun beaming onto her face.

She turned around to catch Julia's reaction. At first, those eyes were shut due to the change in intensity of the light, but she quickly realised there was no heat from the sun.

"The fuck?" Julia said, opting to shorten what was quickly becoming her catchphrase.

Clara grinned, as though sharing a revelation that would forever change the course of humanity.

"If you think that's something," Clara said. "Take a look at what's behind the Tower."

The werewolf complied, curious as to what could be so interesting. The first thing that caught her eyes was the Tower itself, tall and foreboding, stretching out, into the blue as though someone pierced the sky with a black arrow.

Julia must have gawked at Clara's former home for a solid five minutes. Clara could see it in those eyes that Julia remembered that was not the most impressive feature.

At first blush, there was nothing special about a mountain tall enough to pierce the clouds. That is, until someone saw those thick, black clouds, composed primarily of volcanic ash. Upon further inspection, there were also bright veins of red running down its sides.

"Magma?" Julia asked. "That's a volcano?"

"One of the biggest in history," Clara answered.

"Mount Saint Helens?"

"Vesuvius."

"Vev—The one that destroyed Pompeii?"

Julia revealed a great deal about herself. She often acted like an ignorant biker chick, but this girl clearly had an extensive education. However, this sight defied reason for a simple reason.

"Well…" Clara began. "That will happen… eventually."

The angel pointed down the hill towards a sprawling, Roman, port city. A place that would *soon* be buried in ash and debris for millennia.

"Fuck me…"

"No greater words have ever been uttered here…"

CHAPTER 30

THOSE GREY EYES

S o, this *tower* of yours is located in Pompeii?" Julia asked.

This was an instance of seeing not always equating to believing. Julia may be faced with all the signs as to where they were, but her mind needed time to digest the impossibility of it. *Doesn't help that the answers are more nuanced.*

"For this moment in time," Clara answered, as they neared the city.

They were walking at a brisk pace, in part due to the eeriness of it. There was no warmth to the sun, nor any wind, and a total absence of animal life. These elements could leave someone unnerved, especially if they happened to be a predator with their senses heightened accordingly.

"You mean it wasn't here before or after?" Julia asked.

"That's my understanding."

"That's seriously fucked up."

"That's one way to phrase it…"

It was a tactical choice to prevent their enemies from being able to strike directly. The volcano also ensured that no one would dare to lay siege to the Tower. *For the sliver of time it exists in this reality.*

"Have you ever encountered other people?" Julia asked.

"Only residents of the Tower."

Even that was a rare sight. Those like her who pushed the boundaries of orthodoxy were rare. *Were rank and file hunters always like those we encountered during the evening meal?*

That was a question that Clara did not wish to answer. Alas, the more she learned, the more she realised her mind formed an idealistic version of this place… *and those within.*

They were alone on the road, but the first sign of habitation soon reached her ears. There was music hanging in the air, and by the sounds of it, it was live.

There was a distinctly feminine voice singing in Latin, accompanied by an instrument reminiscent of a fiddle. The melody was faint at first but grew in prominence with every step.

"That's… music?" Julia asked.

"Sounds like."

"That's not—(*normal, is it*)?"

"No, it's not."

This experience was entirely new to Clara. Her home as an acolyte was always well below capacity, but at least four generations were born here since being isolated. The music also made sense, as a way to inject sound into the city.

They soon came upon a red-haired maiden, and a black-haired man equally blessed with youth. In Clara's mind, they were both young enough to be hunters but their clothing differed from the uniforms in significant ways. *Given our failure rates, these are probably rejects.*

A crowd was formed in a half-circle facing the couple. No one had acknowledged their presence, as their eyes were fixed on the performers.

Their clothes looked to be hand-me downs. There was little colour variation, but many had taken the time to alter their clothing so they would stick out.

"In a world without variation," Clara whispered. "These two are a breath of fresh air."

"I wish I could understand them," Julia said, louder than intended.

The maiden was now singing a song from the Hebrew Bible, something about a young couple yearning for one another. While hunters did not expressly acknowledge the existence of this part of the Bible, some enjoyed delving into the prose. *The religious schools' equivalent of a nude magazine in class.*

Upon hearing Julia speak, the maiden looked up and took in a sharp breath. The interruption was brief, but enough to pique the curiosity of those within the audience.

They collectively turned their heads, with their eyes going right past Julia. The fact the werewolf was wearing blue jeans and a white T-shirt should have caught their gaze, but something more unusual was just at her side.

The group erupted in a cacophony of chaos. Some gasped, while others appeared to be on the cusp of hyperventilating. However, what was most telling were the words that slipped out unfiltered.

"A hunter here?"

"The high and mighty have graced us with their presence."

"Why can't they leave us alone?"

Which changed as more details registered in their minds.

"*Are those wings?*"

"*She's not wearing a shirt!*"

"*Scandalous!*"

"*Those grey eyes…*"

Much more came out in the chaos, but Clara could not filter out the cacophony entirely.

"*That's her?*"

"*The one who died?*"

"*It can't be.*"

Clara took a bow and unfurled her wings. This further energised the crowd. *Even the entertainers are joining in on the excitement.*

"*She's come back from the dead!*"

"*You can't escape death!*"

A voice cut through the chatter and silenced them all. It was the singer, every syllable played out like a musical note in the hand of a skilled musician.

"Welcome to Pompeii, Clara Grey."

Clara smiled, her mind struggling to accept that anyone knew of her at all.

CHAPTER 31

IRON ELEPHANT

There should have been an ellipsis after '*Welcome to Pompeii*,'" Clara said.

They were headed deeper into the city after some of the locals *celebrated* her return. These citizens were decidedly not hunters.

"How so?" Julia asked.

"Just a vibe, really," Clara said. "They see me as an aberration, and it's not the wings."

She could tell from their mannerisms that most were uncomfortable having a hunter in their midst, especially one in *uniform*. *Although, several men complimented my wardrobe.*

"Dunno… the men *really* wanted to get to know you a LOT better…"

These were artists, misfits, malcontents, those who were just a little *off*. As acolytes, these traits would be filtered out quickly during training.

Clara never did find out what happened to those who failed out in her time. *These have nowhere to go.*

"Whereas no one at the Tower showed any outward interest..."

"You can't smell them—(*like I do*)." Julia said.

There was a tremble in that voice, as Julia found herself back in that dark place at the mercy of those men. Her eyes were distant and glassy, while her breathing grew shallow.

Clara was not sure how to deal with the situation. Trauma like this ran deep, and she had little experience in handling it. *Especially my own.*

"Julia?" Clara asked.

When no response came, Clara tried to take Julia by the hand. The werewolf reacted violently by tearing her hand away. Those eyes were quickly filled with rage. In a matter of heartbeats, the fire died down and her lower lip trembled. Clara only swooped in when it became clear that Julia's legs were about to give in.

"Sorry—(*I forgot where I was*)," Julia said.

"No need to apologise," Clara said. "We can't all behead the source of our torment."

"I did that and more. It didn't do fuck all."

"No. The difference is they won't be able to do it again."

There came an awkward pause.

"Cold comfort," Julia said.

* * * *

"What did you mean back there?" Julia asked.

Clara looked up from an assortment of copper jewellery that would never find an owner. This was an open-air market, filled with fish, meat, clothes, and accoutrements. As an acolyte, Clara loved to take in the opulent artistry of the era. *Historians would kill for such a find.*

"People who never made the cut at the Tower," Clara explained. "Individuals who once had a chance at a great life in the real world."

"I knew I liked them," Julia said.

While more than a light ribbing, it also matched her own thoughts on the encounter. These hunters scared her, but she was equally leery of any group so easily accepting of her.

"I'm a hunter!" Clara said in mock anger.

The next booth served as a grim reminder of the Roman Empire's darker side. Shackles, locks and other accessories for the affluent slave owner. *How did I forget about these?*

"Then I'm a fucking direct descendant of Lupa," Julia said.

The young woman once again managed to surprise Clara. If there was ever a woman needing their mouth washed out with soap, it was her. *Yet she knows about Romulus, Remus and the wolf who nursed them until they were discovered.*

"Meaning?" Clara asked.

"Shit—Sorry."

Clara's choice to play on her own ignorance was a subtle reminder that the werewolf was outing herself. *That might have changed the tone of their celebrations.*

"You weren't wired right," Julia said, after rolling her tongue three times in her mouth.

"Really?" Clara asked, her voice booming out like thunder.

That was an interesting development. Angels did not possess the wrathful-god voice. *Does that mean Hecate is back?*

The angel tried to channel a bit of power to make her eyes come aglow, but nothing happened. She hid her disappointment, but her eyes widened after spotting the look of shock on Julia's face.

"What the literal fuck was that?" Julia asked.

"Pardon me," Clara said. "It must have been the angelic equivalent of a burp."

They both knew it was not, but also realised there were risks to Clara being too specific. Hunters may welcome an angel, but not one who was effectively a goddess vessel.

"If it's any consolation," Julia said. "I thank God every day that you're the exception to the rule."

Had Clara been wired correctly, she would have killed every werewolf that night, and promptly freed Evelyn of her head. *Abominations to a hunter had to be put down, and ultimately, a few ended up being powerful allies.*

"Awww," Clara teased.

Clara stopped dead in her tracks when she noticed something. Her movements became slow and deliberate with her head aligning itself with the object of interest. It was made of iron, and resembled an elephant. The artistry put into this *creature* was exquisite, but it was the purpose that bothered her.

The black scorch marks along the beast's belly were a clue as was the hatch in the rear. They would lock someone inside like a cell. *That doesn't end there.*

They then lit a fire under the belly and let the heat build up inside. It was said that the grim deed was done once steam came out through the snout.

If that was not disturbing enough, the distinctive scent of wood smoke lingered still in the air. *A definitive sign that it's been used recently.*

"I hope that's not what I think it is?" Julia asked.

"I'm afraid it is," Clara answered, before clenching her jaw. "It's also known as a brazen bull."

"What—(*for*)?"

That was a good question, but it also explained why so few lived beyond the Tower.

"The iron gauntlet of a tyrannical leader…" Clara answered.

That was a sobering thought. However, Julia quickly realised there was something more to it than scaring the population into complacency.

"And?" Julia asked, in a whisper.

"Population control…"

CHAPTER 32

LONG OVERDUE

On the way back to her quarters, Clara made sure to get Dorothy's attention. The young acolyte's eyes were half-shut, while her facial features remained slack. *She must have had a good nap.*

"Thank you…" Dorothy said. "What's your title?"

"I've been given plenty of titles over the course of my life," Clara began. "Most of which can't be used in polite company."

The acolyte's mind was either too muddled from waking up, or she had no inclination towards Clara's brand of humour. Such a shame, as the angel considered laughter to be an effective way of fighting off the horrors of life.

"Clara will do," she said.

The permission to use a superior's given name nearly made the acolyte's eyes pop out of her head. While Clara could not remember being so smitten by world-hardened hunters, she concluded that it must have been true at one point.

"Thank you… Clara?" Dorothy said, as though testing if there would be repercussions to following directions.

"No need," Clara replied. "Everyone here started as acolytes… present company excluded…"

The acolyte did not outwardly appear to react to those words. There came a notable pause, albeit brief, in her breathing. *Hopefully, this opens her eyes.*

They were escorted to their quarters, and the acolyte took up position on the right. This left their escort with a view of both ends of the hallway. *If only she knew about Julia, she'd keep her distance.*

Before closing the door, Clara decided to test a hypothesis.

"Have you ever heard of the brazen bull?" Clara asked.

Dorothy's eyes rolled towards the ceiling as though the answer was carved into the rafters. Nothing in her body language or vitals implied this reaction was an act. *At least I'll get a truthful answer.*

"Something to do with a china shop?" Dorothy replied.

"Cute," Clara said. "Have a good night."

* * * *

Clara turned around and realised that Julia had a book in her hands. It was a leather-bound tome common around the Tower. *How did she get her hands on it?*

"Horny?" Clara asked.

Julia shot an intense stare at the angel, the glow in those eyes indicated a flaring temper. The werewolf was clearly uncomfortable with their deception. Clara made a note to find other ways to make some noise in the future.

"Oh… yeah… baby…" Julia replied.

Clara scrolled through the audio and found the beginning of another scene. The runtime gave them the opportunity to chat. *After I apologise.*

"Look, I'm sorry—" Clara said.

"For a great subterfuge?" Julia asked. "It's… fine… I just need to get over my hang-ups."

There was something to that tone that implied there was more to it than words. *I wonder if it's harder for her on account of being an apex predator.*

"I'm here if you—(*you want to talk*)."

"I *really* fucking don't."

Her voice spiked enough to drown out the audio. She bared her teeth and backed her head by a couple of inches.

Julia's lips enunciated, "Sorry."

"What are you reading?" Clara asked.

With no desire to talk, it made sense for Clara to get to the point.

"I'm not sure," Julia said. "It's old and written in another language. I think Agnes left it."

Clara nearly asked how Julia knew the latter, but the werewolf tapped her nose three times with her index finger as a hint.

"Can I see?"

Julia surrendered the book without hesitation. The leather was old and so was the binding. Books like this were rarely removed from the library, but rules did not deter a determined acolyte.

"*As lectorem de hyptohesibus huius operis,*" Clara read in Latin. "Which translates to the reader concerning the hypotheses of this work."

"Wait… You can read Latin?"

"Yes… I'm that old."

Clara stuck out her tongue and Julia chuckled. It was nice to see a healthy response to an attempt at humour.

In between the pages, there was a library card. That was odd as she did not remember the monks using anything like this when here. While the initials were all different, everyone was written in the same ink, as was the stamp.

Someone had been careful, the dates were plausible, but it was the time of return that caught her attention. Out of the eleven entries, every single one was within the same hour. *While most acolytes are scrambling to get to their lessons.*

There were numerous instances which she considered discounting due to their ubiquity such as J and M early within the initial set. However, they all contained an A and the final letter denoting the family name was always an M. *Curiouser and curiouser.*

"We've been invited," Clara said.

"To?"

"The library… Where else would you return a book?"

"Smart ass!"

"Of course! We have a while to wait. So, take the bed and get comfortable."

"You aren't going to sleep?"

Clara wiggled her wings, making it clear that she had her own way of getting some rest.

"Right," Julia said. "I'll toss you a pillow."

"Thank you," Clara said, before dodging the pillow. *The gal can throw!*

CHAPTER 33

MICE IN A MAZE

Here ow the fuck do you know where we are?" Julia asked, as they took another turn down yet another nondescript passageway.

"I've been down these halls thousands of times," Clara replied.

While the Terminus was designed to confound those who entered. The Tower was a lesson in security through obfuscation.

No floor was designed to be straightforward or obvious. This served several purposes, the first of which was to deter any incursion. *Like fighting a war in a maze.*

Clara was not entirely certain that the ability to drive an acolyte crazy was not a feature rather than a bug. She knew of several students who ended up hopelessly lost, left to cry in some forgotten part of this place.

"Besides," Clara said. "I wouldn't have made it without being able to navigate these halls."

There was a pause, Julia's jaw muscles pulsated as though attempting to chew on the gristle of the idea.

"You had a fucked-up childhood," Julia said.

"…It could have been worse…"

Clara had no desire to dwell on what might have happened had she stayed in that mining town. There was nothing for her there, and she was certain that her life would have been wasted. *The candle which burns twice as bright.*

"That's the sad part," Julia said.

One had no choice but to play the hand they were dealt. *As long as you leave the world in a better state.*

They took another turn and this time they faced three, large, stone arched entrances. It made no difference which one she picked, as all three led into the library. *All to divide and conquer.*

As they approached, the immensity of the room became apparent. The scent of old books and leather overwhelmed Clara's senses, curling her lips into a smile. Libraries and archives had always been her favourite places to explore as an acolyte.

The shelves were so tall that there was a platform at the half-way mark along with ladders for each level. The ceiling itself was vaulted for additional strength.

Clara glanced at the werewolf, whose pace had slowed. The werewolf's jaw was hanging loosely, and those brown eyes were wide. *This was all pretty mundane to me.*

"Holy fuck!" Julia said. "Wait… is this another fucking maze?"

There came a chuckle while Clara nodded in agreement. The library was real, but most of the books here were archives. Few students had any business here, and that was precisely why they were here.

"Stay close," Clara said.

"No shit…"

The next three minutes were made up of several twists and turns. Julia never lagged more than a metre behind, afraid of getting lost within the depths of this place.

"Here we are!" Clara said.

"It's a dead end."

Julia was, in fact, correct, this was *technically* a dead end. They faced a wall, and the only obvious way out was the way they came.

Clara returned the book to its rightful place and found its companion seven books to the right of the slot. She ran her index finger down the spine of 'De Revolutionibus Orbium Coelestium,' or '*O the Revelations, Revisions of the Heavenly Spheres*' and instructed Julia to do the same.

The binding came aglow each time someone interacted with it. This was a good sign, as it meant they were authorized to enter. The effect may as well have been magical, because no one could explain how it worked.

"Close your eyes," Clara said.

"Why—"

"Don't ask, just close your eyes and let me lead you."

Julia actually gulped and took a deep breath. When she closed her eyes, Clara took her hand and walked forward, through the rows of books. Soon she was one with the bookshelf, followed by the stone wall behind it.

Visually there was nothing to see. Her eyes could not pick up colours and patterns from inside an opaque object. This was a leap of faith, like the one Julia had taken by letting Clara lead her through.

When everything opened up on the other side, she ensured they cleared the wall before letting go. They travelled through solid objects and found themselves in an entirely different room with no visible windows or doors.

The space was linear and expansive, which featured several smaller alcoves built into the walls. There was furniture, weapons, and clothing everywhere. *Everything a gal needs for waging war on their enemy.*

"Where the fuck are we?" Julia asked.

Julia's heart rate spiked, the sudden change in scene must have triggered a wave of anxiety… *or is it due to the confinement?*

All around here, there were steady heartbeats, several by the sounds of it. Either this was a trap, or a test to prove that Clara once belonged.

"Girls," Clara said. "Would you care to answer that question?"

Several appeared out of the shadows. While most were girls, there were also women among the group who were clearly full-fledged hunters.

"Welcome to *Les Filles de Jeanne d'Arc*, Clara," Agnes said.

Clara had never seen so many here. In fact, this space could be segregated, enabling students to utilize the same space without anyone else being aware.

CHAPTER 34

DAUGHTERS OF A SAINT

I'm honoured," Clara said.

She bowed deeply and used her wings to add some flourish. She found it odd that hunters, who killed anything that was not outwardly human, tolerated her wings. *I'm sure there're enough zealots in their ranks to chance an attack.*

"So, what brings us here?" Clara asked.

The use of the word *us* was purposeful, it reinforced that Clara was one of them. They had to cut this short, and idolatry would get them nowhere.

"What do you mean?" Agnes asked.

There were older hunters lurking in the shadows. Clara presumed they were keeping an eye on the exchange, observing Clara's every tick and response.

"Let's dispense with these games," Clara said. "Everyone seems to know who I am, including those *living* in Pompeii. *I was never famous—in life.*"

232

"You survived an encounter with Drusilla, one she arranged for you and another hunter to be captured," Agnes responded, without skipping a beat.

Clara survived that incident by sheer luck, she happened to guess correctly from which side Drusilla would attack. However, Clara did not have the time to confirm the kill and the vampire got away. *Allied forces had to pull back after their defensive line was decimated by the vampire.*

"You're credited for killing a vampire in the middle of a battlefield... in the nude."

That sounded more impressive than it really was. She did it to distract the idiot long enough to get the upper hand so the sun would set him aflame.

"Discovered a plot by a former acolyte to lure and torture members of the Tower for information," Agnes went on. "You dealt with that situation handily."

Only if *handily* included falling under the spell of her first crush. *I was lucky that the failsafe kicked in.*

"Foiled a plot to domesticate ghouls, and saved a fellow hunter who they left to succumb to their wounds."

If not for the aid of a creature that ought not to exist, Clara would have been caught in that trap. *Odd how the Tower always explicitly denied the existence of ghosts.*

"Stopped a serial killer by posing as a woman of the night."

Time and preparation, although it turned out that Evelyn and her sire were there for the same reason. *For all I know, they tilted the scale in my favour.*

"The one who single-handedly killed Drusilla—(*at The Grand*)."

"You can't possibly know that," Clara said. "Besides, I died that night."

Hunters officially disavowed the existence of old gods. Clara risked breeding distrust among the group by bringing up the name Hecate and their involvement.

"That's why you ascended," Agnes said.

"You had agents reporting back?"

"We did."

"Why was I—(*cut off from the Tower*)?

"Because *you're* a lone wolf," one of the elders said.

Julia chuckled upon hearing that answer. *If only they knew there's an actual wolf in their midst.*

"We knew you would complete your objectives at all costs. What you lacked was the ability to follow orders."

"Awkward," Julia whispered, before clearing her throat to conceal what she said.

That part was true, and Clara embraced that aspect of herself.

"And who would you be?" Clara asked.

"She is—"

"I asked her, Agnes."

"Amelia Wright," the elder said.

Elder was perhaps a bit harsh as a label. In her time, any hunter who reached their forties was considered an elder. Women that age were proverbial matriarchs and seen as candidates to one day take over as the Reverend Mother. *There's a bunch of them here.*

"Pleasure, I'm sure," Clara replied. "So, that confirms that I was little more than a weapon."

Clara had grown to accept that she was, first and foremost, a pawn. *Point in the right direction, pull the pin, and stay out of the way.*

"What else would you expect?" Amelia asked. "Do you prefer working with the likes of *them?*"

That meant they had up-to-date information on what was going on within her reality. Her heart sank, and if she was not actively monitoring her vitals, there would have been a noticeable dip in heart rate.

"So, you have agents in place even now?" Clara asked.

"You thought the financial assets you tapped into were there as though by magic?"

"The Tower always used administrators and bureaucrats to handle their affairs."

"That's a fair assumption," Amelia said. "Even a bureaucrat can shed some light on your *chronicler's* history."

That was enough for Julia's heart rate to skyrocket, but the werewolf did not betray herself. The angel always suspected the prison system knew what Julia was. That explained why they sent her to a nameless prison in a remote area.

Formally, Julia was convicted for her connection to a gang that terrorised the city, leaving a swath of dead and wounded in their wake. People wanted blood and Julia served as their scapegoat. *The people demanded 'justice.'*

Amelia could just as easily be alluding to Julia being a felon. It was fortunate that the werewolf did not rise to her own defence, and was probably biting her tongue. *Her colourful language sure does brighten up the place.*

"I stand by her record," Clara said. "I can't think of anyone else I'd rather have at my side."

"Did Evelyn tell you that?" Amelia countered.

Clara's eyes flashed blue for a fraction of a second. It was enough for several to back away. *How did that happen?*

"All of that time observing, and no one bothered to write a note? I'd have been happy with a naughty poem scrawled on a bathroom stall…"

The angel suspected they needed her and not the other way around. *Why else go through all these precautions?*

"Do you ever get to the fucking point?" Julia snapped. "Why don't you two just fuck and get it over with?"

Clara's face broke into a smile. While unexpected, this might be the opportunity they needed. Julia was surprisingly adept at dealing with complex social matters, even if her instincts were to hack at them with a cleaver.

"I'm game if you are, Amelia," Clara said.

A few let out a giggle and one of the hunters even burst out laughing. Social masks like hers came with a lot of practice… *and we need them to hide the trauma.*

That *invitation* made Amelia twitch. Clara doubted it was the sexually suggestive statement. Hunters often worked in pairs, and made *sure* the pair was not sexually compatible.

This was frustration related to her *grand plan* to outmanoeuvre the angel blowing up in her face. Hunters were used to the likes of *them* and built up their arsenal based on engaging them. *That's probably why Evelyn and I get along.*

"Is that why you brought the werewolf?" Amelia asked.

"Not at all," Clara said. "I look out for those I take under my wings."

"Fine… we need you…"

"For?"

"To get out of here."

That was not a surprise, but it was notable because it was said aloud. The revelation did bring up a question. *If they can communicate with the outside world, why do they need me?*

CHAPTER 35

DERRINGERS AND TOMMY GUNS

T hree?" Clara asked.

In the span of a century, only three hunters escaped the Terminus. While they refused to quantify how many made the attempt, Clara guessed the number would even make a bloodthirsty general cringe.

Upon graduation, which was something Clara never officially did, many volunteered for the chance. Clara imagined that being born and confined within the Tower taxed the mind. *This place is designed to drive you insane.*

"That we know of," Amelia admitted.

"They weren't embedded with a failsafe?" Clara asked.

They were walking two and two through the main chamber, passing by individual niches. The place had not changed, which Clara found comforting. Amelia and Clara took the lead as equals, while Julia and Agnes kept busy chatting about their respective worlds.

"What's that?" Amelia asked.

Clara mulled over how to best describe the purpose of this device. It was possible that they knew it as something else entirely.

"Something that triggers a psychotic break if you are at risk of being turned by the likes of *them*," Clara replied nonchalantly.

While Amelia did not respond, a glance in an accelerated state showed they all bore the signs of confusion… *just me? Really?*

"We've never heard of such a device," Amelia said, after looking back to confirm the acolyte had the same opinion.

"Wonderful device…" Clara said, with a straight face, even though every word dripped with sarcasm. "It saved me from being raped and tortured, and it also sent me on a rampage that decimated most of the city's vampire population."

"A dozen or so?" Amelia asked.

"They are far more numerous than we believed," Clara said. "I've seen battlefields littered with fewer dead."

Since the hunters were not going to be open with her, Clara would not delve into the minutiae.

"What else has changed?" Agnes asked, before clamping her mouth shut.

Clara smiled, enjoying being around another who did not heed the rules. If there was any group that excelled at this, it would be this one.

"Werewolf populations have rebounded and are now found in cities," Clara began. "Ghouls are interbreeding with captive, human females…"

While much could have been said on the latter, Clara considered it a mercy to leave the rest to their imagination. She really hoped that they would not press her on that subject.

Clara spotted a way to let Julia and Agnes blow off some steam. They came upon an arsenal of weapons, of various calibres and styles. They even had one of the derringers that she used back in the day.

Her fingers went over the barrel before picking it up by the pearl grip. The familiar texture and feel took her back to a simpler time before dredging up all the times she got herself into trouble.

"Safe as always?" Clara asked, in Latin.

Amelia nodded before that smile faded away, whereas Agnes was already smirking. Clara tossed the weapon to the acolyte while eyeing a Thompson submachine gun.

"Shoot me," Clara said, imitating a drill sergeant.

"Yes, Sister," Agnes said.

It was the first time someone referred to her as a nun and Clara honestly hated it. The sisters were always old, stiff, and formal. *At least I'm old.*

Agnes aimed for the chest and fired. Julia's eyes expanded in size, as the powder charge went off. It was a good shot, a quarter of an inch off from where her heart was. Yet it bounced off the clothing and landed harmlessly on the stone floor.

The second shot did the same, even with an impact against her forehead. Neither projectile left any visible marks. *She's pretty good with the weapon.*

"What the fuck!" Julia said.

Those eyes did not shrink, either from the initial scare or the fact that bullets bounced off Clara... *Good thing she has a strong heart.*

"We use these for training," Clara said, after grabbing the submachine gun with the loud, rattling drum. "Watch."

Clara trained the barrel on an assortment of furniture and unloaded the full drum. By the end of it, the group was left deafened, facing furniture littered with bullet holes.

"Five... four... three... two..."

On the call of *one*, the furniture began to repair itself. Bullets popped out of the frame and stuffing, as the material healed. Right before their eyes, everything returned to its original state.

"That—That's fucking badass," Julia said. "Can— *(I try)*?"

"Of course," Clara said, before tossing the weapon to Julia. "Agnes, would you mind assisting?"

"Of course, Sister," Agnes replied.

Julia smiled upon seeing Clara's jaw bulge for a fraction of a second.

"Do you mind if Amelia and I walk on for a bit?"

"Yeah," Julia replied. "Not too far?"

"Agreed."

"Let's fuck some shit up!" Julia said.

Agnes was too disciplined to add anything, but that smile said plenty.

* * * *

The sound of gunfire was interspersed with giggles and laughs as Julia and Agnes tore up anything they came across. Clara smiled, wondering if this was the kind of *therapy* the werewolf needed. *Senseless destruction with no repercussions.*

"Thank you," Amelia said.

"For?" Clara asked.

Clara figured that Julia was bored of their shop talk. *Besides, lethargy could trigger unexpected behaviours at a critical time.*

"You didn't come up with that so we could chat privately?"

"Julia knows my darkest secrets, many of which would make you turn pale," Clara said. "We were always free to speak openly."

"It's not—(*our way*)."

"Your way…" Clara said, at the same time. "I'm fully aware and we might have wasted the evening getting nowhere."

"True," Amelia said. "We are products of our *upbringing*."

"Fed lies and half-truths to ensure compliance…"

The hunter cocked her head but remained silent. Clara hoped that Amelia would provide some insight by either confirming or denying that statement. *Instead, we are back to playing games.*

"Let's cut to the chase," Clara said. "What do you want me to do?"

"We want a way back to the world."

"It's no picnic out there. I'd say humanity is worse off than it was during the Roaring Twenties."

"Better to be free than forever trapped in a cage."

"I died out there," Clara said, without a hint of humour. "Arguably more than once."

"People die here too," Amelia confessed.

"So, I've observed," Clara said. "To be honest, we are not sure if we can find our way back."

"How… How did you end up here?"

"Julia."

By now, they were in one of the more remote areas of the space. Most were congregating closer to the entrance, as though ready to exercise the better part of valour.

"How did she end up here?"

"She followed my trail."

That logical loop forced Amelia to take a pause. The hunter cocked her head and furrowed her brow. Clara smiled, waiting for Amelia to reason it out before interrupting.

"That doesn't make any sense."

"The Terminus is a quagmire of temporal pockets and eddies." Clara said. "I'd argue one… one… all tailor-made for me."

All the different choices she might have made and the repercussions that came with it. *Even Julia commented that she detected my scent in three, other pockets.*

"What do you mean?" Amelia asked.

Clara had to be careful here, since this was little more than a conjecture. *It could be attributed to the fact that I was the one in transit during the attack.*

"Julia reflected that she could not interact with the pockets," Clara said. "Most were set before she was born, and she could not *snap* into that reality."

"Do you suppose our volunteers—(*had the same problem*)?"

"Most certainly," Clara said.

In the background, there came a blast. Clara snapped her head to investigate and saw the charred remains of a couch. Julia was in tears, overjoyed that Agnes handed her a grenade.

"Cute," Clara said.

When the angel turned to face Amelia, something caught her eye. It was a formal portrait, and judging by the colouring it had been done recently. Even a glimpse was enough to send a chill down her spine. *You'd think I'd seen a ghost.*

Amelia touched Clara on the shoulder. It took all she had to not react adversely. Instead of ignoring what she saw, the angel aligned herself entirely with the portrait.

Clara's heart was at a gallop, her palms were clammy and wet. She forgot to breathe, forcing her autonomous functions to take over…

"Clara?"

"Who's that?"

"That's—was the reverend mother," Amelia said.

"Augustine?"

Blood flushed from Amelia's face. They might have managed to surprise Clara by bringing up details of the world beyond Clara, but this was an insight into their domain. *I'm only supposed to know how things once were.*

"How do you know?"

"She was Reverend Mother, when I was alive," Clara said.

There came a pause as Amelia processed what was said.

"Impossible! That would make her…"

"At least forty years older than me," Clara said. "I'm over a century old."

"That's crazy," Amelia said.

"Not so much. Why are there no old hunters in Pompeii or here?"

"Horsefeathers!"

"You took the words right out of my mouth."

CHAPTER 36

THE HEART OF THE TOWER

Clara's eyes flashed blue, bright enough that Agnes and Julia immediately turned towards them. The angel calmed herself, wondering yet again how she could tap into powers that should be lost in the temporal tempest within the Terminus.

"Died?" Clara asked, after taking a deep breath.

"Three months ago," Amelia repeated.

Two sets of footsteps were heard approaching at a run. Clara did not even turn around, knowing that one was Julia and the other was most likely Agnes.

While the acolyte had to catch her breath, Julia appeared no worse for wear. *If they didn't already know, that would make them curious.*

"What happened?" Julia asked.

The werewolf had a British concussion grenade with her. Had they been anywhere else people might have been uneasy. Upon realising what Julia had in her hand. Her cheeks turned red as tomatoes, and she casually placed it on a counter. *Luckily, she never pulled the tape.*

"Do you remember me talking about the Reverend Mother from my day?" Clara asked.

Julia's eyes rolled up towards the ceiling and her head followed. This time, the answer must have been up there.

"Sounds like a mashup of Roman emperors..." Julia began. "Augustus... Constantine... so... um... Augustine?"

For Clara, this was an odd way of remembering a name, but it was nonetheless effective. Clara beamed a smile, finding that Julia was rather adept at hiding her strengths. *I wonder if this was her way of surviving with a werewolf gang.*

"Quite right!" Clara said. "Guess who died three months ago?"

Clara's body and arms flowed as though she was showcasing products in a game show. Her arms pointed towards the painting, surrounded by candles and keepsakes.

"Wait," Julia said. "Is that how long we've been gone?"

Given how long it took for Julia to reach her, that much time may have actually elapsed. *Evelyn will be pissed!*

"Were you given a cause of death?" Clara asked.

"None..." Amelia said.

It paid for hunters to be open to the idea of coincidences being just that. Still, these seemingly random events were piling up faster than firewood in preparation for winter's bite.

"Doesn't that strike you as a bit odd?" Clara asked.

"Fucking suspect," Julia answered.

"Tell her," Agnes said.

It was surprising that the acolyte would openly direct a superior. *Hints at the importance of it.*

Amelia lowered her head until those eyes focused on the tips of her toes. After a deep breath, Amelia looked up at Clara.

"A new Reverend Mother should have been selected immediately," Amelia said. "Agnes is keeper of the scrolls, and realised they went missing after Augustine's death."

"Did you study these scrolls before?" Clara asked, with a grin.

"I did," Agnes said. "I wanted to know what I was up against."

"Smart girl," Clara said.

"So, you don't think she's dead?" Julia asked.

"Why would I?" Clara asked, in return. "The timing alone borders on a statistical impossibility. The pockets I ended up in were, in many ways, designed to trap me."

"Or teach you a lesson..." Julia said.

There was truth to that, but to what end? Clara learned through those encounters that the Tower had no problem using pawns to further their goals... *or torturing those they suspect of being against them.*

"I doubt their goal was to make me more distrustful of this place and its leadership."

Amelia and Agnes shot the angel a curious glance. Few hunters would speak as freely as they were. *They're dipping their toes in the shallow end, and I dove in below where the light reaches.*

"Right," Amelia said. "What now?"

"It's time I met with the dearly departed," Clara said.

"Are you sure that's wise?" Julia asked.

"Of course not," Clara answered. "I sense we won't make it out of here unless I do."

Everyone had a grim look, as though attending a wake. Clara grinned, but she needed to do a lot more than that to lighten their spirits.

"Agnes," Clara said.

"Yes, Sister."

"You strike me as someone who likes to explore."

Amelia shot the acolyte a hard stare and the latter's cheeks flushed. *She has nothing to be embarrassed about.*

"That was encouraged in my day," Clara said, to relieve some pressure.

"…I am, sister," Agnes replied.

"Do you know of any good hiding places in Pompeii?" Clara asked. "Say… where people might hide from the Tower?"

"How do you know—(*about that*)?" Amelia asked.

"I've seen what happens when someone breaks the rules," Clara said.

"…I do, Sister," Agnes replied.

"Excellent," Clara said.

"We need to have—(a chat)."

"No, we don't," Clara countered. "I want you two to find anyone who is sympathetic to our cause. Evacuate them to safety."

The rest of the plan was straightforward because it involved someone with wings.

"Do you want directions—(*to find the place*)?" Agnes said.

"No," Clara said. "If I fail, you might still have a chance."

"How will you find us?" Amelia asked.

"I'll have a chat with Death…"

While Julia did not react, the girls certainly did.

"What about me?" Julia asked.

"You need to go with—(them)."

"But—" Julia protested.

"I can't keep you safe up there," Clara admitted.

The werewolf grinned, not for lack of concern, but because she had a good quip.

"Evelyn will kill you if you don't come back," Julia said.

"All the more reason to succeed…"

If anyone had the means of tracking her down… *even in death*.

"How will you get to her?" Amelia asked.

Clara wiggled her wings and chuckled as the hunters' eyes widened in sync with their mouths.

"Oh," they said.

CHAPTER 37

THE VAN HELSING CONJECTURE

Clara knew that Reverend Mother Augustine was familiar with all the shortcuts and secret passages. *This was the woman who snuck up on me in Pompeii after spotting me from her office…*

Convention called for her quarters to be sealed off at the time of her passing. Clara suspected that alternate egress points were also blocked to prevent anyone curious from learning the truth. *This might be a reason why the brazen bull was used.*

That left the path least travelled, which in this case was the one never taken. Hunters could not fly and there were no insects or birds. *Better hope my wings work in this place.*

There was also no wind, but obviously there was breathable air. Had an atmosphere been omitted or static, there would be no one left. *The only ones who can avoid breathing are like Evelyn.*

She supposed that a resourceful hunter might try to scale the walls of the Tower. Up close, the black stone was nearly seamless and Clara suspected the structure itself might resist the attempt. *Walls and structural elements are known to heal themselves.*

Tired of these games, Clara walked straight for the main doors. Staff, students, and hunters alike all began to follow in her wake, there was a buzz in the air, humming with curiosity.

She wondered if Les Filles de Jeanne d'Arc were working their way through the rest of the Tower. *The news will be like dropping a grenade on the table during a heated poker game.*

Clara made every effort to show no outward emotion. A smile or frown could be falsely interpreted and spark a confrontation. *We need this to be an evacuation, not outright panic.*

They walked on until she passed two, armed acolytes and was in the open. Clara turned around and looked up. The Tower appeared to stretch on forever, but she caught the glint from the highest point.

"She's enjoying—(*the view*)," Clara whispered.

"You're not the only one who's trapped." Ray said.

Clara recognized that voice immediately. This was the man whose likeness was perpetually marred by the sunlight. The one who delivered a cryptic message before disappearing in the blink of an eye.

He was the reason why she delved into her past and was now standing at the base of the Tower.

"But?" Clara asked, to speed things along.

"You are about to meet the one who holds all the keys. You must claim these for yourself to free the others."

This was by far the most this *man* ever said. Normally, he shared no more than a line or two before vanishing, but he was still here.

"Are you trapped?" Clara asked.

The man did not immediately respond, but she swore the silhouette was smirking. *It's a shame that the glare prevents me from seeing much of him…*

"By the very forces you once served," Ray said.

The man looked up as though he had been discovered. Clara had to wonder what group was at play, as the Tower and Heaven could be applied in equal measure.

"How do I—*(free you)*?"

"No time—If you ever need refuge," Ray said. "Seek what withers away and dies in the light."

As expected, the man vanished, leaving nothing more than the blinding sunlight bereft of heat to keep her company.

She closed her eyes, letting her wings spread out. As she turned around, her shadow stretched out until it was absorbed by the black stone. Clara tightened her jaw, focused on her destination and ran.

Wind was not necessary, but it helped. In the absence of it, she had to take off much like ducks did over the water. The angel gained speed until her flaps had an effect. A hundred paces away from the bastion of all hunters, Clara broke free from gravity's grasp and took flight.

Below, a sizable group had formed, staring at the winged creature accomplishing the impossible. Clara ignored them but felt a momentary surge of power. *Due to these hunters skirting idolatry.*

The surge itself was an important clue. If the goddesses were gone, then Clara would not have been able to flash her eyes blue, slow time, shoot with uncanny accuracy, or experience surges in power. The latter of which was often a direct result of gaining fans, admirers… *or worshippers.*

The trouble started shortly after arriving at the Terminus, which coincided with the Reverend Mother's *untimely* death. After that, she jumped from one alternate reality to another until Julia pulled her free.

Augustine had been a hunter before her time as Reverend Mother. Ninety years was an awfully long time for a human, let alone a hundred and thirty. Despite mounting evidence, a part of Clara wanted to dismiss the entire situation as a work of fiction.

It was natural for the mind to dismiss such drastic changes in its worldview. Clara never questioned the existence of ghouls, werewolves, vampires, and other things that went bump in the night. Her exposure as a child ensured that she was a true believer.

"The Tower is a different matter," Clara said, under her breath.

Clara circled the Tower very much like buzzards did with searching prospective meals. With every loop, she gained altitude, but the size of the crowd appeared to be the same. *I'd love to know why they are congregating.*

"Augustine has been at this for centuries," Clara whispered. "So, what changed?"

The realisation struck her like a solid slap to the face. It cleared out the cobwebs from her mind and enabled her to connect the dots.

"Hypocrite," Clara swore. "It fits."

Clara now soared above the Tower's roof, giving her a view of the windows leading into the Reverend Mother's quarters. These were sure to be protected against direct attack. *This leaves me with the skylights.*

She felt a new weight in her pocket. A quick probe revealed a grenade, like those used during the Great War. She smiled, gained altitude and tucked in her wings to enter a dive.

The angel built up speed and flew over the surface of the dark roof. Upon nearing the skylights, she pulled the pin and rolled it along the glass surface until it came to a halt by the edge. All the while, Clara slowed down time, as reaction times were key.

One...

Clara flapped her wings to ascend at a rapid pace. While this slowed her down, the gain in altitude ensured she would be outside of the blast radius.

Two...

She reached her apex and twirled around in midair to align herself with the last point. Next, she tucked in her wings to build up speed.

Three...

There was a bright flash of light followed by black smoke and a blast wave. The sound echoed through this land, sounding as though lightning had struck.

By then, Clara was hurtling through the atmosphere towards a very small point in space. As judged by the size of the opening, she folded in her wings and kept her arms tight against her body. *Just like threading the eye of a needle at terminal velocity.*

"You have one shot Clara, make it count!"

"Wait?" Clara whispered. "Was that Artemis?"

Clara felt her point of balance change and adjusted her trajectory just in time. She tore through the opening as it was about to heal itself closed. There was a twinge on her left wing and she realised that some of her feathers were plucked. *I may have cut that one a bit too close.*

For a human, the following would have been impossible. Given her heightened reaction times, she opened her wings to create enough drag, swinging her feet forward until they were perpendicular to the stone floor.

The next step was to drastically reduce her velocity, at this speed Clara was liable to break something. With three, massive flaps of her wings, she arrested her momentum and made contact with the floor as though it were a dance.

There came the sound of clapping in the corner. It was a part of the Reverend Mother's quarters containing a desk, chairs and a couch, all adjacent to the hearth. The woman she once looked up to in life was seated comfortably in her chair, that face neutral despite the *praise*.

"Reverend Mother," Clara said.

"Clara Grey," Augustine said. "You're supposed to be dead."

A telling statement, but Clara would not let the *heart of the Tower* lead this exchange.

"I did," Clara said. "That's why Drusilla was removed from the board."

"That's not the *death* I was talking about," Augustine replied.

"Oh? Did you mean trapping me in a series of alternate realities?" Clara asked.

While that answer was rather obvious, the Reverend Mother did not react in the slightest. As an acolyte, Clara remembered the matron behaving more like a human. *She reminds me more of a natural-born angel.*

"Or was that after Heaven sent Gabriel and his lieutenants after me?"

Now that got a response, although it was so slight that even a vampire might miss it. Clara was operating at such a heightened speed that everything in this conversation was taking an eternity. She could feel her powers waning, but refused to give Augustine an advantage.

"That was a... *neat*... trick," Augustine said. "Hecate never could get along with herself, let alone anyone else, and yet you're running the roost."

There was vitriol behind every word. It was not so much as praise as an admission that someone was now a viable threat... *to whom? Why hasn't she attacked?*

The longer they spoke, the more Augustine's mask cracked. Clara was not even trying to rile up the woman. This loss of composure stemmed from deep-seated anger, focused exclusively on the fallen angel. *This is not exactly a happy reunion.*

"I was expecting a medal, actually," Clara said. "Hunters are supposed to rid the world of threats to humanity."

"I decide who dies!"

"Clearly, I missed that lesson."

"How dare—(*you*)!"

"Kill Artemis? The goddess who loved to hunt down men on her personal, hunting grounds?"

"They deserved it!"

"As did she," Clara countered. "Hunters do not interfere in the matters of humanity, nor do we take innocent lives."

This exchange was educational and further showed Clara that her formative training as a hunter was nothing more than a lie. *I should've caught on after encountering my first ghost…*

"Thieves? Murderers? Rapists?" Augustine asked.

"It's for God and society to judge the merit of their crimes…. *You* taught us this."

The act of hoisting the Reverend Mother by her own petard had the desired effect. The mask shattered, with that scowl and flared nose, Augustine was losing all composure.

"*You have one shot!*" Artemis exclaimed.

Clara would not reach into her pocket as that risked giving away her advantage. She would also need to return in sync with time soon. *Just a minute more.*

"How dare you apply rules to the likes of me!"

There was one thing she loved about the old gods. They were both the best and the worst of what humanity had to offer. In her opinion, they were creatures governed purely by their impulses.

Not that reason and logic were the be-all and end-all. Passion was a powerful motivator; one Clara used on numerous occasions. That same drive could poison the mind, pushing someone to the brink of insanity. *Zeus must have been a peach.*

"I'll have my revenge!" Augustine added.

Clara's lips curled into a grin. Those steel-grey eyes shone brightly in defiance. This angel had taken her lessons as an acolyte to heart.

"All this time, you were using us as a means to advance your own agenda."

That explained the ledger she found years ago in the abandoned wing leading to Pompeii. Someone had kept a tally of old gods, their whereabouts, and their fates. It seemed that someone was clearing the board. *Leaving room for those closely aligned with Heaven.*

"For the good of humanity."

"Right…" Clara said. "I'm sure Drusilla saw it that way."

That name had a visible reaction on Augustine's face. It made sense, since Clara's involvement with that vampire led to several, life-altering changes in her career. *I wonder if the failsafe was embedded in case Drusilla managed to sway me.*

"How dare you!"

By this point, the matron's veins were bulging from her forehead. Her face was distorted, and red, heralding what would soon come to a head.

"Now…" Augustine said, after taking a deep breath.

It did little to help the matron to regain her composure. Even that single word contained oscillations as though raw power was looking for an outlet. *It would fucking help if I knew who I was dealing with.*

"*Nemesis,*" Silver whispered.

That explains it! This was the goddess of vengeance, who, by some accounts, was raped by her father. She was using hunters not only as pawns, but as a source of power. All the while, exacting her revenge one god or goddess at a time. *Meaning Hecate kept silent about their suspicions.*

"Do what you came here to do," Augustine ordered.

"*What?*" Clara said. *Why does Nemesis wish to meet her end?*

Then the idea seeped into her mind, like a thimble full of black paint falling into a gallon of white. The idea was so insidious that Clara found herself thinking that she would rather go on a honeymoon with Drusilla.

"You came here to deal with me," Nemesis said. "So—(*just get it over with*)."

Clara did not hesitate, nor permit the goddess to say more. The angel had no choice as she was on the cusp of losing her advantage.

The angel reached inside her pocket and found an all too familiar pearl-encrusted grip waiting for her. She smiled, drew out her trusty derringer and took aim.

She pulled the first trigger, sending out a golden bullet in slow motion. The air and dust within the barrel were pushed out, followed by a few grains of gunpowder which sparkled when exposed to the air.

Next came the projectile with a left-handed spin followed by the remaining powder that lit up in a bright flash. Clara was deadly with firearms, but this weapon would make her the stuff of legends.

As though by coincidence, the ground trembled on impact. The effect forced her wings to adjust to maintain balance. *One doozy of a coincidence.*

The bullet flew true and struck Nemesis right in the abdomen. The bullet did not exit out the back and instead lodged itself in the goddess's small intestine.

By then, Clara was already back in sync with time. The drain had taken a lot out of her, but she was fine. The same could not be said for Nemesis whose golden blood was already pouring out from the entry point.

"What—(*have you done*)?" Nemesis asked.

"I sentenced you according to your crimes," Clara answered. "A slow and painful death that will hinder any attempt to halt the evacuation."

There came a tremor, more acute than the last. This confirmed her hunch that Nemesis was the reason they remained anchored in time. *My rise in stature was leading to a comparative drop in her powers.*

"Why?"

"I'm tired of getting dragged into these endless, family squabbles," Clara said. "You'll die alone as this tower crumbles around you."

Before the goddess could reply, Clara disappeared.

CHAPTER 38

ASHES! ASHES!

Clara appeared in the main hall and was greeted by an ear-splitting screech. The angel was surrounded by hunters, many of whom had forgotten everything they learned. *The Mount Vesuvius eruption brought out the worst in people.*

"She's everywhere!" An acolyte yelled, while those big, blue eyes darted from one place to another.

Clara could not see the threat, until she embraced the chill touch of the grave. The transformation always left her feeling uncomfortable while making her translucent as a ghost. In this case, it proved to be beneficial.

"To echo Julia… what the fuck?" Clara asked.

The hall was chock-full of Eleanors. Clara had witnessed several instances of the angel of death appear in one location before. Still, sighting four instances in a graveyard was more benign than what was going on now.

"What else could I expect?" Clara asked.

This pocket of reality would not hold together for long. If she did not intervene, panic would spread throughout their ranks like wildfire.

"Eleanor," Clara called out.

Many noted her transformation. Given that she was embracing death, many assumed the worst.

"Clara," an Eleanor said, from behind.

It took a great deal of self-control to not react. If she did, the situation might further devolved into chaos.

"One second," Clara said.

She prepared herself to adopt her best goddess voice.

"ENOUGH!" Clara yelled.

The walls shook and many covered their ears.

"YOU are hunters," Clara said sternly. "Act like it."

That surprisingly had the desired effect. Clara hated leading, but sometimes people needed a reminder.

"Evacuate to Pompeii," Clara said. "Leave everything behind, your lives are worth more than the entirety of this tower."

The room went quiet, save for the worsening tremors. Hunters and senior acolytes quickly took charge, and dozens of living souls poured out of the main hall, leading to several instances of Eleanor fading out of existence.

"You cost me several souls," Eleanor said.

"They can't escape you forever," Clara said.

Eleanor chuckled, before replying, "Some have managed to do so for centuries."

"A reference to me?"

"Not at all," Eleanor said. "You died; I was simply prevented from performing my function."

A reminder that someone in Heaven intervened personally.

"Does that mean you won't interfere?"

"I cannot claim souls early."

Now that was an interesting choice of words. Clara made sure to keep that sentence in mind.

"Do you know where Julia is?"

"No one hides from the dead."

Now that the *living* was down to a trickle, Clara could see hundreds of souls appear out of the walls, and floors. *They've been trapped here all this time*?

"Some have been here for nearly a millennium," Eleanor said.

When Clara loosened her grip on her psyche, Eleanor could pick up on her thoughts. It was said that gods often did not wish to go through the tedium of conveying direction to their constructs. *I prefer to humanise the experience.*

"Indeed." Eleanor replied. "I know where they are."

"Safe?"

"Is anyone safe under the shadows of an erupting volcano?"

That said a lot, still, Clara would not find Julia in time without assistance. *I won't be able to slow down time for a while yet.*

"Take my hand, Goddess."

Clara did not hesitate. As soon as contact was made, Eleanor snapped her fingers, and they popped out of existence.

CHAPTER 39

MOBIUS

J esus fuck!" Julia swore, as two, otherworldly creatures appeared from out of thin air.

"You might have been right forty years ago," Clara said, with a chuckle.

The werewolf looked at Eleanor and her complexion turned green. No one else appeared to be able to see the angel of death.

"Clara asked me to bring her to you," Eleanor said.

"You're not here for me?" Julia confirmed.

Eleanor glanced at Clara, and the latter realised that the werewolf must have *embraced death* one time too many. Because both Clara and Eleanor were not visible to the rank-and-file hunters, Julia was effectively talking to herself.

Clara smirked and returned fully into the world of the living along with Eleanor.

"You made it!" Agnes said.

Clara smiled but then raised her hand to ensure she had everyone's attention.

"Thank you for the sentiment," Clara said. "However, I believe we have bigger things to worry about."

They were in a large space, underground by the looks of it. While on the surface it was a blessing, the cloud of hot gases would either cook them alive or consume the air they breathed. *Death.*

While the space had been cleared, the impressions left in the dust indicated that items were moved out in a hurry. The scent of fish and brine was powerful enough to make Clara want to take shallow breaths.

"Just ducky," Clara said, under her breath.

"*Clara?*" Silver asked. "*We need to talk…*"

* * * *

Clara found herself standing inside the convocation hall. The five goddesses were all seated at the table. *At least no one is fighting.*

"Artemis," Clara said. "Thank you for lending me your *bow.*"

While Clara inherited goddess's powers, she did not have to be a god killer.

"Creative," Artemis said. "I was expecting a headshot, but this *may* work in our favour."

"May?"

All the goddesses went pale, which was surprising to see on the already deathly pale Ethereal. Clara saw the skull and bones behind the translucent skin. *Fits right in during the day of the dead.*

"If her power doesn't transfer to you," Silver said. "We're not sure what will happen."

"Horsefeathers," Clara said. "You mean that I'm the one who caused Pompeii to fall?"

An interesting concept. While Vesuvius did blow its top, the added power from the death of a goddess might have amplified the effects. *Killing tens of thousands in the process.*

"Pompeii was always lost," Silver said.

"Meaning that time is immutable?" Clara asked.

"We believe so," Silver said.

They may be ancient, but their knowledge had limits. *We only know what we experience, learned in passing, or studied.*

"Chronos would have known for certain," Ethereal said.

In this state, Ethereal was far more haunting. She usually sucked the joy from a room, but now Clara wondered if her soul was forfeit for just being in the same room. The past tense told her all she needed to know.

"Right…" Clara said. "Options?"

"Go back and kill Nemesis?" Sparky said, in an excited tone while repeatedly making stabbing motions.

"We'd end up stuck here tied to this little prison," Ethereal countered. "…nitwit."

The latter part was whispered but it reached Clara's ears just fine. At least others were considering more productive options… *hopefully.*

"Assuming Clara could hold back that persona for long," Silver added, to prevent her sisters from fighting.

"I thought the same," Clara said. "New body, new skills, and a new generation of even more fanatical hunters."

Everyone went silent. All except for Bastet, who was purring. *That doesn't help me, since cats purr when they are happy or nervous.*

"Other than slowing and speeding time relative to myself or in a bubble…" Clara said. "Anything else?"

"At your current power levels," Silver said. "You would only be able to protect this space for a day, and with luck, two."

"Unless someone distracts her," Ethereal said.

This was the equivalent of holding back the water after a dam bursts. She might be able to hold the waters at bay in the near term, but eventually the volume would overwhelm her. *They say it can take years for lava flows to cool.*

"That's out then…" Clara said. "…too early?"

"Clara?" Silver asked.

"Just something that Eleanor said," Clara said.

Beyond those windows, there was the angel of death. She never noticed it, but those black eyes were focused exclusively on her. *As though she knows about this convocation.*

"Eleanor?" Clara asked.

"Goddess," Eleanor said, from behind.

To put it mildly, Eleanor's appearance inside her head was *jarring*. The instance ahead of her was still there, apparently frozen in time like everyone else. *Except she's not, because those eyes are moving!*

"You know how to get us out of this mess…" Clara said, after turning around.

This kept Eleanor in her field of view but left the goddesses at her back.

"No, goddess," Eleanor said. "You do."

Clara cocked a brow upon hearing the answer. She took a deep breath before looking at the goddesses to see if anyone else had insight on the matter. She gave them time to answer by circling around the table and focusing on every single set of eyes.

She stopped at the head of the table, leaving her with a view of everyone in the room. The answer made no sense, but only because she was missing some context.

"Ethereal," Clara said. "You created Eleanor. How does she experience time?"

"The same way we do," Ethereal answered.

That made sense, because she bore the limitations of her maker. Clara felt there was a variable at play that they had yet to account for. *There's more to her than meets the eye.*

"We've done this before…" Clara said.

"I have," Eleanor corrected.

Eleanor could be anywhere when needed. This was Pompeii and the angel of death would be here to collect souls. *Why does she know me then?*

"You're all part of the whole and… linked," Clara said.

When the walls between this existence and reality faded, the contemporary and past versions of Eleanor synced up. *This left Eleanor with insight about the next thousand years.*

"Isn't this around the time she began to malfunction?" Sparky asked.

"You can't be—(*be serious*)," Silver said.

"It was always you!" Ethereal exclaimed.

"You knew exactly where I was going when we met at the outskirts of that church," Clara said.

"Of course," Eleanor said. "This moment never takes place unless you thread a *narrow* path in life."

The rest was obvious. Clara would invariably ask Eleanor for help, convincing the angel of death that these souls could only be claimed after they were born and reached their age. *One cannot claim souls before they are created.*

Eleanor would agree to intervene in exchange for something. An item of value, for someone who did not seek wealth, love, or anything humans coveted.

"You reasoned it out?" Eleanor asked.

"You want my soul?" Clara whispered. "I wasn't even sure I still had one."

Clara could not see her own soul, and besides, she was an angel. She assumed it was forfeited in the transition.

"No," Eleanor said. "I wish to guide you for judgement when your journey ends."

"What if I live forever?"

Eleanor's dark eyes twinkled, and she smiled.

"Everything dies," Eleanor said. "As everyone in this room can attest."

"*Touché,*" Clara said. "I accept your terms."

"Thank you," Eleanor said, before snapping her fingers.

CHAPTER 40

SPRING FORWARD

In Clara's mind, the angel of death had just snapped her fingers. However, this world *felt* different somehow.

The passage of time became more obvious when she looked through the portholes and focused on the surroundings. For one, there were stalactites above their heads, and the walls were visibly worn and cracked. That was her first clue that this was not a case of where she was… *but a matter of when.*

"I'm jealous of your ability to manipulate time," Clara said.

Eleanor smiled and bowed her head slightly. The angel of death was not accustomed to being praised by her masters. *I'm not sure that she'll ever relax around me.*

"I simply took you out of time," Eleanor said.

Clara saw no need to question why the angel of death did not delve into the details. *It's sobering enough to think we ceased to exist for nearly two millennia.*

"Back to the last time we met?" Clara asked.

"One hundred days after," Eleanor replied.

"That…accounts for my time trapped after breaching the Terminus?"

"Correct," Eleanor said.

The angel of death's black eyes twinkled, before a smirk crept upon her face. Clara realised that a part of her must have left an impression on Eleanor. *Which Hecate characterised as defective.*

"Check your coat pockets when you return to your conscious self," Eleanor said. "I believe you dropped something."

"Real—(ly)?" Clara asked.

Eleanor was gone from her mind, which left Clara and the goddesses at a loss for words. It was humbling to be surrounded by five, old gods and still have no way to get out of that mess.

"Right," Clara said, before clearing her throat. "Any signs of Nemesis?"

The goddesses looked to one another, and while nothing was passed on verbally, they somehow came to a consensus. *I'd love to know how they managed that.*

"No sign of another's presence," Silver said.

"Good riddance," Artemis added.

All the while, Bastet purred while chewing on her claws to remove the sheath. Like a common household cat, Bastet's claws were always kept sharp. *One the size of an average lion and with the strength of a bear.*

"Any hint of her," Clara said. "I want to know."

The reasons did not need to be mentioned. If Nemesis planned to have Clara kill her, then it logically followed that she expected to rule the roost. *I'd throw myself in a volcano before giving her a second lease on life.*

"Evelyn would kill me…" Clara said.

"Clara?" Silver asked, while the rest of them looked at her as though she just passed gas in church.

"Oh…" Clara said. "I was just thinking of a conversation we had… anyone have something to bring up?"

The room was silent as a tomb, or at least those not infested with ghouls. Clara smiled, and bowed respectfully to them.

"Thank you for sticking with me," Clara said. "Meeting adjourned."

* * * *

Once Clara returned to her conscious self, she first became aware of her breathing. The scent of fish lingered still, further driving the urge for Clara to breathe through her mouth. *It's hard to imagine that smell is the first thing to come through when the walls of a reality collapse.*

"What just happened?" Julia asked.

The werewolf's senses were more attuned than those of a human. Naturally, she would be the first to notice that something changed in the time between heartbeats.

"Do any of your phones work?" Clara asked.

"Why would they work?"

Clara sensed something vibrate in her pocket, a double pulse every second repeated several times over. All the while, the hunters looked at her as though she was possessed. *Well, that answers Julia's question.*

The werewolf reached into her bag and found one that powered on, but it had a three percent charge. Insufficient to connect with the network… *Even if you try to make an emergency call…*

"Shit," Julia said. "Yours works…"

While there were no overt questions to avoid raising suspicion, the werewolf was clearly confused. Clara lost everything she had after jumping through that bubble. *I couldn't take a single selfie this whole time.*

"Thank Eleanor," Clara replied.

The reason why they had a signal was a different matter. Clara reached in her pocket and toggled the screen, noting that it was nearly fully charged. So far, there were well over seventy notifications where nearly every message was from a single account. *Evelyn was clearly worried...*

"Clara," Amelia said. "What happened?"

"*When* may be the more appropriate question. At least the where is obvious..." Clara said.

Many sighed in relief for having escaped the bubble. No one wanted to ask the next obvious question.

"We need to find a way—(*out of this chamber*)," Clara said.

"Judith and Theresa," Amelia said. "Check the exit."

The two acolytes stiffened and went for the main doors. Meanwhile, Clara did not see any harm in dialling one, one, and two before pressing send. The phone screen switched to making a call, but there was nothing beyond that. *The signal is too weak for voice, but enough for text messaging.*

The girls were not getting anywhere fast. Even after enlisting the help of the male acolytes, they could not get the wedged doors apart.

Clara walked over, and those in the way naturally ceded space to her. Meanwhile, she handed her phone to Julia, who guessed what Clara was trying to do.

"Stand back," Clara said.

She suspected the doors were compressed by rubble on the other side. That meant debris could come tumbling in if she loosened the proverbial logjam.

With a firm grip of both hands around a large, black iron handle. Clara then gave it her all, and the door barely budged. That changed when she opened her wings and added a hard flap.

The handle tore clean away from the door. Clara landed fifteen paces away, with her ass absorbing most of the blow. *That's going to leave a bruise!*

That was enough for the rubble to roll in like a wave. Clara thought nothing of it, but caught sight of an orange construction cone. *They must've excavated this area.*

The room came alive with excited chatter. Everyone wanted to know what was going on and what to do next. Clara had a small army at her disposal, but that mattered little when they were effectively buried alive.

Sure, Clara could opt to transport herself out of this space. Even as drained as she was, the faith this group had in her would allow Clara to reach Rome. *I'd be pushing my luck with Paris.*

"Shut it!" Julia yelled.

Those words tore through Clara's mind. Her thought soon shifted to reasons why the werewolf needed the hunters to simmer down.

Nevertheless, the effect proved beneficial. The noise level dropped considerably until Clara easily picked up individual heartbeats and breathing… *wait?*

"Dogs," Julia whispered.

What did she mean by that? Clara focused until her mind filtered out the individual heartbeats, leading to several unusual sounds reaching her ear. Clara was not naturally attuned to claws scraping against stone and debris. *Julia runs with wolves.*

"How many?" Clara asked.

"Three and their handlers," Julia replied.

She supposed that even werewolves feared hunting parties. *Although some might see it as an invitation.*

Other sounds became more obvious given the context, such as the dull thump of boots against stone. Something that may have been shouting, although the sound propagation through the rubble was problematic… *at best.*

Amelie and Agnes hovered nearby, waiting for direction from Clara. Outwardly, Clara and Julia appeared to be deep in thought with their heads pointed towards the exit. No one else would ever hear what was going on, not until they were on the cusp of being saved.

"Sister," Agnes whispered.

Clara opened her eyes and turned around to better focus on the hunters. There was prep work to be done, but what they really needed was a cover story.

"We believe a rescue party is headed for us," Clara said.

There was surprisingly no reaction from the hunters. They had fallen back on their training, and Clara would be able to finish what needed to be said.

"We need to act as though we are part of a tour group visiting the ruins," Clara said.

That meant concealing any weapons and provisions they packed away. A bit of dirt on their faces and clothing would also help. Clara assumed they would have been down here a while.

Meanwhile, Clara and Julia indicated they would handle the authorities. The latter may not know Italian, but the werewolf spoke in a manner that was expected for tourists from her region. *I'll have to watch my use of outdated slang.*

The next step was easy. As the hunters organised themselves, Clara's wings melted away, her shoulders were soon bare, so Julia helped to patch up the holes to make her uniform look complete.

Agnes had difficulty spotting Clara when she returned with an update. The two versions of Clara did have resemblances, but the biggest difference being her muted beauty, enabled her to blend in.

"Thank you," Clara said, upon confirmation their plan was underway.

Meanwhile, her phone vibrated again. The pulsating tone was missed by everyone else in the room, but Clara caught it with ease.

The list of notifications was massive. Most of it was written in code, like they had done before when lacking a secure means of communication. Every line was effectively randomly generated, save for the first which hinted at a biblical reference to give Clara a key to work with.

Clara ignored those because she did not have time to go through the process of breaking down the intended message. *I'll get to it when things settle.*

However, that last message was more obvious, devolving to an earlier code.

> **Evelyn**: Have you made your declaration of independence.

This slang was a reference to getting a divorce but could be extended to Clara's mission. She typed up her reply and hoped it would send.

> **Clara**: Got the bum's rush from the clip joint after an off-time jive. I don't have any mad money for a dimbox.

She pressed '*Send*' and then '*Retry*' six times. On the seventh try, it showed the message as sent.

The response did not take long and was comparatively blunt.

Evelyn: I'll handle the bulls. A dingle dangler passed on your coordinates. Listen for my name.

Upon seeing that last line, Clara was left with more questions than answers. The vampire was resourceful, but this went beyond the pale. No matter, as the sign that things were going their way brought her great assurance.

Until receiving the news, Clara had unwittingly been holding in her breath to the point of hearing her heart pounding in her ears. She relaxed so much that Julia caught the change.

"All good?" Julia asked.

"Seems we have help from the outside."

"Evelyn?" Julia asked. "How——(*would she even know*)?

"No clue, but it feels as though she had plenty of time to prepare…"

"Really?" Julia asked.

"Were traffic cones common in the Roman Era?"

"Now you're being mean," Julia teased. "I never finished high school."

"You too?" Clara asked before winking.

* * * *

An hour later, there came the sound of stones being moved. Clara asked the hunters to organise into a line to clear out the rubble from their end. The place was abuzz, and even she found it difficult to maintain composure. *I need to keep up appearances.*

Another hour went by before light bled through, along with cool, outside air. Clara hoped that no one thought to ask how they managed to survive being trapped in here for so long. *This should have been our tomb.*

At the top of the third hour, they sent a team of paramedics into the chamber. The rescue team needed time to stabilize the entrance, and this permitted the medics to apply first aid as needed.

What the medics found was a group of healthy men and women. Julia naturally stuck out as her clothing differed from the uniforms the rest wore. Clara approached at the earliest opportunity and explained they were touring the site when all hell broke loose.

Of course, Clara had no idea what happened. Her woes began nearly two millennia ago and there was no end in sight. It was fortunate the bored medics were more than willing to talk up a storm while waiting for an all-clear.

They said the skies filled with volcanic ash that bathed the ruins in shadow. This brought several to the site to witness this bizarre phenomenon.

What followed next was a bright flash of light and a shockwave. Several were left temporarily blinded and in need of immediate treatment. The local authorities wasted no time in mobilising emergency crews to assist.

Then a tower '*with no reference in the historical records*' appeared out of thin air. While pristine and standing tall as '*the day it was built*,' in the blink of an eye, it turned to rubble.

In the days that followed, books and news archives began to appear with references to similar sightings in the past. It was as though the books themselves were being updated to account for this disconnect. *Every sighting was on or around the same date and time.*

Rescue teams were still busy digging up bodies. Some appeared as though they died recently, while others looked right at home among the dead in Pompeii. *A tear in reality that will eventually become a ghost story.*

"That's bad—(*assed*)," Julia tried to say in response to that.

A quick glance from Clara was enough to silence the werewolf. While the angel agreed, she would not give them enough clues to believe anything other than this group being incredibly fortunate. *You'd think some divine entity played a hand in it.*

Of course, that all went to hell when the senior medic, with '*Esposito*' on his nametape, looked right at Clara and said with a flirtatious smile, "I can see why Evelina has only eyes for you, Chiara."

Hearing the Italian equivalents to their names was enlightening. Clara never considered there could be localised variations, as she always went by Clara or used region, specific pseudonyms.

The angel knew that Evelyn anglicized her name a few centuries back. Phonetically, it was practically the same as the French variant, Éveline. *It all depends on the local flavour of the speaker.*

Clara's face broke into a shit-eating grin. Since this was all part of the plan then there was little reason to continue playing this game.

"Quite right, Julia." Clara said. "Absolutely badassed."

Julia snickered before tapping on her nose. That could mean several things, but Clara soon picked up the scent of vanilla wafting in the air. It was faint and the paramedics were the source. *Why else would they volunteer to potentially get trapped?*

"Anything we need to worry about, *Signore?*"

"No, *Signorina,*" Esposito said.

This man had all the elements that made him handsome. Short-trimmed black hair, chocolate-brown eyes, and a square jaw. What might dissuade any potential *signorinas* was the intense stare, but the sight of those pearly whites revealed his impish nature.

Clara noticed they were in no rush to treat the minor first aid cases they did have. *They are leaving that to the hunters.*

"Excellent," Clara said, before her eyes glowed blue, bathing the room in electric light. "You're surrounded by trained killers… and we hold grudges."

The man gulped and Julia chuckled. Meanwhile, Agnes approached the group quietly. As judged by the sound of muffled cheering, the first hunter made it through safely.

"Sister," Agnes said.

"I know," Clara said. "That's great news. Ensure you are among the first and help keep them organised."

The acolyte took in a sharp breath while water welled up along her eyelids. Clara was putting a lot of faith in an acolyte. That much was true, but she also knew the acolyte would deliver.

Clara had the choice of getting an address and finding her way to Evelyn. It would avoid a lot of questions, but that meant leaving the hunters alone to fend for themselves. A group that came into life entirely isolated from the real world.

These were effectively cloistered nuns and brothers who could take on ghouls, vampires, and werewolves. That was a recipe for disaster if not properly managed, and while Agnes and Amelia were capable, they were also creatures out of time.

She glanced at Julia, who cocked an eyebrow. She had a plan in mind, but it was too early to play her hand. Either way, she needed to run it by all those involved. *Hunters are xenophobic at the best of times.*

"What?" Julia asked.

"Nothing," Clara said. "Just a crazy idea."

"I hope the world is ready for it…"

It was surprising how true those words were.

CHAPTER 41

SURFACE

Clara was exhausted, based on a culmination of her powers being drained, physical weariness, and trauma. *No one should learn firsthand that martyrdom was the right call.*

Still, returning to the real world helped her recharge. She wondered if Evelyn was busy reviving the legend of the Valkyrie. *Not that I'm complaining.*

Based on Julia's eyes being half-shut and her head swaying in sync with the bumps on the road, it was clear that the werewolf also needed downtime. *Is it ever a good time to have a chat with her?*

She had to make the time, assuming that Evelyn gave them more than a minute to breathe. From her point of view, they were gone a short while. *That's why all of this preparation and comes across as miraculous.*

That was partially true, because Clara divulged the location of the Tower early on in their relationship. *Evelyn must have made the connection when a mysterious tower appeared out of nowhere.*

Clara suspected this level of planning must have involved blackmail, extortion, and sizable *donations*. Evelyn had a way of getting what she wanted even when every door was shut. *She probably bankrolled the search and rescue operations.*

Despite being fatigued, Clara knew that Esposito and his partner Rizzo were taking an indirect route to their final destination. They switched vehicles already and guessed they would change a couple more before arriving.

Clara personally witnessed Evelyn enact this plan before and knew Marc did not tolerate lapses in security. If she guessed right, the elder vampire was keeping tabs on their progress. *He might even have eyes on us.*

That was why Clara let Julia drift off into the dream realm. For a moment, the angel was envious, but her opportunity would come up eventually. *Just spending an hour in the setting sun did wonders for me.*

The driver looked into his mirror. He smiled and Clara slowed down time as he reached for something. Her precautions were all for naught, since he produced a new set of keys. Five minutes later, Clara picked up the young werewolf and carried her to their next ride.

The men's jaws dropped, and Clara winked as Julia nuzzled into her shoulder. *If you think this is impressive.*

They drove on for another hour and eventually pulled up besides the nondescript storefront. It was now late in the evening and the doors were locked. Clara nudged Julia awake, who rubbed her eyes and stretched out.

"I was sleeping? How long?" Julia asked.

"Over an hour."

"Wow..."

Julia yawned before adopting a faint smile. That glow in her eyes hinted she had been in the sweetest of dreams.

"Sorry, I was dreaming of being back home with mom… Where are we?"

"Somewhere in Naples," Clara answered.

"Really?" Julia asked before those eyes widened and came aglow. "I've never been overseas…"

"If you're up to it, I'll take you on a grand tour of Europe."

Clara liked the idea of revisiting the wonders of her youth in the modern world. *Two women on the prowl, looking for a good time, with neither having the time for any bullshit.*

"I'd like that…" Julia said.

They were escorted to a gate that led into the alley with a locked hatch. Esposito unlocked it, and Clara spotted the hand-carved steps. *Into the depths we go…*

CHAPTER 42

UNDERGROUND

D id you know there was an underground network of tunnels here?"
Julia asked.

"No. Most of my time in Italy was spent hunting ghouls in Rome."

Some of these tunnels must have served as aqueducts, the surfaces were
smooth as a river stone. They also passed crypts, places of worship, and what
looked to be the ruins of shops. *This must have been an underground city.*

Some of the sites were still frequented by tourists, but the escorts led them
away from such places to avoid witnesses. At the end of a long tunnel, they
came across a barricade followed by a sudden drop into an abyss.

The men walked straight through the barricade and Clara followed. When Julia
hesitated, the angel smiled and took her hand.

"It's fine," Clara said. "I'll explain later."

Julia followed suit but forced Clara's arm all the way back. After taking three steps over the void, they found themselves in a large chamber, empty save for what appeared to be an oversized mirror with an oval top and bottom. The dull glow from the object was enough for Clara to visually confirm they were otherwise alone.

"That's fucked—(up)!" Julia said.

"It's a vampire gate," Clara said.

That meant Evelyn was not in Naples. *She might still be in Italy.*

"Five minutes," Esposito said.

Clara furrowed her brow, because she realised that Rizzo had yet to say a word. *Not even a whimper, sigh, or even a fart…*

So, this was a roundabout way of delaying their arrival to line up with a certain destination. Unlike the Terminus, vampire gates rotated through their destinations. While this made them more versatile, they were also more dangerous. *People have lost body parts for crossing the threshold too late.*

"Close your eyes," Clara said.

"Why would—fuck!"

The room came awash in a bright, white light and the opaque surface of the oculus now showed a vivid image. She had seen a couple of destinations before, but she never had the time to take in the *sights.*

Clara saw this destination before, notable for the underwater ruins of a temple. Fish were swimming by and there was very little light other than what the oculus was putting out. These were not clownfish or anything that lived in a reef. *This is not shallow water.*

"That's not an aquarium?" Julia asked, while rubbing her watery eyes.

"No," Clara said. "Don't touch."

"Really?" Julia said. "I was hoping to take a selfie with a snaggletooth."

"Cute... I mean you... not the fish."

* * * *

It was interesting to observe the military precision required to make this happen. The oculus changed another time and they were unsurprisingly greeted by the image of Evelyn.

The vampire was, as always, dressed to the nines, and this dress left little to the imagination. Clara's jaw dropped at the sight of her. *She never disappoints.*

Julia did not appear to be bothered, but a surprise was waiting for them both. Evelyn ran through the gate and instead of going for Clara, the vampire went straight for the werewolf. Within the blink of an eye, Evelyn was hugging Julia to the point of pushing all the air from those lungs.

"*Merci!*" Evelyn exclaimed. (*Thank You!*) "I owe you so much for what you've done."

Clara realised that Julia was stiff as a board, almost humming with anxiety. After the werewolf realised there was no way to extricate herself from that monstrous grip, she returned the hug.

"It's... nothing..." Julia wheezed.

"Oh, *non!*" Evelyn said, while Clara chuckled. (*Oh, no!*) "Sorry. I forget my own strength when I'm excited."

The vampire chose that time to turn towards Clara and wink. The movement was so fast that Clara might have missed it if she had not been operating at a heightened speed.

"Glad to do it," Julia said, after taking several deep breaths. "It was educational."

"We posed as lovers," Clara teased.

"*Vraiment?*" Evelyn asked. (*Really?*) "If Clara has any new tricks to show in the boudoir, I'll know who to thank."

Julia's face was flush with blood. Part of her showed extreme discomfort with an equal part of rage, but Evelyn's cool kiss to the cheek took the bite from that temper.

Clara caught something unusual. The vampire hid it well, but she was unconsciously reacting to something. Vampires were known to be affected by the faithful. The devout could make vampires step out of their way without realising it. *Like anyone would do when exposed to an open flame.*

As an angel, Clara's effect was more pronounced, she watched crowds of vampires move out of her way like the bow of a ship would cut through the water. *That happened at a rave and no one realised why.*

Older vampires like Evelyn could temper such urges, at least long enough to eliminate the threat. *Something really powerful is among us.*

Evelyn's head shifted towards Clara long enough to make eye contact. Those soft lips with red lipstick were moving…

"*Do you feel it?*" Evelyn asked, without making a sound.

Alas, Clara was blind to that particular sense as she was herself a creature of faith. Still, she had been out of sync with time for a reason. *Now!*

"Three minutes—(*Signorina*)," the man said.

Evelyn turned around so fast she appeared to be facing in both directions simultaneously. Julia reacted accordingly, sniffing for a threat but found none. *Nothing in the air to alert her senses.*

Meanwhile, Clara felt her reserves being drained. There was barely enough left for her to maintain her temporal state.

"You're not Mattia Esposito," Evelyn said, while distancing herself from him. "…You just look like him."

The man smiled, but the effect was as chilling as it was calculated. When Clara switched her vision to peer into his *soul*, she saw the light of creation emanating from the body. On instinct, her wings tore through the velcro as they reformed.

"Get behind me!" Clara ordered.

Clara would beat herself up later for not acting on her suspicions until now. She had a very real threat to deal with. Esposito's skin stretched to the point of being translucent, like a water balloon filled to the point of bursting. The man then literally blew apart from within.

Clara's wings moved to shield her from the worst of it. Those black feathers were covered in blood, viscera, and pulverised bone. What was left was truly a sight to behold. An angel with perfect, white wings, full armour, and a sword of heavenly fire.

Meanwhile, his partner collapsed to the ground as though a marionette with his strings cut. *I never knew we could possess people or use mortals like puppets.*

While Clara never laid eyes on this particular archangel before, his name, Uriel, and his visage were burned into her mind. The only reason they would program him in was sobering. *In case of war, break glass...*

"You have—(*violated our laws once again*)," Uriel said.

"Gabriel wasn't up for a rematch?" Clara asked.

There was no facial response, most archangels could barely interact with humans. They lacked any behavioural elements to do so, save their appearance.

"He has yet to recover," Uriel said, using a tone that made Ethereal sound warm and cuddly.

"Shame," Clara said, before wearing a grin.

She pulled two, identical, golden pistols that felt exactly like her trusty nines. Clara backed away towards the oculus, hoping the shadow from her wings was enough to protect both Evelyn and Julia. She only stopped once the gate was at her side.

"Get behind the oculus, and stay in its shadow!" Clara ordered.

"Do not bother, they are on my list as well," Uriel said.

"Really?" Clara asked. "You'll have to get past me."

"Not a problem."

Something blue streaked past Clara's peripheral vision, right where Uriel's head ought to have been. One moment, the archangel was on the receiving end of a bad case of electrolysis and, in the other, he deflected the bolt of energy with his sword.

Before Clara had a chance to engage, three golden arrows in a tight group flew by. His wings moved to deflect, but the arrows of a goddess could not be denied. The first one went clean through and through, while the others sailed past him.

Both Sparky with a hyper-caffeinated look and Artemis with a stone-cold glare popped out from out of her shadow. Uriel did not appear to be worried, even as Clara fired off two bursts from her pistols.

Even with every shot aimed at his centre of mass, every single one hit the wall behind Uriel. The archangel appeared to smile, one that was more fitting for a deranged prisoner in an asylum.

Clara, Sparky and Artemis kept up their attacks. Their movements were slow and deliberate. Like all defensive battles, the attacker only needed to get lucky once. *Uriel is eternal and just as patient.*

The first to break ranks was Sparky, whose beam faltered.

"My turn," Uriel said, while a second set of wings appeared. *That explains the biblical references.*

Uriel flicked his sword, sending a shower of flames towards the goddess of magic. She evaded the attack, but the fire nonetheless scorched her gown. *She was only running at a twentieth of her normal power.*

There came a snap, the echoes lost in this expansive space. The ground beneath his feet cracked from the strain, leaving deep impressions of his sandals embedded in the stone. Gravity, as usual, won out in the end, forcing him to his knees.

Ten more arrows were loosed and struck him through both his knees. With another arrow nocked, Artemis held back the bow string, waiting.

"All good?" Clara asked Sparky.

The goddess pressed her hands against her knees while wheezing. After several deep breaths, she looked up with those bloodshot eyes and nodded.

"You can't hold me forever!" Uriel said.

That was true, but Clara needed him to send a message. Killing an archangel would further rile up the hornet's nest. *Time to get creative.*

"Gals," Clara said. "He thinks we want to contain him."

Everyone chuckled, but even Silver was beginning to show signs of strain. Uriel grinned, his teeth shining brightly in the silver light of this destination. Clara was too busy keeping her pistols trained to pay attention to the minutia.

What she did not expect was the sound of Julia dropping to her knees. She heard it all before, it was the sound of bones dislocating, increasing in length, and reattaching themselves. *She's turning!*

"Oh… *merde,*" Evelyn said. (*Oh… shit.*)

Silver, the goddess of the moon, used her ability to manipulate gravity to pin the werewolf against the far end of the chamber, Julia was high enough to ensure the vampire was out of reach.

"You are destined to fail," Uriel said.

"Because there are only four of me?" Clara asked, her voice trembling.

"Because you cling to your humanity—(*instead of embracing your true potential*)."

A shadowy figure dropped to the floor coinciding with a drop in gravity. Despite the height of the fall the catlike creature made no sound. But what followed next was loud and clear.

Ten, sharp claws fitted on two, oversized paws began slashing at Uriel's back and wings. Golden blood splattered everywhere, coinciding with both Artemis and Clara firing off a volley.

An arrow struck Uriel in his sword arm, while Clara struck his other arm and thighs. *That's going to slow him down.*

"Make that five," Clara said.

"Fools," Uriel said. "I only need a moment to—(*heal*)."

That was potentially true. They always operated out of sync with time and he had yet to utilise his powers. *I'm pulling up for a drag race in my hayburner with an empty tank.*

"Sorry, six! Do you have any idea how many dead there are here?"

Ethereal popped in from the ether and brought with her a legion of undead. The goddess of necromancy and the dead certainly had a way of inciting the dearly departed... *and her sisters.*

They swarmed the angel. Angry and tormented ghosts were capable of wreaking havoc. Not only could they ignore the effects of gravity, but also exert their rage physically on Uriel.

He tried to fend them off, but his wings were in tatters, further reducing his combat effectiveness. They began to move him towards the oculus, their progress slow at first, but they quickly built up momentum.

With one final push the undead sent him through the gate. Uriel ended up exposed to the harsh conditions of the moon, deprived of heat and air. *I wonder if archangels need to breathe.*

Alas, the sunlight was enough to heal the archangel, doing so much quicker than Clara thought possible. She trained her pistols at the portal, followed by Artemis. To help out, Ethereal merged with Sparky giving her a proverbial second wind. *This is going to suck hard.*

Silver had to stay out of it, or risk the werewolf breaking free. Meanwhile, Evelyn was doing her best to try to reach through to Julia, but being natural-born enemies meant the attempt was doomed to failure.

There came no sound as Uriel yelled at the sun, leaving a cloud of ice crystals behind. Clara focused on the archangel to create a time distortion surrounding him. Instead of a blur, he approached at the speed of an Olympic sprinter.

"Ready," Clara said.

Everyone took aim, leading their target.

"Steady," Clara added.

There came the sound of the bow string straining from being held back.

"Now!"

They gave it all they had, but the change between an Earth atmosphere and one with a near-vacuum was the problem. Bullets were deflected or deformed from the transition causing them to fly off randomly.

The arrows fared better through the transition, but without an atmosphere, they lost stability and buried themselves into the regolith.

The blue bolt transitioned well and struck the ground. It was only enough to cause the archangel to hesitate. Clara involuntarily winced, because hand-to-hand combat was next. *I'm running on fumes!*

Fortunately, the gate cut out just as the archangel's sword arm crossed the threshold, along with a part of his face and chest. When the light died out, there came a wet *plop* as the discarded flesh hit the ground.

"Hunters always said these gates were dangerous…" Clara said.

"You got lucky!" Ethereal said.

"*We* got lucky," Clara corrected. "Take the win."

Clara realised that a sword was still attached. That fiery light was now extinguished, leaving black steel behind. She freed it from Uriel's hand and gripped the handle. The sword began to glow, but the flame was dimmer, with red, orange and blue highlights.

She had no idea why the sword was glowing at all. She was disconnected from heaven, but the biggest mystery is why those colours made up the flames.

"Do you think Marc will like this sword?" Clara asked.

"Any sword would make his day, but one once wielded by an archangel?"

"The man of war might even end up smiling."

"That might actually break him…"

"True… I'll save it for his birthday," Clara said, with a smirk.

Meanwhile, Silver released the werewolf, who was now nothing more than a naked, young woman. Julia was unconscious, which was rare for adult werewolves. Clara knew for certain that their kind rarely changed halfway through a cycle unless they were ancient. *It must have shocked her system.*

Evelyn hesitated a moment but picked up Julia as though carrying her bride across the threshold. Meanwhile, Artemis reached for the backpack and gave it to Clara.

"Thank you," Artemis said.

"The feeling is mutual," Clara replied. "You'll need to teach me to wield a bow like you do."

"I'd like I—" Artemis said, as the room filled with a blinding light. "That."

Clara smiled as did Evelyn. At the sight of Marc, her vampiric partner was humming with energy. She covered the distance to Marc in the blink of an eye.

Seeing no reason to delay, Clara followed suit with a flaming sword in hand.

"*Non*, Marc," Evelyn said. "You can't have it."

When Clara saw Evelyn in the light, she realised that her wings proved to be an ineffective cover. Evelyn bore all the signs of someone who had been out in the sun too long. *That's usually fatal.*

Marc gave Clara a hard stare and the latter smiled meekly.

"I'm fine, Marc," Evelyn said, to soothe his soul. "It's nothing a late-night snack won't fix."

Clara chuckled nervously, because it would be a challenge to explain what happened…

CHAPTER 43

BREAKFAST WITH AN ANGEL

C lara awoke in the late afternoon. It was obvious, considering the ambient light in the room, but something was missing. *Where is she?*

The angel sat up while folding in her wings, the heat radiating from the sun meant she could walk around in the nude comfortably. *It's not like she hasn't seen me naked before.*

The hardwood floors in here were old, ancient even. That fit in with the rest of the space, hinting that this little apartment had been here for centuries.

She took in a deep breath, and her senses picked up on the scent of hardwood and orange-scented oils.

To her left, there was the bathroom with the door open and the lights out. The connecting door appeared to be a recent addition. *They just can't make it like they used to.*

The marble, and brass fittings were decidedly modern as was the style of lights. *Evelyn needs her amenities.*

Clara walked down the hall, headed for the kitchen. There came the sound of a paring knife cutting through the flesh of a fruit. Sure enough Evelyn was busy slicing a pear, along with a small plate of meats, cheeses, and fruits.

"Good afternoon," Clara said.

"Oh!" Evelyn said, after jumping up about a thumb's width. "You're surprisingly quiet these days."

"I blame Bastet," Clara said.

From Clara's index finger, a large, razor-sharp claw retracted. She then proceeded to slice through some sausage. Clara grabbed one end and presented the other to Evelyn. The latter licked the tip before wrapping her lips around it and sucked it in entirely.

"So that's why you purr when I get you excited."

"Only for you," Clara said, before adopting a grin. "What are you doing up?"

"I wanted to prepare some breakfast for you," Evelyn replied.

This was more of a delaying tactic, as Clara had plans to meet up with Julia later today. A fortnight had passed since they emerged through the gate and found themselves in the Parisian catacombs.

Marc arranged for the hunters to be smuggled into the country a couple at a time to avoid suspicion. The last one arrived in Paris last night, and Julia was ready to announce her decision.

The choice to take an active role in forming a new order of hunters could not have been an easy one. The werewolf was just as likely to sever ties with Evelyn and Clara entirely. *That would be understandable.*

She also had the opportunity to go on more adventures. Clara felt that this was the least likely outcome, because few willingly followed a martyr into danger. *No matter how good I look in a dress.*

The angel hoped that Julia would accept her offer to shape a new order of hunters. Marc even managed to find a few, *open-minded* vampires willing to train… *and accompany them on hunts.*

The idea had merit, since vampires did serve along the Western Front during the Great War. Marc headed a group that countered Drusilla's attempts to shift the tides of war in their favour.

Marc even offered to watch over their operation in the short term. Clara wanted to pinch herself to confirm she was awake, but Evelyn said it was genuine.

"Besides, it might be for the best…" Evelyn said. *"Marc has more confirmed kills than you…"*

"I wasn't keeping score," Clara remembered saying.

Evelyn pulled Clara in closer before kissing her on the cheek.

"He was," Evelyn said, before giggling.

* * * *

"Clara?" Evelyn asked.

The angel opened and shut her eyes several times in rapid succession. The world slowly returned to the forefront of her mind and she realised that those piercing, green eyes served as a lighthouse guiding her back to reality.

"Sorry," Clara said. "I wasn't home for a moment."

"De rien," Evelyn replied. (*It's nothing.*) "You're worried about her."

"…I swear you can read my mind," Clara countered.

The vampire giggled, her breasts bouncing up and down with the motion. She turned around and grabbed the cutting board that she prepared for breakfast.

"I enjoy the challenge of not being able to read you," Evelyn said. "That said, she has been your special project for a while."

"What if she walks away?"

"It's her choice and she's big enough to live with the consequences."

That was true enough. Still, Clara had a soft spot for the woman whose life she unexpectedly destroyed three years back. Sure, that set the werewolf on the eventual path of redemption, but the guilt lingered.

"You still struggle with that last part," Evelyn said. "Viens, you need to eat before venturing out in this Parisian spring."

"I'll make it up to you when I get back," Clara said.

"I'll never have enough of you, *mon amour.*"

The vampire now clearly owned expressing her love. Clara liked it, loved it even, but she could still not work up the courage to reciprocate.

"Was the bathroom once a bedroom?" Clara asked.

"Oui," Evelyn replied. "That was Marc's room when he whisked me away from the bordello."

"You lived here?"

That explained the strong adherence to maintaining so much of the original architecture and style.

"*Oui,*" Evelyn said. "As a human, and for a time after I was turned."

"He owns it?" Clara asked.

"*Non*," Evelyn confessed. "Marc's surrogate sire did for centuries. A decade after he went missing, I was informed the man bequeathed the property to me."

She supposed that Marc would not have a strong reaction to such a slight. Clara suspected the reason for this *gift* was due to a connection with Evelyn that her *man of war* could never have.

"Explains a lot about the design," Clara said.

Clara noticed early on that there was never any direct light. They either faced the wrong way, or something obstructed the light's path. *It also puts into context the spartan kitchen, and the lack of dining room.*

"Precisely," Evelyn said. "Anyway, eat up. You need your strength."

Clara's reserves were plentiful, but she was uncertain of the cause. While her online viewership dipped due to her absence, she could feel raw power coursing through her veins. *Uriel would have had a serious fight on his hands.*

"*It's the hunters*," Sparky said.

"*They are so few*," Silver countered.

Clara tuned out the goddesses and smiled. Evelyn had taken the time to do something special and it was time to focus on what mattered…

EPILOGUE

THE VAN HELSING INVERSION

Clara was seated at a little bistro located along one of the canals. She was in her plain-Jane form, nondescript and able to blend into a crowd, worlds apart from her true appearance. *The wings are a dead giveaway*.

She wore a simple, jean skirt, a light-white blouse, and combat boots. Most were too busy looking at the sights, or lost in the eyes of their partners to pay her any heed.

"She's late," Clara said, before taking another sip from her third glass of the house red wine.

That part did not bother her. Given the chaos she went through recently, the angel was thankful for the lull. On the table, there was a menu, she went over it enough times to commit the contents to memory.

"The breeze is nice," Clara said.

In spite of it being a hot, spring afternoon, the wind carried with it a cool breeze from the water. She smiled while keeping her eyes closed, letting the sunlight soak into her skin.

Through her eyelids there was a red glow that changed as something dark crept across, her field of vision. Her skin cooled, and her heart sank. *I haven't felt like this since I was a child.*

Hunters were expected to control their emotions, push them out of the way and charge without hesitation into the fray. This creeping sense of dread was entirely alien to the fallen angel.

She opened her eyes, and spotted one of the servers standing dead ahead. The man was blond, featured a flawless face, and had piercing, blue eyes. Despite the appearance of a warm smile, it was those eyes that bothered her. *They are as cold as glacial ice.*

"Your friend hasn't shown?" the server asked. "Who would turn down an angel?"

Upon hearing that last word, the contents of Clara's stomach soured. She concealed a burp and, on a hunch, looked past the flesh and peered into the man's *soul*.

Clara could see souls, or the lack thereof. Humans were like shining beacons of light, an image of themselves in astral form. Those who strayed further from the light bore the scars of their actions.

Souls could heal by embracing the light. She had seen souls flayed to within an inch of their lives recover nicely after sustained efforts to better humanity. *I've only met one so far who managed this feat.*

That was why Clara said that people should leave the world in a better state than they entered. Every act did not require a Herculean level of effort to get past Saint Peter. Sometimes it was a simple matter of showing compassion, helping out a neighbour, or ridding the world of a monster.

The darkest soul she ever set eyes upon was that of her sister. Ada had been manipulated and twisted to feed off her jealousy and hatred leading her to turn away from the light. As a vampire there was nothing left of her soul other than bleached bones. *It's what else that I saw that bothered me.*

Her sister's skeleton writhed with dark snakes, as though they crawled out of a tarpit. To this day, the image of her sister in that state left Clara with an uneasy feeling. *Like this one.*

What stood before her was worse. There was no skeleton, nor any hint that the server had once been human. The body was composed of tens of thousands of these snakes, writhing, and moving about as though controlled by a singular consciousness.

"I bring—(*word from my employer*)," the server said.

The fallen angel reacted entirely by instinct. Large, sheathed claws extended from her fingers, looking very much as though they belonged on the paws of a large feline. She then swiped the server's arm, leaving deep gashes that were initially invisible.

Given a few *heartbeats*, black, viscous blood oozed from the wounds. Clara pushed back on the seat, sending the chair sliding back until she gained enough distance to stand. All the while, two growths formed around her shoulder blades, deforming the blouse until these protrusions tore through the fabric.

Within another heartbeat, Clara's wings were fully formed, replete with black feathers. They opened to their full size and several passers-by gasped at the sight of the *Valkyrie in* their midst.

"*C'est elle,*" a random woman said. (*That's her.*)

Clara did not take her eyes off the server, even as the blood was absorbed back through the skin which sealed the skin up entirely. *That's just how vampires heal.*

However, it was the sizzling sound and the acrid scent of something burning that caught her attention. A quick peek at her hand revealed the claws were smoking, the oily blood reacting as though it was acid.

"Horsefeathers," Clara said.

She scraped her claws against the side of a concrete barrier with enough force to tear off the sheath and arrest further corruption.

"You'll need to do better than that," the server said.

"*What is that?*" Clara asked her voice resounded solely within her mind.

"*Abaddon,*" Ethereal, the goddess of the dead, said.

"What the f—(*uck*)!" Clara swore.

* * * *

Clara found herself in an expansive space designed to look very much like a Greek or Roman Temple. Ahead, there was Abaddon visible from two viewports revealing what her eyes saw.

"As in the demon?" Clara asked.

Ethereal nodded as did the five other goddesses. They were all seated around a large, stone table, each occupying a chair on the sides, whereas Clara was to sit at the head. *I prefer to stand most times.*

"How do I fight him?" Clara asked.

"You can't, not as an angel," Silver, the goddess of the moon, said.

"…light and dark…" Clara said.

She had been forged in the light and was never meant to be exposed to the polar opposite of herself. *We aren't supposed to exist in our pure states.*

"What…" Clara said, while the idea gained detail in her mind. "What if I bled on him?"

"That's an attack that only weakens yourself," Artemis, goddess of the hunt, said.

That was true, but she was left with the suspicion that a key detail was left unsaid. Clara closed the gap between her fingers and made a rotation motion. *That might need some prompting.*

"The sun," Silver said. "Demons can't normally venture out in broad daylight."

"Like vampires," Clara said. "He has backing? Someone from down below?"

"Or above," Ethereal said dryly.

The other goddesses glared at the goddess of the dead and necromancy for that cheer-sucking tone. Clara had to smile though, as that was precisely the kind of thinking she needed. *Two archangels failed, so they pulled some strings.*

"Just ducky," Clara said.

At the outer edge of the viewport, Sparky spotted something and began to cheer. Clara's eyes flowed to that area and spotted what appeared to be Julia, showing up late for their meeting.

"That's the key!" Sparky, the goddess of magic, said.

"You've taken a few too many flights—(*over to cuckoo's nest*)." Ethereal said.

"The moon," Sparky added.

This led Silver's eyelids to open wide. As her face came aglow, it left Clara with the impression that she was staring at the face of the moon itself.

"I can turn her," Silver said.

"Can she fight him off?" Clara asked.

"… yes," Silver replied.

"That's not exactly a definitive answer," Clara said. "She's not a pawn to be discarded."

"I'll need to be freed to use my powers," Silver said. "It'll work."

302

"Okay," Clara said, but before a smile could break across the goddess's face, she added, "She must consent."

"That will take time," Silver said.

"Sparky and I will make sure you have time," Clara said, before winking at the goddess of magic.

Clara looked at every other goddess in the eyes. Breaking Silver apart from the whole was a risk, and she had no desire to broadcast to the world that she served as a vessel for several, old goddesses.

"I can't afford the media catching wind of your presence," Clara said. "Now, let's have some fun."

* * * *

Time was nearly at a standstill while they worked out a plan. Before Clara returned in sync with time, she consciously separated Silver from the whole, doing so in such a way that another instance of herself appeared in a back alley near Julia. The transition appeared to be no more than a shimmer, although she suspected that Abaddon would pick up on the change.

"I simply have a message—(*to deliver*)," Abaddon said.

Clara raised her left arm, pointing a finger straight at the demon. A brilliant bolt of blue energy left her fingertip and arced towards the target. It was powerful enough that the air crackled leaving the lingering scent of ozone.

The demon raised his hand. The bolt struck him dead centre of his palm. While the skin turned blue, and bled onto a portion of his arm, the damage left behind was no worse than a cigarette burn.

Abaddon did not hesitate to fire back. A similar bolt of red energy shot across the distance between them. Clara, now operating at an accelerated tempo, sidestepped the beam... *better not take any chances...*

This exchange happened back and forth. While Clara's powers were fed directly by the celestial Sun, she sensed they were not being replenished.

"Are you done?" Abaddon asked.

Clara fired off another quick beam, followed by another. On the third attack, her finger only sparked, which sent the contents of her stomach straight to her toes.

"Is that all you—(*got*)?"

There came a long, woeful howl from above. Clara glanced upwards and spotted a werewolf bathed in the silver light of the moon. Abaddon turned around just in time to watch the three-metre tall creature leap from the roof with claws outstretched.

While angels were not known for their emotional outbursts, demons apparently had no such limitation. His reaction began with his eyes opening wide, followed by his lips parting to reveal his clenched teeth... *genuine surprise and a healthy dose of fear...*

Abaddon moved out of the way by merging into his shadow and reforming at the tip of it. Meanwhile Julia barely made a sound when she landed, only light clicking as those claws struck against stone.

The werewolf took a fast and powerful swipe. Her claws cut through Abaddon's chest, covering her claws in thick, viscous blood. However, the werewolf did not react to the interchange. She swiped again but the demon moved out of the way. *Just barely...*

Abaddon looked past the werewolf and straight at Clara. The man was no longer smiling, his nature shining through. *I've seen warmer faces on a serial killer's mugshot.*

"Your loss..." Abaddon melted into shadow which was absorbed by the tiny crevices in the street.

Julia pounced and slashed several times, the equivalent of pounding sand. This further enraged her, leaving Clara to wonder if this threat was about to change for the worse.

"*You know where to find me*," Abaddon whispered.

Clara turned around but found nothing. She focused on the situation ahead of her, wings wide open. The werewolf's muscles twitched, while its drool dripped from its lower jaw. *This could end badly!*

"Now!" Clara said.

Just like that, Clara disappeared from sight without making a sound, taking the enraged werewolf with her. That left those in the street gawking at their phones.

"Did you get that?" A random spectator asked their partner.

LEXICON

A Snap   Something which is quick or easy.

Ab-so-lute-ly   Agreement in the affirmative.

Absent Treatment   Dancing with bashful partner.

Airtight   Someone who is extremely desirable or
                            attractive.

Attaboy   A congratulatory statement.

Balled Up   Confused and/or messed up.

Baloney   Complete nonsense.

Baby   Another word for sweetheart. Can also
                            be used to denote something of high
                            value or respect.

Baby Vamp   A woman considered attractive or
                            popular.

Bank's Closed   Not interested in kissing or fooling
                            around.

Barneymugging   Euphemism for sex.

Beat It   Another word to go away.

Batty   Driving someone crazy.

Bee's Knees   Excellent or very high quality.

Berries	Someone attractive or pleasing, or another word for great.
Berry Path	Euphemism for a woman's genital area.
Betty	An attractive woman.
Billboard	A flashy man or woman.
Bimbo	Slang for a tough guy.
Bingo	Used to express satisfaction at a sudden positive outcome.
Bird	A term for odd or strange which applies to either gender.
Bird Cage	Elevator car.
Biscuit	A pettable flapper.
Black Tuesday	Also known as the Great Crash of 1929.
Blower	Slang for the telephone.
Blowhard	A braggart and/or a bully.
Bootleg	Alcohol that has been illegally produced.
Bronx Cheer	Loud sputtering noise to show disapproval. Also known as a raspberry.
Bub	Often used as an insolent term of address.
Bull	Slang referring to a police officer or another branch of law enforcement.

Bump in the Night	Unexplained and frightening noises at night, purportedly caused by ghosts.
Bumped Off	To have someone killed.
Bum's Rush	To be forcibly removed from an establishment or locale.
Cable	Message sent by telegraph.
Cash	Euphemism for a kiss.
Caper	A criminal act which normally involves an elaborate plan.
Cat's Meow	An excellent person or thing.
Chassis	Slang referring to the female form.
Cheque	Euphemism for saving a kiss for later.
Chippy	A woman who is the polar opposite of frigid.
Clip-Joint	A dance club filled with rich or sophisticated patrons.
Coffin Varnish	Moonshine.
Cool His Heels	Forced to wait.
Copacetic	That which is wonderful, fine or alright.
Cupid's Bow	The way a flapper uses lipstick to make the bow more prominent, while their lips appear smaller.
Crashing the Party	The act of getting into a party in which one was not invited.

Daddy   A young woman's boyfriend or lover, especially if he's rich.

Dame   A lady.

Dapper   A flapper's father.

Dead Hoofer   A lousy dancer.

Declaration **of** A divorce.
Independence

Di Mi   Dear me.

Dimbox   Slang for a taxi cab.

Dingle Dangler   Someone who insists on calling.

Doll   An attractive woman.

Doozie   Something that is hard to comprehend.

Dough   Slang for money.

Drugstore Cowboy   A man who tries to pick up women on a street corner.

Dumb Dora   A woman who is considered lacking in intellectual prowess.

Ducky   Great or wonderful. Can be used sarcastically to imply the opposite.

Edge   A term applied to the feeling of intoxication.

Electric Cure   As in, electric chair; a way to end a problem for good.

Face Stretcher	An older woman who adopts youth fashions or wears heavy makeup to conceal her age.
Fancy Smancy	A derogatory way to refer to something high-class.
Finale Hopper	Someone who arrives after everything has been paid for.
Fire Extinguisher	A chaperone.
Flapper	A stylish, brash, hedonistic young woman with short skirts & shorter hair.
Flat Tyre	A dull witted, insipid, and disappointing date.
Flivver	A Ford Model-T or any old car after 1928.
Flour Lover	Girl who is too liberal with the face powder.
Four-Flusher	A term applied to cheats, swindlers, and liars.
Gams	A woman's legs.
Getaway sticks	A woman's legs.
Giggle Water	An alcoholic drink.
Goofy	To be in love.
Hayburner	A vehicle that uses a lot of fuel.
Heater	Slang that is applied to firearms.

Heebie-Jeebies	Nervous or anxious.
Helluva	Alternate pronunciation for hell of a.
Hen Coop	A term referring to a beauty salon.
High-Hat	A snub.
Hit on All Sixes	Going full throttle or all out.
Hoity-Toity	Marked by an air of assumed importance.
Hole	Slang for solitary confinement in prison.
Hooch	Another term for bootleg alcohol.
Hoofer	Slang for a dancer.
Hoofing	The act of dancing.
Hoosegow	Slang for prison.
Horsefeathers	The equivalent of a modern swear word.
Indoor Aviator	Also known as an elevator operator. This is a play on the fact that their lives are composed of a series of ups and downs.
It	Slang for someone with sex appeal.
Jalopy	An old car or a beater.
Jane	A term applied to any female.
Juice Joint	Another name for a speakeasy.

Keen   Attractive or appealing

Kick the Gong Around   Smoking opium.

Killjoy   A person who spoils other people's fun or enjoyment.

Knee-Duster   Slang for a skirt.

Kodak Moment   A memorable moment that one would wish to capture on film.

Mad Money   Cab fare home if she gets in a fight with her escort.

Make Do   Working with what one has.

Malarkey   Talk that is nonsensical.

Middle-Aisle   The act of getting married; walking down the middle-aisle at church.

Moll   A gangster's girl.

Mistress Grundy   A priggish or extremely tight-laced person.

Munitions   Face powder and rouge.

Mustard Plaster   Someone who is not wanted and will not leave.

Neck   The act of kissing with passion.

Nobody Home   Describes someone who is dumb or dumbfounded.

Nertz   Used to express disgust, defiance, disapproval or despair.

Nervous Nellie	Timid or worrisome.
Off-Time Jive	To be inappropriate, impolite; to have bad manners.
On the Lam	Someone who is fleeing from the authorities.
On the Up and Up	Legitimate and above board.
Ossified	Someone who is intoxicated.
Palooka	An average or below average boxer.
Peashooter	The term for a firearm, normally of smaller calibres.
Petting	To make out or foreplay.
Petting Party	A party where young couples make out.
Piece of the Action	Share of the profits or advantages generated by an activity
Pill	A person who is generally unlikable.
Poufter	An effeminate male.
Pushover	Individuals who are easily convinced or seduced.
Quiff	A term applied to sexually active females.
Racketeering	Service offered for a problem that does not actually exist.

Real McCoy	A term applied to an item that is genuine.
Ritzy	Based on the Hotel Ritz; implies elegance.
Rock of Ages	A middle-aged woman, usually over thirty.
Sap	Someone who is easily fooled.
Sapphic	Slang for a lesbian.
Says You	A reaction of disbelief.
Shell-Shocked	The term employed during the Great War referring to Post-Traumatic Stress Disorder (PTSD).
Speakeasy	An illicit drinking establishment dealing in bootleg alcohol.
Spifflicated	Someone who is intoxicated.
Spiffy	Something that is elegant or opulent.
Stewbum	Someone from the dredges or an old drunken hobo.
Sure-Fire	Will not fail.
Swanky	A term similar to ritzy.
Talkie	Original term for movies where actors speak.
Take for a Ride	The final drive someone will take before they are murdered.

Tapped Out	Slang used to imply that one has no money.
Tarte	Slang for a prostitute.
Tits	Slang for breasts.
To a Tee	Something which is made properly or to exact specifications.
Toe-to-Toe	Being in direct confrontation or opposition.
Torpedo	A hired gun or enforcer.
Tough	Too bad.
Townie	Someone from the city.
On the Up and Up	Open and honest.
Upchuck	Slang for the act of vomiting.
Wallflower	A person who stands apart from others during a dance or party.
Waterworks	Crying.
What am I, Chopped Liver?	Frustration or anger at being ignored on a social level.

BIOGRAPHY OF BACKGROUND CHARACTERS

Evelyn Chartres' novels are part of an interconnected universe. While some stories stand alone, recurring characters and places are mentioned to tap into the rich, cohesive tapestry of the series. This section lists characters who shaped the narrative through their influence on the main cast but do not take an active part in the story.

These biographies provide backstory for new readers and serve as a refresher for those familiar with the series.

ADA

Ada, the eldest Grey sister, stayed in the company town and married a young miner. When a cave-in claimed his life, she was left destitute and turned to prostitution to survive. Her gravestone claims she died a year later from a breech birth, but the truth is darker.

Drusilla, a vengeful vampire thwarted by Ada's sister, Clara Grey, sought Ada out. Offering power and purpose, Drusilla turned Ada into a vampire. Over decades, she wove a web of lies, convincing Ada that her youngest sister, Clara, had stolen her valour to ruin her life. Consumed by resentment, Ada embraced her new existence, becoming Drusilla's loyal disciple.

After Drusilla's death in the Roaring Twenties, Ada vanished. She resurfaced when Clara, now an angel, returned to Earth. The vengeful Ada seized control of Drusilla's empire, and channelled its resources into a relentless campaign of revenge against her sister. Their conflict culminated in a showdown at The Grand, leaving the storied hotel in ruins.

Clara, unable to kill her sister, waled away from the conflict, leaving Ada's ultimate fate uncertain.

ADRIENNE

Adrienne Smythe toiled as a waitress in a gritty, dive bar until she crossed paths with Joseph Black, the enigmatic leader of a biker gang. Their passionate, whirlwind romance soon led to a pregnancy, immersing her in the supernatural, surrounded by a fierce pack of werewolves.

As mother to William and stepmother to Julia, Adrienne seized a pivotal moment when Clara Grey, dubbed '*the Harpy*,' murdered the pack's alpha to seize power. With cunning guidance, manipulation, calculated coercion, and a penchant for violence, Adrienne elevated her son William to the role of alpha while orchestrating Julia's exile from the pack.

Although humans are insignificant in the eyes of a werewolf, Adrienne boldly assumed the role of den mother, maintaining an unyielding grip over William and, through him, the entire pack. Driven by a burning desire for vengeance for her husband's death, she set in motion a chain of events that culminated in her death.

DRUSILLA

Drusilla was born in Rome during Emperor Diocletian's reign. As daughter of a prominent senator, her comfortable life collapsed when a slight against Hera sparked a mob's wrath, forcing her to flee.

She was saved due to a runaway, Christian's sacrifice, which led to a secret conversion. Drusilla joined the Tower, a group set on purging Rome of pagan gods and vampires. As a founder, she devoted herself to the cause but was overlooked for leadership in favour of the Reverend Mother Augustine. Jealousy and the discovery that the Tower's mission rested on a lie broke her faith. She left the order.

Turning to darkness, Drusilla became a vampire, known for beauty and cruelty. Over centuries, she sought to destroy the Tower, seeing it as a barrier to dominating all *lesser* creatures. In the Roaring Twenties, she finally succeeded in isolating the Tower but was hunted down and killed by a hunter who died in the act.

EDITH STONE

Despite the tragic loss of a close friend and fellow acolyte of the Tower, Edith Stone excelled in her studies, earned prestigious appointments, and became a senior member of *Les Filles de Jeanne d'Arc*.

During the Great War, Edith hunted alongside Clara, confronting a surge of ghouls spawned by the conflict's mass casualties. In their first year as partners, they were lured into a trap set by the vampire Drusilla. Clara's quick thinking saved them, but Edith faced the consequences. The Reverend Mother demoted her for the mission's failure. Humiliated, Edith vanished entirely from the many eyes of the Tower.

By the Roaring Twenties, a disillusioned Edith resurfaced, aligning with a group of women resisting their government's religious oppression. Her lover was brutally killed by Drusilla, days before Clara showed up to investigate the Tower's isolation. Their reunion was cut short, leaving the state of their relationship unresolved.

Edith's death remains shrouded in mystery. In an alternate reality, she slays Drusilla and ascends to heaven. Eighty years in the future Earth, Clara and Edith share one final encounter, where Edith chooses to make the ultimate sacrifice for the sake of humanity.

MARIE GRÂCE DE FOIX

Marie Grâce de Foix, better known as Grace, is a former French countess who escaped the Bastille during the French Revolution. In New France, under Evelyn's guidance, she was turned into a vampire. Over time, Grace becomes Evelyn's trusted agent, switching between roles as assassin, spy, or saviour as needed.

Once a countess of stature, Grace's appearance, fixed at thirteen, clashes with a modern world's view of teenagers. She leans into her youth, posing as a moody teen, and relies on a blood-bound couple acting as her parents to maintain her cover.

ABOUT EVELYN CHARTRES

Evelyn Chartres is the *nom de plume* for a self-published Canadian author. The writer of ten, Gothic fantasy novels, Evelyn released her debut novel, *The Portrait*, in 2016, and her latest, *The Van Helsing Conjecture*, in 2025.

A fan of the phrase '*live to eat*', Evelyn shares her recipes on evelynchartres.com. These recipes have a loose focus on French Canadian cuisine, which feature deep-dish meat pies, seafood, and desserts that are rarely seen outside of *La Belle Province*.

Evelyn is currently living in Ottawa, Ontario, and is busy laying the foundations for her next book, Man at War.

Follow Evelyn on Bluesky
https://bsky.app/profile/evelynchartres.bsky.social

Follow Evelyn on Facebook
http://www.facebook.com/theportraitofawoman

Follow Evelyn on Instagram
http://www.instagram.com/authorevelynchartres/

Follow Evelyn on X
http://x.com/EvelynChartres

Visit Evelyn's Website
http://evelynchartres.com

ALSO FROM EVELYN CHARTRES

THE PORTRAIT

"A vision from the past becomes a writer's deadly obsession."

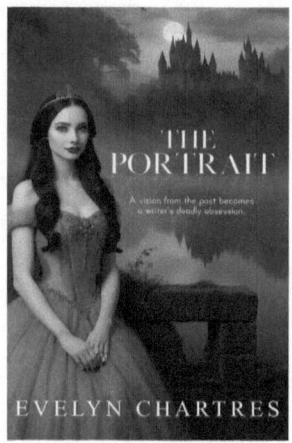

Available below:
https://bit.ly/3HG4ec0

The Portrait is a Gothic fantasy about Victoria Frost, an author who develops an unhealthy obsession for her character. As events unfold, her infatuation sours, forcing Victoria to question her sanity. Is she simply slipping into madness, or is there something else at play?

The Portrait features a mixture of contemporary and historical scenes brought forward as Victoria explores the world of her muse. Using both prose and art, every scene yields a new piece of the puzzle, providing insights into the origins of her character's portrait and its featured model.

Discover how a vision from the past becomes a writer's deadly obsession.

The Grand

"Even things that go bump in the night need a place to unwind."

Available below:
http://bit.ly/2DzPqgE

You will find The Grand nestled atop a cliff that overlooks a cursed valley. Surrounded by foreboding mountains, this ritzy-French palatial-style hotel is a place where a roaring party's success is measured by its body count. This hotel does not cater to the rich or famous. Instead, its staff and facilities serve a clientele with a more *discerning* palate.

The Grand is a collection of Gothic fantasy stories with an overarching storyline that incorporates supernatural themes. The Roaring Twenties serves as a rich historical, linguistic, and cultural backdrop.

Centred on the victims, each story brings a unique perspective to the hotel, the staff, and their esteemed guests. At The Grand, it is best to remember: Even things that go bump in the night need a place to unwind.

The Van Helsing Paradox

"A gal has to look out for herself, after all."

Available below:
http://bit.ly/3inTKyT

Clara Grey's parents once said that the world was a dark and dangerous place. There was more truth than fiction in those words. There were things that lurked in the shadows which defied the laws of nature: perversions that fed on the dead, terrorised the living, or escaped the chill touch of the grave.

Clara is a member of the Tower, a religious order of hunters who work outside the confines of the Church. As keepers of the arcane, her order takes an active role in countering such threats. Alas, the life of a hunter can be short, and many go missing before they are ready to serve. So, what does it take to succeed against all odds?

Explore Clara's origin, a child born before the dawn of the twentieth century. Witness her rigorous education, how she faces adversity, and fights in the Great War to become the derringer-wielding flapper she is.

Throughout her tale, keep in mind: No matter the threat, a gal has to look out for herself, after all.

The Van Helsing Resurgence

"While the Roaring Twenties are long gone, a heroine's work is never done."

Available below:
http://bit.ly/2XvgFQF

Clara Grey was a hunter and part of a secret organisation known only as the Tower. During the Roaring Twenties, she sacrificed herself to destroy a powerful vampire. As a reward, she joined the ranks of Heaven's army, and for ninety years, Clara yearned to take an active role in the mortal realm.

In an attempt to alter the course of history, scientists trigger an experiment with devastating results. The effects are felt not only on Earth, but in other realms as well.

Clara and an echo from her past are sent to Earth to investigate the case of a stolen soul. For this transgression, Heaven could go to war, but they chose to send Clara—and Edith. They fall to Earth, focused on their mission.

Both had been isolated from the mortal realm for generations. In their lifetimes, monsters were on the decline, but learn how much the modern world has changed. While navigating this alien land, will they adapt to their surroundings to fulfil their mission? Or be swallowed up by the evil that lurks in the shadows?

Before reading on, be sure to remember: While the Roaring Twenties are long gone, a heroine's work is never done.

The Van Helsing Incursion

"Hunting things is child's play when compared to juggling relationships."

Available below:
http://bit.ly/3eFuGCH

During the Roaring Twenties, Clara Grey hunted things that went bump in the night. On her last mission, she paid the ultimate price to rid the world of a powerful foe. As a reward, she ascended to Heaven and joined its ranks as an angel.

Ninety years after her death, Clara fell to Earth, intent on saving a soul. While successful, killing an old god in self-defence barred her from returning to Heaven. Lost in the modern world, Clara was forced to seek unlikely allies to navigate through these uncertain times.

Four months later, Clara has settled in with Elizabeth, a young woman she saved shortly after descending to Earth. For a gal who had sworn off anything that hinted at normalcy, Clara learns that being average takes more effort than she suspected.

Alas, repercussions from choices made on that fateful mission have not been idle. Her enemies trigger a chain of events that force our fated femme fatale to act. Is Clara prepared to deal with the fallout? Will her allies come to her aid? Or must she stand on her own?

Before reading on, be sure to consider: Hunting things that go bump in the night is child's play when compared to juggling relationships.

The Van Helsing Impetus

"While she failed at normal, she's still a force to be reckoned with."

Available below:

https://bit.ly/421tmRM

Clara Grey is a fallen angel, one who tried her hand at having a normal life. That experiment came to an abrupt end when werewolves kidnapped her gal. While victorious, tales from that fateful night became the stuff of legend. Now known as 'the Valkyrie,' she is a wanted fugitive.

She has been on the lam for months, using a nondescript persona to evade the authorities. All the while, Clara is tormented by voices from a goddess that she thought long dead.

Clara has never faced an enemy that can strike from the shadows, forcing her to align herself with the things she hunted in life. Even with an army at her back, does she have what it takes to defeat her foe?

Before reading on, be sure to consider: She may have failed at being normal, but she's still a force to be reckoned with.

High Water Mark

"When humanity has been driven into the sea, what lurks above the waves?"

Available below:
http://bit.ly/3CxZXlh

Anna is a humanoid mermaid who spends her days with the local timekeeper until a podmate comes to her with a proposal. They hatch a plan to head out into the watery ruins of humanity in search of lost technology and materials. For a young mermaid living in the dregs of society, the promise of riches from such a find is just too good to pass up.

Armed with nothing more than an old map and some rusty road signs to follow, they are soon reminded that adventure often brings forth more than its fair share of rough waters. Her friend gets captured, leaving Anna alone in a world where mermaids are nowhere near the top of the food chain.

Follow Anna as she makes landfall and learns why her ancestors abandoned the surface. Lost in a world that is perpetually covered in a thick fog, Anna must navigate through what remains above the high-water mark. What will she find? An ally? A foe? Or will she find nothing but death and destruction?

Before reading on, be sure to consider: With humanity driven into the sea, what lurks above the waves?

Dark Hearts

"She may look like the Little Red Riding Hood, but she really is the wolf."

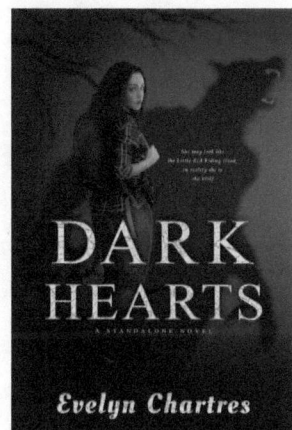

Available below:
http://bit.ly/3pZ211H

Julia is a werewolf who turned against her pack and saved an innocent life. As a reward for her good deed, she ends up in prison, but thrives while others like her waste away.

On the eve of a full moon, an unknown benefactor arranges for Julia's release. Faced with the prospect of returning to the city that nearly killed her, she opts to disappear into the surrounding woods.

This is the opportunity she needs to find herself and reconnect with the wild. As her past resurfaces, the supernatural and dark elements within humanity take notice of her.

Before reading on, be sure to consider: She may look like the Little Red Riding Hood, but she really is the wolf.

Man of War

"While good intentions pave the road to hell, jumping off comes with a price."

Available below:

https://bit.ly/4ccXzmd

For centuries, Marc has served as Evelyn's unwavering protector—a vampire of shadow—unfeeling, fiercely loyal, and a force to be reckoned with. But what of the man?

Man of War unravels the first century of Marc's life. It traces his origins as an impetuous French Viscount who finds refuge in service of king and country. Watch as he wages war against the world, those beyond the grave, and with himself. Focus on the women who forged his very being.

Set against the backdrop of seventeenth-century Europe, this dark fantasy immerses the reader in a rich historical, linguistic, and cultural tale. Before reading on, consider: While good intentions pave the road to hell, jumping off comes with a price.